T0365675

RETRIBUTION

DONNELL HARRIS

authorHOUSE

AuthorHouse™
1663 Liberty Drive
Bloomington, IN 47403
www.authorhouse.com
Phone: 833-262-8899

Published by AuthorHouse 01/17/2023

ISBN: 978-1-7283-7777-3 (sc)
ISBN: 978-1-7283-7776-6 (e)

FOREWORD

SINCE LEAVING BALTIMORE A LITTLE OVER TEN YEARS AGO, MALIK (KING) HAVE been living a very surreal and tranquil lifestyle. Steadily complimented by his bosses for his professionalism and recognized among his peers as worthy of their trust, he never consider politics until he was approached three years ago, but he stayed firmly embedded where he had taken roots and without any regrets. He was rising to heights he never imagine considering what transpired in Baltimore to have him migrate to the outskirts of Atlanta. A simple phone call from a soft sultry voice from his past brought disheartening news concerning the murder of his mentor and big brother Road Block. He was now on his flight home. He never thought he would ever walk the streets that earned him the nick-name Lion, again. Lion has been peacefully lying dormant, but there was a stirring in him, now. He could hear the subtle growls of him awakening and it stirs ignited his fears. Once he is released upon the streets of Baltimore and get the scent of blood, he won't extract his claws until those responsible for the murder of his brother and mentor have paid their restitution to his "RETRIBUTION."

"RETRIBUTION"

IN THE PARK HEIGHTS SECTION OF BALTIMORE, MARYLAND, FIVE OF THE BIGGEST drug distributors and one of the most notorious hit men in the city was having a private meeting. They all had aspirations of controlling the city, but they also had the same problem that neither of them would ever attempt individually. How to deal with Road Block and his partner Monster? Since coming up through the ranks affiliated with the East Side Boyz at the age of twelve, he had suddenly become the main man. He owned the East Side. Once you cross the bridges from the west side to the east side on North Avenue or the bridge leading to Orleans Street, he controlled it all. Creeping in from University to Greenmount, all of his also. A dime of coke or dope sold in any secluded alley was a part of his shit. Up Greenmount Avenue from North Avenue to Woodbourne Avenue or down towards Latrobe Homes and stretching towards Somerset Homes and Douglass Homes, Road Block controlled it all. The C & J crew up on Collington and Jefferson was his pride and joy. As expected with a Kingpin, he controlled his turf with an iron fist. He had stretch out everyone that had tried to step to him or try to take what belonged to him, especially his corners. Every motherfucking squad that step up to them received their just dues while he nor Monster ever received a scratch. He and Monster were very well educated and trained to the etiquettes of the streets by Boogie.

With the sudden murder of his mentor Boogie and the double life sentence that his right-hand man Ace received from the Feds, Road Block shouldn't have been as organized as he was at the age of twenty-five, but he had listened and learned his lessons. When he suddenly came out of the gate after being a sergeant in arms for Boogie for five years, the quality of his product couldn't be fucked with. The little distributors on the east side of the city were looking to patch up with him and he received them with open arms. They would take their product out of his territory and find a hole somewhere on the west side to grind or at the very lucrative Lexington Market down town. His pride and joy crew were those boys up on C&J (Collington and Jefferson). With the undercover addicts creeping from Johns Hopkins and the city workers going to the Northeast Market for lunch between the hours of eleven and two, those white professionals felt safe walking one block over after understanding that if anything happen to any of them on their watch, their block would be shut down by five-o and they wasn't having that. Stick boys knew not to touch them or feel their murderous wrath. They were pulling in well over twenty G's a day and stretch out every person that tried to tap into their business if diplomacy didn't work. In no time at all with his connection down in Miami, Road Block gradually became the main distributors.

He has four of the most notorious and ruthless lieutenants controlling his four principal areas. Coming from out of Hagerstown and Jessup Correctional Facility as young hungry soldiers, they have known one another since elementary school and are now very loyal to him because of what he naturally did for them while they were incarcerated. During their five-year vacation, he hit their books every two weeks while taking care of their immediate families. Anything that they wanted or desired, he tried to provide especially when a C.O could be persuaded by nondeductible dead presidents. At a rate of a thousand dollars a ride, female CO's was making that nondeductible money under the cover of darkness in the stairways near their posts. Their moans, groans and pleads would filter through the vents while inmates was asleep or so she hoped but sly smiles and stares met her the very next morning. When each of them step out from prison, he had a SUV waiting for them with a phat ass young lady and fifty G's. The most important thing about what Road Block built was that none of them was affiliated with any gang running around in the streets or behind the wall. So, trying to put a wedge between this tight knit set of friends would be suicidal to say the least. Never say a disrespectful or derogatory thing about any of them in the presence of the others. A minimum of a right hook would be your payoff. A minimum. The East Side Boyz under Road Block tutorage weren't anything to taken lightly if you want to see the morning sun rising.

"Alright! Alright! Calm the fuck down, shit!" demanded Ice Pick staring around the table. In front of him was his claim to frame, an ice pick and a glass of Cîroc. Dress in a gray three button Johnston suit with a dark gray round collar shirt, his gold diamond cufflinks reflected from the light as he twirled a Havana cigar between his fingers. "We've been having these meeting for weeks and I'm personally tired of having them" he admitted slightly snarling. "Are yawl going to step up or what?"

"Stepping up isn't the problem, we are here again, right?" Byrd informed him calmly while slightly grinning. "The boundaries you're trying to establish are the problem. The park at 23rd and Greenmount and the area surrounding it is very profitable, but you're trying to claim it for yourself especially around York Road and Woodbourne. That, I'm not feeling."

"What the fuck do you suggest Byrd?" he asked staring at him coldly. They have never liked one another since hooking horns while attending Roland Park Middle. He didn't know the little nappy head girl he was hollowing at was his little sister. When she ignored his advances, he did what a lot of fifteen-year-old would do, say things he didn't mean. So, he attacked her nappy ass head and shabby looking clothing causing the other little boys and girls to laugh at her. She never coward or ran from his verbal assault. She stood there glaring at him. Not a single tear escape her young eyes. Well, all the laughter stop when Byrd showed up. Yeah, Byrd won the fight but that wasn't shit. Their beef at the Baltimore City Detention Center (Old City Jail) occurred when Byrd got out of his lane to assist a guy from Roland Park. He knew the guy was being extorted. Although they were still teenagers, about eighteen, they hook horns again. Byrd got deep up in his ass and beat him just enough that he never tried getting pay back. They cease their beef and form a unify front when the East Side Boyz tried stepping up on them. Only then, did they join forces. So, this business adventure was on a very fragile foundation.

"Let Mookie and Sunshine split the area while you and I contend with the boys in Latrobe and Flag House."

"What!? Hell no!" he reputed his suggestion adamantly. "Fuck that!"

"Why not?" he asked with a coy smile.

"I don't want to fuck with those East Side knuckleheads."

"Nobody here does" he assured him still slightly grinning. "But you're the one initiating this thing. So, it's only natural that you take one of the toughest spots and I'll accommodate you by taking the other one. My only question is which area do you want?"

He didn't answer right away. He just snarled over at him. He had more than enough soldiers to make Latrobe get down or get laid down including Church Square. Those little pockets along Greenmount up to Broadway will fall right into place or get what is being administer. But Flag House, includes Chapel Hill and Douglass Homes will require a persistent violent presence for their lucrative business. A lot of bodies will have to be stretched out before those boys simply lay down. Taking Flag House and Latrobe would be like the East Side Boys invading Murphy Homes or Lexington Terrence, do you see that happening easily? The little clique on Collington and Jefferson (C&J) is one of the most ruthless of them all for its location, but the money being made by Northeast Market couldn't be ignored. If C&J would take out their own people for dipping into the profit, what fucking chance do a motherfucker from the west side have in making them boys bow down? None. The profit from that area would be three times the amount that they would be making but not before the final body count. "I'll take Latrobe" he finally answered ignoring Byrd's smile. "Anything else?" he asked looking around the table then focus on Byrd. "Well, I have seen that look before. What the fuck is it now?"

"Just one thing" replied Byrd pulling from the blunt he was smoking.

"And what the fuck is that?" he asked sarcastically.

"Have you forgotten about Lion?" he asked slightly hardening his eyes as he stared over at him.

"Lion!" he suddenly chuckled. "Fuck that little nigger" he snapped slightly snarling. "Nobody seen his little ass since he skipped town over ten years ago."

"Touch his big brother and I'll guarantee you, he will return" he said with conviction in his voice and eyes.

"Lion? Who the fuck is Lion?" Sunny Boy asked looking confused.

"A nigger that don't mean shit!" Ice Pick snapped.

"That's his motherfucking opinion" Byrd replied staring at him then at the others.

"Who is Lion, Byrd?" asked Mookie staring at him from over the rim of the glass of Brandy he was drinking.

"Road Block little brother" Byrd replied catching his eyes.

"I didn't know Road Block had a little brother" Bash said staring at him closely. Byrd doesn't show concern except where it is warranted, and he have always been like that since they were kids. While he stayed close to the drug game, he became addicted to the euphoric smell of gunpowder and became a top-notch hitman. When he was locked down for five years at Jessup, he refined his skills as a hire assassin, but he never forgot that

Byrd always hit his books. So, if there is a need for apprehension, he was going to take it as good advice.

"Most people don't Bash and those who are foolish enough to forget about him are playing themselves short" he replied staring straight into Ice Pick eyes.

"Where is he?" inquired Black.

"Nobody knows Black" replied Byrd returning his stare. "If I knew, I would send a four-man hit squad to take him out before touching Road Block" he informed them with a menacing stare. "He was locked down for three years at Jessup for a murder until DNA proved it wasn't him. The suppression of evidence by the prosecutor's office also didn't hurt in obtaining his freedom" he slightly smiled then allowing it to slowly dissipate. "The civil case against the police department and prosecutors' office is how I think Road Block got started."

"I always wonder how he stepped out so large?" mention Boo-Boo.

"I think Lion met somebody while he was inside and set him up" Byrd shared.

"Was he in the game too?" inquired Mookie.

"No way, Road would have beaten him down" he slightly smiled. "I need yawl to not just hear me, but listen to me, understand?" he asked staring around the table as they nodded yeah. "Fuck what Ice Pick is saying. There is a tremendous difference between Road Block and Lion. Listening can save your motherfucking life while just hearing me will have you stretched the fuck out" he urged them not expecting a response. "Ice can play Lion short all the fuck he wants, but I'm advising yawl, don't. He can be very vicious" he stress staring them in their eyes individually, again.

"Man fuck that little motherfucker!" Ice said waving off his comment snickering. He was bringing apprehension in their eyes, and he didn't want or need that. He wanted his dream to come to reality. "He can be stretched out next to his motherfucking big brother if he does come from under that motherfucking rock, he's been living and trying to make some motherfucking noise" Ice told them slightly laughing while nudging Bash.

"Big talk, Ice" Byrd replied leaning forward and staring in his eyes. "Remember this gentleman" he told them ignoring Ice. "Road Block's blood run through his veins and he's a Baltimorean. Don't sleep on Lion or he'll rip your motherfucking throat out" he warned them again then lean back in his chair smoking his blunt and reflecting.

Lion was just eight years old when he found out that Road Block was his brother from another mother. He thought that the massive guy just took an interest in the dusty looking loner, but he revealed to him who he was and how they were related. A look of surprise came to Lion's face as he looked up in admiration of his big brother. While visiting their father in Hagerstown two-years ago, he informed Road Block of his presence and last known address. He made it his mission to hunt him down and eventually he did after two years. He too thought he was alone, also. Although Lion was fifteen years younger, they were still blood brothers.

Once his mother was reintroduced to Road Block, Fridays after school until Sunday around noon, they were together. Road took his big brother role to heart. He educated him on anything that his young influential mind might conceive or ponder over. Lion could be found sitting at the Billie Holiday monument on Pennsylvania Avenue reading his first book. "Dope Fein" by Donald Goins. Why he chose to travel all the way over on the west side just to read was just another of his mysterious ways. Road Block wanted a five-page report from him after reading the book and what lessons he received from it? These graphic novels grabbed his young attention because he was witnessing and surviving in the same described environment. He devour all sixteen of his novels and craving others. Iceburg Slim had him reading his novel twice while constantly making mental notes concerning women.

When he first peeked on Lion at Northeast Market a year later, his whole appearance had changed. New wardrobe, fresh fades, but he was always carrying a book or sitting by himself somewhere reading. Living in the hood, perceptions are perceived by your actions. If those that you hang around with is doing mischievous or delinquent things, more than likely you'll take on their traits or character. You'll quit school before reaching high school because of the alluring tones from the streets or quit not much longer after you succeeded in getting there. Obtaining a juvenile record from putting in full time work on the corners, Lion knew that Road Block was had decremented his young ass. As most juveniles learned their trade, they eventually graduate to an adult criminal and obtain nine numbers that will follow them for the rest of their lives. In the hood, you will definitely learn the streets or be eaten by them especially if you intend on playing around in them.

With Lion, he gave the perception of an up and coming square. A pure geek. Someone who was going to be the target of his peers especially those overly mischievous juveniles. Who would have thought he would be a lion in sheep clothing? He damn sure didn't. He had made the same mistake as so many other corner boys did by misjudging his cover. With what they were contemplating, he needed them to understand who would be coming to town and ignore the dumb shit coming out of Ice's mouth.

"Byrd! Byrd!" shouted Ice Pick staring at him with a perplex expression. "Huh?"

"Where the fuck is your head!? Damn!" he asked snarling over at him.

"You really don't want to know where my head is" he told him slightly grinning.

"Are you ready to do this or what?"

"I said I am."

"Then I'll set things up, the 5th Regiment Armory is having its annual Old School Party in about a month on a Saturday. Is that cool with yawl?"

he asked looking around the table. They all nodded their heads yeah except Byrd. His mind was back on Lion.

As the plan was put into motion, Ice Pick contacted his people in Cherry Hill. His people guaranteed him he could get some exceptionally reliable soldiers who are hungry and wouldn't give a damn who the target was. For their plan to work, they first had to initiate phrase one. They had to spring traps on Road Block's lieutenants first. Since they already had their names, their mission is to find the apartment where they live away from their families or girlfriend. Ice Pick men had started cruising the streets on the East Side under the cover of darkness regularly. His squads hit every little corner bar and lounges that ran along Monument Street and up to Patterson Park and Milton Street including the weed spots. They hit the spot regularly making their faces known. Hooking up with the adventurous teenage girls that consider themselves playmates for the drug dealer's and with them willing to spend money for their entertainment, they gradually and discreetly acquired the addresses from the young tricks then eventually dissipated like the morning dew on grass.

Vengeance is a motherfucker even if a woman is involved and if the East Side Boyz ever put it together, who these evasive guys were and how these young tricks were played to extract information; their blood would be spilled in the streets also. So, revealing that you were discussing someone's business to anybody especially perfect strangers using "burners" cell phones almost guarantee you a bullet to the back of your talkative head and rightfully so. If it's not your business, you need to act like it or the price you will have to pay could cost you dearly.

They definitely had to hit his lieutenants at the same time. If any of them are away from their fuck apartments on Saturday, their plan would be shot to hell. No communication between them can happen. If Road Block gets the word what was transpiring from one of them escaping or surviving the assassination attempt, they had two options on the table. Ride and die together or get the fuck out of town. Getting low only puts your loved ones in harms' way. Once he extract the information he needed from any survivors before putting a slug in their heads, he would go through their sets like a motherfucking possess tornado. He would only subside his wrath once he get his massive hands around the conspirators necks individually and squeeze the life out of them while staring in their eyes. He would touch these assassins family members with extreme bodily harm until they surrender themselves to him within a week. Their women are not excluded because there are a lot of gangster bitches in the city trying to get feed also. This would continue until their family members begged them to stand up and be a got damn man and surrender to the penalties to be paid for whatever the fuck they did. The thirty-eight cents it cost for a bullet Road Block would gladly keep spending until retribution is obtained.

Days before the reunion and with the information obtained, Ice Pick snuck into Cherry Hill under the cover of darkness. He approached Bridgeview Road by Carver Road then found a parking spot across the street from Cherry Hill Middle School and extinguish the engine with the radio still playing. He sat there in the dark smoking a cigar while listening to Magic 95.9. The only evidence of him sitting in his car was the illumination caused by him pulling from his cigar. He reflected on every scenario that could possibly materialized and had every one of them cover or so he hoped. He could give a damn about Lion or any motherfucking scenario he could bring to the table. If Lion do come back home trying to roar over his lost, he will show him that he was still just a cub and have a double funeral for his dumb ass. His only main concerns was Road Block and his right-hand man, Monster. As far as Lion and anybody else was concern, fuck them.

Growing up together, Road Block was raised in Flag House housing project on E. Lombard Street while Monster was raised in Perkins Homes on S. Bond Street. While attending City Springs Elementary on S. Caroline

Street, they became aware of each other not because they were massive compared to their school mates but because of the "beef" between the two neighboring housing projects. Everybody living in Flag House who was going to attend elementary school had to attend City Springs. There was no way of avoiding that or the things they had to subject themselves to, daily. So, each morning around seven-thirty, little squads from Flag House would walk up Lombard Street or Pratt Street to infiltrate Perkins. With the heart of Perkins being less than three blocks away, they could start up their shit and always get reinforcement almost instantly when necessary. How is a child supposed to get an education when they knew every morning, they had to defend themselves or humble themselves to the antics of the Perkins Boyz?

Road Block had always walked to school alone or somebody was riding his coat tail. Although only eight-years-old, he was as tall and thick like a teenager. Already standing about five feet seven and a solid one-hundred-fifty pounds, his nick name fit him perfectly. He would ignore the little slick things that filter out of his peers mouths like calling him Baby Huey. He never heard of the cartoon character until he looked it up and smiled at the reference. Down in Flag House as an only child, he understood early that he had to protect what was his or it would be taken. His absentee father had brought him a bicycle for his sixth birthday, and he was riding on cloud nine. He would ride it on the seventh floor with its training wheels on for a week before he finally obtained his balance and took them off. He would cruise around his court yard for hours after getting out of school before the inevitable occurred about eight months later. Three guys requested a ride one day and he naturally refused. He had seen this same strong-armed tactic used on other naïve guys or passive guys before he had even acquired his bike.

"Come on, Baby Huey. We aren't going to keep the damn thing" lied Bumpy trying to smile but all he saw was a snarl.

"No because yawl won't give it back" he replied peeking over at their smiling faces.

"Yes, we will" cosigned Skippy.

"Nope" he replied, still staring over at them.

"Well, supposed we take it" Bumpy asked glaring over at him.

"Then I suggest you get ready to give up some ass while yawl are trying to get mine" he counter allowing the bike to hit the ground as he kept his eyes fixed on them.

"Man, give me that damn bike, fat boy" insisted Tuck reaching for it but he never made it. A straight right hand had him suddenly kissing the pavement. As Bumpy and Skippy leap into action, Road Block was eating their punches for lunch, but each time he landed a punch, neither was in a hurry to receive another. As he step forward with his hand up, they surprise him by retreating. As the incident made its way around their isolated community, the older guys described him as being like a road block as they tried to get around his massive frame. Thus, his nickname. Road Block.

Monster was the product of another illiterate mother getting addicted to drugs much too young. With three different fathers for her four children, Monster was the only boy and oldest child. He was constantly put into unwanted positions being the big brother for his three sisters. The little boys around the complex was constantly saying nasty things to them according to them and he had to step up or they would have continued to fuck with his sisters. It was a vicious display during an incident in late July that earned him the name Monster. His sister Monica was coming back from Patterson Park pool when a couple of guys that live near Spring Court got a little too frisky and had her running home crying. Seeing her and getting the information he requested, he headed straight towards the Court. As soon as he turned the corner, two of the guys took off running but the other four remained and stood their ground with confidence. He never said a word as he approached but his eyes revealed all of his intentions. As they rush at him, he hit the first guy with a right-hook, and he instantly disappeared while receiving several punches. Although they were easily three years older than him, you would never have known it by the way he was handling them. It was when he had them crawling on the ground and starting to submit when he grabbed that baseball bat, he was unmerciful and vicious like a rapid Monster then casually walked away leaving them nursing broken bones and abrasions. Since that day, nobody ever bother any of his sisters after that menacing and psychotic display.

In fourth grade, the "beef" between them seem to have intensified. At first, guys and girls from Perkins could safely go down to Attman's for their delicious corn and roast beef sandwiches on rye while the guys from Flag House could safely go to the supermarket up on S. Broadway. Repeated violations of this simple truce and it was on and popping again. Teenagers were using grade school kids to get their roast beef or corn beef sandwiches while they stare on from two blocks away. If something were to happen to their recently brought sandwiches, what could they really do? They had watched helplessly on numerous occasions as a group of guys would stand on the corner of Lombard and Centre eating their recently brought merchandize while laughing up at them on the corner.

At the height of their beef in sixth grade, Road Block was still walking alone and so was Monster. As the other guys patch up to fight one another after school, they never participated. As kids, they didn't run home to stay out of harm's way or anything. They would stand on separate corners smiling at the show. They had done this so often that they eventually became aware of one another. They had stumble upon each other down by Fawn Street and E. Falls Way sitting on a bench over-looking the Chesapeake River. They acknowledge one another but kept their distance. The sun had already started to descend when Road Block started heading home sight-seeing up Eastern Avenue. He was so engrossed in a winter coat that he was admiring that never saw Monster walking pass. As he proceeded further up, he should have turned on High Street, but he didn't. As he near S. Exeter Street, he saw Monster getting in a slight beef with some guys from Chapel Hill. Normally, he would have kept it moving because Chapel and Flag never had a beef but instead.

"Hey, Cuz" he greeted him coming to stand next to him. "I really could use a work out tonight" he smiled over at the six pre-teens.

"Na, Cuz" he smiled over at him. "I'm sure these guys couldn't handle what we are putting out."

"I know that, but I'm hoping that they don't" he replied still smiling at them. "Well, gentlemen. What is it going to be because we got school in the morning?"

The guys stared over at the two book ends then decided to leave it alone. There was no doubt in their minds that these two guys could very easily tare the fur off of their frail, little asses. So, they continued down Eastern Avenue as Road Block and Monster walked up.

"I've seen you around school. My name is Road Block."

"Mine is Monster" he shared as they shook hands.

From this simple incident, their friendship gradually emerged. They started hanging out together after school for a few hours, but during the weekends, they would venture into one another's set and dare somebody to try to get with them unless they were coming individually. A couple of guys up at Perkins decided to try their hand with Road Block. He was handling his own until another guy tried to interject himself then so did Monster. Word got around their elementary school quickly that they were partners. If you mess with one, you had to contend with the other and running wasn't in their D.N.A. Even when they caught a slight beat down from a group of teenagers, those same teenagers never came back for seconds when they noticed them a couple of days later after licking their wounds. Their little reputation reach up through Chapel Hill and eventually to the guys living around C and J. Their names were being spread on the ghetto grapevine but long before their faces were recognized.

They would walk up to Northeast Market on Monument Street just to get out of their neighborhood and walk around. Guys from their set wouldn't dare venture to the places that they did. They had gotten into fights down at Latrobe Gardens and Johnston Square simply because of where they were walking. Strangers don't take leisurely Sunday strolls through these complexes like it was a natural occurrence. The funny thing about the incidents where they got their asses, kick. They always went right back the following day looking for a repeat. The second time the results were completely different once Road Block suggested how they should approach their combatants. With Monster staying on his right side, he could utilize his left-hook while Monster could use that sludge hammer of his. They never took more than two steps backwards and this simple ploy work as they weren't stumbling over one another and more importantly, knew where the other would be located.

By the time they started Dunbar Middle School, seniors and eight graders had already heard about them. No hazing or antics was directed at them as most freshman had to endure. They tower over their classmates as they walked the halls. Entering their classes for the first time, all of their teachers look at them like they were a freak of nature, and they would just surrender faint smiles. One thing became apparent quickly, both were about their academics. Big dummies could never have a reference with them. Both graduated Dunbar Middle as honor roll students.

During their freshman year at Dunbar High while they were walking towards the cafeteria, they were approached by the junior varsity coach about playing football. With Road Block unnatural speed and beautiful foot work, they tried him out on the blind side of their quarterback and their allegedly best defensive end couldn't get around him or get a finger on the quarterback. The coaches stared at one another with impish grins. They tried Monster out at defensive end because he like rushing the quarterback. Whatever the coach whisper to him seem to have lit a fire under his ass. Teams had to double team him allowing the linebacker to blitz uninhibited because he was destroying guys trying to block him one on one. By the time they were graduating Dunbar High, Road Block and Monster had numerous of college football scholarships on the table waiting for their graduation day. Road Block was the number three offensive tackle in the United States while Monster was rated the number one defensive tackle.

While growing up together, they never used their size to intimidate individuals, but they despised bullies. They have come to several people aides as teenagers and earned the respect of the young guys roaming the streets. Witnessing them fighting six guys one day, they ate the guys punches for lunch while damn near destroying them with a single punch. By the time they were seventeen, mid-level drug distributors were introducing themselves to them.

According to stories coming from the east side, this was how they met their future mentor, Boogie, and his partner Ace. They were playing in a Pop's Warner game down on Dunbar Football Field. Boogie and Ace had just left Latrobe when the sounds of people cheering caught their attention. Crossing Madison Street, they initially wanted to take a peek, but found themselves climbing up into the stone bleachers and took a seat. Road Block and Monster made their presence known almost instantly. They appeared to be adults playing among children. Watching Road Block pulling, the half-back didn't have to push him. He had tremendous speed for his size. Double teaming Monster on defense gave a linebacker an open invitation to rip the quarterback's head off. Even at a youthful age, his strength would easily over-power his opponents. Hearing their names being mentioned by those in the stands is how they learned their names. Seeing them casually walking through Collington Square, Boogie pulled his silver color fully loaded Land Rover over ahead of them and climbed out.

"Gentlemen come here" Boogie called dress in a blue three-button Armani suit while holding a cigar.

"What's up OG?" they asked admiring his clothes while staring up at him.

"I'm Boogie and this is my partner Ace. How old are yawl?"

"We are thirteen" Road Block informed him.

"Yawl have an excellent future a head of yawl in football and motherfuckers already know to leave yawl alone" he informed them slightly hardening his eyes. "If things ever change yawl path, yawl need to reach out to me" he informed them staring down in their eyes. "Do yawl hear me?"

"Yeah, OG" they both replied returning his stare.

"I hope yawl do" he slightly snarled then turned and climbed back into his SUV. Pulling away from the curb, Jay-Z's "Empire State of Mind" filter out.

"What the fuck was that all about?" Monster asked watching the vehicle turning down Patterson Park Avenue.

"He's planting seeds in our mind" Road Block replied staring also.

"Planting seeds?" inquired Monster slightly confused.

"Yeah, man" he smiled across at him. Monster wasn't about the streets like he was acquainted. "He's hoping that his seeds grab roots, and we reach out to him one day."

"For what?" he asked still dumbfounded.

"Employment" he replied slightly smiling and leading him up the streets.

Although Ice knew what they were initiating could be very extreme and detrimental to their health, the payoff was well worth the chance. If shit goes does go south, he was contemplating a contingency plan. A self-preserving contingency plan. He was so deep in his thoughts that he never saw the person walking up on him in the shadows until the passenger's door was suddenly snatch open and illuminating the interior.

"What the fuck!"

"What's up Ice Pick!?" he asked snickering seeing the surprise and startle look on his face while getting comfortable.

"What the fuck is up with you Meeks!" he snapped not liking him sneaking up on him.

"Relax, man. Damn" he continued to snicker while unconsciously wiping his nose. "So, what's up?"

"So, everything is a go."

"What about our money?" he asked unable to hide the greed in his eyes.

"You will get your damn money after the job is complete."

"What?" he asked staring over at him like he had lost his damn mind. "Na, that definitely won't work."

"What do you mean that won't work? I thought you and I had a got damn agreement?"

"Oh, we do" he assured him returning his stare. "My partners understands how dangerous this job is also and requesting a down payment which is only fair. Just in case they don't make it, their families will have something to show for their actions. I know you can understand that, right?" he asked with a little smirk.

"How much are you suggesting Meeks?" he asked flatly.

"Half."

Ice knew this would be the option that faced him. He was just hoping that it wasn't mentioned. If some of them had lost their lives before getting paid, he would have gotten over like a thief in the night and he still wouldn't have sent no flowers to their funerals either. "Okay" he finally said.

"I thought you would" he replied and couldn't contain his snicker. "When can we expect that?"

"Tomorrow afternoon" he replied not liking his snickering. "I'll have two of my men give you a call. Where you want to meet?"

"Do you know where the community center is located?"

"They'll find it," he replied staring in his eyes.

"Then, I'll see them tomorrow" he said reaching for the car handle.

"Oh yeah" he said grabbing his full attention and staring in his eyes. "You nor your boys want to get low on me after receiving this down payment."

"Man, nobody is going to play you" he replied grinning.

"If yawl do" he replied ending their conversation and watching him climbing out of the car. He scan the area before moving.

Ice watched from his side view mirror as he walked back down the street until he disappeared in one of the shadows. He started up his vehicle then pulled away from the curb as Little Jon's "Act A Fool" filter out the moonroof. As he cruised back towards the city, he was in deep concentration. If things didn't go down as plan, he would take immense pleasure in blowing Meeks smart ass away. His reputation in Cherry Hill is well known, but not his heroin addiction he obtained while incarcerated at Jessup Correctional Facility two years ago. If those at the meeting knew of his addiction, they would have never conceded to his plan and back off him. Nobody should trust a junky and especially in a devious and scandalous plan, but he also knew, nobody in the city would dare take the contract they were offering. Mentioning it to the wrong person in the city could get them all taken out before they even had a chance to initiate their plan, but Cherry Hill was another thing. Those scandalous motherfuckers have done so much shit all over the city back in the day. Now, they are forced to remain in Cherry Hill isolated or risk being touched by some very vindictive and menacing people.

Thursday night, Byrd was in his county apartment near Woodlawn. He sat there thinking about Lion again. The more he thought about him the more nervousness crept into his mind. Nobody knew where he had migrated, and Road Block never shared it with anyone including his partner Monster. If he did have his location, he wasn't bluffing. He would have sent a four-man hit squad to hit him up before hitting Road Block, but that option wasn't on the table. He didn't want him creeping into town afterward and gathering any information. The simple knowledge of where the assassins were from would be his starting point. If he get their scent, he will go through Cherry Hill as quiet as a sheep grazing all the while trying to obtain more information. If he does get too close, they must be dealt with extreme prejudice and severally. There were too many ifs and wishes in this plan. Something he despised just as much as he despise the architect, Ice Pick, but the gluttony of money which is the root to all evil and obtaining Road Block's turf would make them instant King Pins. As he reflected on the possibilities smiling, Lion suddenly invaded his beautiful thoughts again and that same eerie feeling came over him, again. A feeling of dread or death knocking at his door. "Touch Road Block and you won't have to go looking for him" Byrd had informed them. He knew he will be coming with the gentle breeze and darkness. He tried to assure them. He guaranteed it.

On the night of the hit, they had decided to meet up at Sister's Place out on Reisterstown Road around ten o'clock. This would be the place of their alibi and the video cameras will attest to where they were that night. From the time they walked through the doors with their expensive attire and jewelry, women follow them with their eyes. They would be caught on tape flirting, partying, and dancing with the mature and receptive women until a little after one o'clock in the morning. According to the Baltimore City Police Department, they were well known as high-level drug distributors who were congregating together in a social environment with unknowing law-abiding citizens. How would those flirting mature women react to knowing they were flirting with some very precarious individuals? They will eventually and nonchalantly finish their drinks after Ice received a phone call.

Saturday night around nine o'clock, four cars entered the east side under the cover of darkness. Cruising up Monument Street, one car turned right onto Milton Street then parked next to a tree near Jefferson Street and killed the engine. The other three vehicles had destinations they had to get to. The two guys inside the car checked their weapons for the fourth time before checking the time. They stared up at the second-floor apartment window. Around nine-thirty, two lights went out and they stepped out of the car while standing in the shadows provided by the tree limbs. With their .38 and .45 clutched in their hands with the hammer pulled back, they stared at the front door. As the door swung open, their target never felt their presence as they crept quietly in the shadows. As he descended the steps, he was just starting to open his driver's door when he suddenly felt them, and his peripheral vision picked up their movement. He knew it was much too late as he tried to reach for his .357 on his waist. Seven bullets rip into his body spinning him around. The force of the slugs pin him against his car before sliding down the driver's door. His hand was still clutching his weapon. Gasping for air, one of the assassins stood over him.

"Good night" the voice whispers to him before extinguishing his life with a single round to his head. The same scenario was unfolding on Patterson Park and Eager, Central and Broadway and by Latrobe Homes on Greenmount. City police officers were running around like a chicken with its head cut off. Arriving at one crime scene just to hear about another two minutes later, homicide detectives were being called in from their homes to respond to certain locations.

"What the hell is going on tonight?" Detective Ron asked inspecting the crime scene. "This makes the fourth suspected high-level drug dealer to get murder in the past half hour."

"Looks like a takeover to me" his partner Det. Shitty said inspecting the bullet wounds. "All the perks seems to have been hit as they were leaving their homes."

"What the hell is going down tonight in this psychotic city?" Det. Ron asked looking for bullet casing. "Is there a party or something?"

"Yeah, they are having a party over at the 5th Regiment tonight" he replied standing up and staring down at the bullet ridden body. "If this is a take-over, the body count will definitely rise" Shitty shared his opinion.

"No doubt about that" he agreed staring at his young protégé. "The four perks have extensive police records but none of them have been arrested in over eight years. So, why now? There is no indication that they were in the drug game again or they would have surely come through the department again" Detective Ron mention scratching his head. "I don't know what's going on, but rest assure, this is not over until the East Side Boyz say so" he told him hardening his eyes.

At the Old School Party being held at the 5th Regiment Armory, Road Block and Monster were waiting on their lieutenants to arrive. They were well over an hour late and both men intuition was starting to ring. It was completely out of character that all of them would be so late especially Romeo. Women and dancing was his two passions. A simple call would have sufficed Road Block or Monster, but none came. Every time a group would appear at the entrance they would stare intensely. Each time it weren't them then they would peek at one another.

"What time is it?" Monster asked checking his diamond and gold Bulova watch.

"It's time to go" Road Block replied getting to his feet. "Something is not right" he said downing his drink while keeping his eyes fixed at the main entrance. The bottles of liquor that they brought with them were left at the table. As they made their way towards the entrance, their eyes stayed fixed on anyone who they felt was a little too close or had their hands hidden. If a person divert their eyes suspiciously, they will peek at him to make sure he wasn't following them. Once outside, they got to the outer perimeter of the crowd then scanned everything around them. They each called one of their lieutenants but didn't get a response. Retrieving their weapons by the State Center subway station trash can, they proceeded up Eutaw Pl. turning left on Dolphin Street. They took in every movement that caught their eyes. Turning onto Madison Street, Road Block's intuition started ringing again. He nudged Monster to put him on point about the approaching group of guys. The group stayed in the shadows as they studied them closely. It was their attire that made both men retrieve their weapons from their waist and clutched it in their hands, Tim's, jeans, and black hoodies pulled up on their heads. The light reflecting off the chrome of one of the weapons is what alerted them as gun fire suddenly erupted from Tiffany Court. The distinct sound of a street sweeper caused both men to dive over the hood of a park car as the sounds of the rounds struck it. Rat-A-Tata as the windows were suddenly shattered. An eerie smile came to both men faces.

"Seems like old times, huh?" Monster smiled over at him.

"Niggers will be niggers" he smiled back at him. "You ready?"

"Let's do this" he said as they each shot three rounds from their Glock .40 over the trunk and front hood then moved in opposite directions using the park cars as cover and a shield. As the assailant's fire where they once were, they suddenly appeared three cars away catching them in a small cross fire. Both guys concentrated on the two guys with the street sweepers. They fired three more rounds revealing their new position but finding their targets. Both guys slumber to the ground. With Lion's persistence to learn how to handle a weapon when he visit him, Road was very prolific with his Glock. He caught another guy sticking his head up a little too high to peek. The round skip off the hood blowing the top of his cranium off. Unable to watch everything, a guy retrieved the AK and sprayed both areas forcing them to take cover again. Three more rounds were discharged before they moved again except neither saw the two guys sneaking between the park cars. As Road looked over the hood, he spotted them.

"Watch your back!" he shouted at Monster. Just as he turned, two guys stepped from between the cars. Before Monster could react, they lit him up. He was dead before he hit the ground. Road shot five rounds at them catching both center masses. The street sweeper was being reloaded as he heard the empty clip hit the ground. The moans and groans of the two guy he just shot could be heard as they tried to crawl for cover. As he moved further down the block, he heard an order being given. "Move!" Footsteps could be heard converging on his location. He had to move as the bullets from the street sweeper follow his shadow. Springing up suddenly, he took the guy off his feet with two rounds, but at a cost. He was hit twice. Once in the stomach and the other on the left side of his chest.

"Aaggghhh, shit!" he groan from the impact while staying low but moving.

"He's down! He's down! Move motherfuckers! Move!"

While clutching his stomach, he kneel between two cars bleeding profusely and waited. As they closed the distance on his last position, he sprung up again catching one fatally and another in the shoulder but catching two more rounds for his trouble. He rolled off the front hood and fell back onto the ground as bullets rain on his position. Bleeding profusely and gasping for air, he felt very weak and disorientated. The rounds inside of him felt like hot pokers. Coughing up blood while having difficulty breathing, he knew he wouldn't see the morning sun rise.

"He's down!" another voice alerted the others.

A smile came to his face as he stared up at his assassins while still clutching their weapons.

"What the fuck are you smiling about?" Meeks asked snarling while clutching a .357 Magnum and standing over him as the others joined him.

"I think he likes you, Meeks" one of his boys chimed snickering as the faint sounds of sirens could be heard in the distance.

"If you think this shit is over, it's not" he whispers while trying to gain his breathe.

"Oh, it's over motherfucker" Meek smiled down at him while pulling back the hammer.

"Not until my little brother come home" he smiled up at him then coughing out more blood. "He will sniff you out like a prey and everybody that's involved will get touched. Remember, I told you" he tried to inform them with an impish smile.

"If he does come sniffing around, he'll be joining you" Meek smiled down at him then started snarling again.

"Nigger, you won't hear him coming until its' too late. Tell the motherfucker that hired you that he signed their fate in blood, but he will be last to feel his retribution" he chuckled staring at them individually with menacing eyes then spitting up more blood while still gasping for air and winching from the pain of his wounds.

"He won't hear us coming just like you didn't" he snarled squeezing the trigger. The sound from the Magnum as deafening as the sirens were getting nearer.

Staring down Madison Street, flashing lights of patrol cars could now be seen getting closer. "Bounce" ordered Meeks. They ran through a court yard then piled into their cars parked on McCulloh Street and left the area. Driving down MLK Blvd., they saw several police cars responding to the crime scene from their rear-view mirror. Ten minutes later, they were in the confines of their beloved Cherry Hill and now nervously laughing. Parking at the community center, they piled out and joined the others that were standing around drinking and smoking blunts. Meeks stepped away from the festivities to call Ice Pick. He waited patiently until he answered.

"Yeah, is it done?" was the first question he asked staring over at his other accomplices.

"Yeah" he replied smiling at a young lady walking pass flirting.

"Are you sure they are dead?" he asked adamantly.

"I personally put one in this guy Road Block's head" he replied lightly chuckling.

"Did he say anything?"

"He was uttering some bullshit" he burst out laughing.

"What the fuck did he say nigger!?" he shouted causing unwanted eyes to fall on him.

"Some bullshit about his younger brother coming home and will sniff us out" he replied still lightly snickering then asked. "Who is his younger brother?"

"Nobody you need to concern yourself with" he replied staring over at Byrd peeking at him.

"If that little nigger become a problem, just give me a call" he offer his service.

"Hopefully, he won't."

"So, when can we pick up the balance of our money?"

"I'll call you tomorrow."

"Alright, I got to go. I have this young freak waving me over" he shared ending their conversation.

As Ice Pick place his cell down on the table, he took a big hit from his glass of Hennessy then lean back in his chair. Only time will reveal if Lion comes to town or remain secluded. He was hoping that he remained secluded. If Byrd is correct, he will be coming, and if he does, they will be waiting on him. If he comes to town trying to make any noise, he will be taken out without any hesitation or remorse.

At three o'clock in the morning, the telephone ringing woke him up.

"Who in the hell can that be?" he asked rolling over and staring at the clock then at the strange number. Only when he stared at the area code, 410, did he recognize that someone from home was calling him. Only two people from home had his number and this wasn't one of them. "Hello?"

"Excuse the hour, please" the woman's sultry voice apologized. "Is this Lion?"

"Lion?" he repeated not hearing his street name in over a decade. "Who is this?"

"Kalila (Beloved). We were in fifth grade together."

"Kalila?" he mention thinking. "Misty?"

"Yes" she lightly giggled. "You beat up Rhino because he was being very disrespectful to me, Malik (Owner)."

"Wow" he chuckled sitting up in bed. "I remember that. How are you?"

"I'm fine, but I'm calling because I have some disheartening news."

"Is my brother, okay?" he instantly asked.

"No, I'm sorry to inform you. He was murder earlier tonight with my brother while attending an old school party at the 5th Regiment Armory."

"What!" he said swinging to his feet to the floor. "What happen?"

"The streets are eerily silent right now."

"Can I reach you on this number?"

"Yes, it's my cellular."

"Thanks for the information."

"Sorry to be the bearer of unwelcome news after so many years."

"So am I, but I do appreciate the call."

"Goodnight, Lion and you have my condolences."

"Thanks, good night, Misty" he said placing the phone back into its cradle. He got to his feet and walked over towards his balcony then pushing open the French doors. He stepped outside staring out at his massive front yard. He's been living peacefully outside of Atlanta since leaving Baltimore. The four-bedroom, five-bathroom Cape Cod house he stumble upon has been his place of tranquility and solitude for almost ten years. Finding this diamond in the rough was strictly by chance. The four thousand square feet house has been on the foreclosure list for three years and desperately needed a complete over-haul. The house was an eye sore for the residence that live on the street. They would take turns cutting the grass. Paying just under four-hundred G's for the house, he invested an additional two-hundred and fifty thousand for the remodeling and furnishing. With certain attributes included, the house was recently appraised for nine-fifty but with a bidding war, it could easily get a little over a million for her. With the steady insistence from his neighbors to see the remodeling, he allowed for a tour one Saturday for an hour. Motherfuckers he knew didn't live in the neighborhood came snooping around. Walking through the finish product, he could see the envy in most of their eyes. Numerous offers was given to him. The one for a million-two almost had him packing his shit, but this was home.

When Road Block received an anonymous letter with only a telephone number inside, he study the area code 404 then looked it up. ATL. He instantly called the number. Hearing Lion's voice after disappearing three years previously, he was overly elated. He informed Monster that he had some place to go for a couple of days and took the first flight out from Thurgood Marshall Airport. When he first came down for a visit, he instantly fell in love with the place and semi-privacy it provided. They would go in the back yard every morning to hit the heavy bag, lift weights and box, like they did when he was younger. He introduce Road Block to the technics of shooting then they would shoot his handguns and rifles in the afternoon at a three-inch-thick metal slab. Road Block seems to fall in love with handguns especially the German made Glock .40 besides becoming very prolific over the years. The time they spent together was always needed by them. Their visits revealed just how much they missed and loved one another. With their father locked away for life and their mother's choosing the crack pipe and dope over their child or children, they formed a strong bond. Road had promise to get out the game the first of the year and move down south. Now, it appears he must return home to bury the only person he absolutely loved then to seek those that were responsible for his early demise.

Pressing 4-1-1. "Operator, how may I direct your call?"

"Yes, ma'am" he replied. "Will you connect me to the Hartfield-Jackson International, please?"

"Just a moment as I make that connection for you."

"Thank you" he replied hearing the phone ringing.

"Good morning, how may I direct your call?"

"Yes ma'am, good morning. I need a flight around nine o'clock in the morning to take me to Baltimore, Maryland."

"We have several flights departing around that time" she informed him. "How will you be traveling coach or first class?"

"First class."

"We have a Delta Flight 124 leaving at nine and it's a direct flight. Would you like to reserve a seat?"

"Yes, please."

"May I have your name?"

"Malik Mohammad."

"Do you desire a round flight ticket?"

"No ma'am, one way."

"May I have your credit card numbers, please?"

"Just a moment" he said getting it then reading the numbers to her then waited for a confirmation number.

"Okay, everything is set for you Mr. Mohammad. I hope you enjoy your flight and thank you for choosing Delta."

"You're welcome" he replied ending their conversation. Staring up at the star filled night, Misty came back to him causing a small smile to crease his lips. When guys used to tease her about her dark ebony complexion back at Tench Tilghman Elementary-Middle on Patterson Park Ave., he use to get piss. Not because he liked her or anything, but because people could be so cruel unnecessarily, and he didn't particularly like it. He stayed in his lane when he witness these antics from those guys even though it was hard for him. The more he stared into her large doe like eyes, she seem to hypnotize him like a deer staring in the headlights of an on-coming car. Allowing him to see her and not just the sensual aspects that he never took notice of before like her blooming breasts, thighs, medium lips, and very sexy smile. Although only twelve and still a virgin, he had sexual desires building for her, but he wouldn't know what to do if she did surrender herself to him. Although they always shared pleasant greetings, neither of them made anything special out of it.

It was the day he was heading to the cafeteria that the shit hit the fan for him and revealed his whole card, a small group had congregated laughing at Rhino humiliating her, again. She stood her ground as usual but was slowly sub-coming to the constant belittling insults. When tears suddenly flowed from her eyes, he witness her vulnerability for the first time, and it touched his heart. He finally broke his humble disposition as something seem to have snapped inside of him as he aggressively approach the crowd.

"Say another harsh word to her and I'll put my foot up your ass!" he said pushing some guys aside and stepping between them while gently pushing her back.

"You need to step off freshman."

"Na, your punk ass needs to step off. Only a bitch ass motherfucker try to embarrass a young lady and weak ass men stands around laughing and giggling at it like little bitches" he told them staring them in their eyes individually. "Now, like I was saying" he stated staring directly back into Rhino eyes. "Say something else slick out your mouth about Misty, Mr.

Big Stuff. Go ahead. I dare your punk ass" he invited him glaring slightly up at him.

"Nigger."

"Nigger!" he repeated invading his personal space and causing him to slightly rock backward. "I'm no motherfucking nigger bitch but I damn sure know how to act like one" he assured him staring up into his eyes coldly. "You or your bitch ass friends couldn't handle the nigger in me" he informed him then peeked back at his friends. "You want to impress your bitch ass boyfriends. Say another word about her while I'm standing here. Go ahead, please" he requested with a slight smile. "Impress your friends Rhino" he urged him.

Rhino stared in his eyes and saw the slight threat, but he was taller and heavier. If he didn't step up, what would his boys think? What will the women think? Being a senior, he didn't want to appear scare of a seventh grader, so he said. "Fuck you and that black, nappy head, ugly ass bitch."

Before the last syllable escape between his lips or knew what was happening or enjoy the smirk that had tried to come to his face, Lion was hitting him with lefts and rights until he hit the floor then step back to allowing him to get to his feet. Shock, he scurried to his feet spitting out blood.

"Come on bitch" he invited putting his hands up to defend himself. Lion evaded his right hand then easily beat him down astounding his friends and on-lookers. A stiff jab follow by a straight right and left hook put him almost to sleep. His body fell towards the floor like a tree that had been cut down. His hands never raise to protect him from hitting face first. Lion stepped over his semi-unconscious body and address his little crew.

"Anybody else got something to say to her or snicker like some little bitch?" he asked staring at the guys coldly with a slight snarl. "I'm Malik and Misty is a particularly good friend of mine. Put it out there you bitch motherfuckers, whoever disrespects her is disrespecting me and you don't want to do that or maybe you do? The option is yours" he said with a slight smirk. "Misty, go to lunch and I do apologize for the vulgarity" he said in a soft voice causing her to slightly smile and stare up at him admirable. She stuck her tongue at Rhino as she walked away as he struggle to gain his balance. Lion was already heading in the opposite direction.

That night while he was home listening to the radio, he kept asking himself the same question over and over again. Why did he do that? He had step so far out of character and that surprise the hell out of him. What will his brother say? Did he do the right thing? All of these questions flooded his mind simply because he step out of his lane. He had caught a couple of Misty girlfriends trying to edge her on towards him a couple of times after the incident, but she was much too shy to step up and he was just as shy to approach her. With the display he revealed easily dismantling Rhino, his nonthreatening geek impression whole card was now shot to hell. He had been flying under the radar since first grade and three months into his freshman year in middle school; a simple act of chivalry or compassion had unclothed him and there was nothing that he could do about it now except wait to see what transpire.

By the next morning, those attending Tench Tilghman had heard of the incident and how easily Rhino had gotten beaten down. Most hadn't heard of Lion and the few that did never knew he was good with his hands. Hearing how easily he took out Rhino, other so-called tough guys came to take a peek at him, so that they didn't make the same mistake while the young ladies wanted to take another peek at this geek hiding the image of a knight in shining armor. He purposely arrived late at school which is out of character. He initially started to play hooky and go to the main library down town or ride the rails all day but thought better of those ideals. If Road Block or one of his friends, and he damn sure didn't know or could recognize all of them, were to stumble upon him, they would have definitely snitch on him immediately and the possibility of Road Block being at one of the next stops was a sure bet. Catching Road Block's wrath or hands as the penalty for breaking one of his rules established to keep him safe from the streets and five-o, he thought better on his thoughts. So, he arrived at school just as first period was beginning.

He was sitting in his seat staring out the window when his peers started filtering into the math class as incoherent whispers filled his ears. Later, as he casually walked through the hallways that morning, he kept catching guys peeking at him or subtly nodding in his direction. Those that have been watching him or slightly knowing him since he first enter the school in third grade was surprised to see it was him that everybody was whispering about. They had only known him as Malik but the perceived geekish sheep was actually a wolf. Profanity wasn't really a part of his daily vocabulary, and he didn't wear his pants sagging off his ass or wore any other type of attire that would give him the impression or image of a young thug in training. His shirts were always press and tuck inside his pants. Dress slacks and soft bottom shoes dominated his wardrobe because of his big brother, he would wear jeans, pull over hoodies with Tim's or Rock Ports during in climate weather only. He seem to favor the winter months and the style of attire it brought. His fade was always kept fresh with a razor shaping his outline.

As students search for his street name, someone revealed that his name was Lion. As he walked into the cafeteria, there was a noticeable pause as he walked towards the food line. After purchasing a tuna fish sandwich and a salad, he brought two bottles of water then went to his usual location to eat by the far-right wall. He bowed his head and said a quick pray before biting into the tuna fish sandwich. Several young ladies walked pass smiling and openly flirting with him. These same young ladies used to lightly snicker at him mainly because of his attire and perceived geekish disposition, but now, they wanted him to notice them and excuse their previous disposition. He was half way through his meal when Misty walked in with three of her girlfriends. As she proceeded towards the lunch line, it was evident that she was searching for somebody by the way she was scanning the room. As he follow her with his eyes, she paid for her lunch with a lunch ticket then found a table to eat at. As they began eating their lunch, her eyes were still scanning the cafeteria. Five minutes into her meal, she stared intensely at his location before finally recognizing him.

"I'll be back" she suddenly announced getting to her feet and grabbing her tray.

"Where are you headed Jamila (beautiful)?"

"To properly introduce myself to my black knight, Chocolate" she informed her giggling then turning and proceeding in his direction. After introducing herself, she didn't have the vaguest idea what to say to him or if he will even be receptive, but that didn't deter her. She was on a mission. The closer she got to him the more her heart started to flutter, and her breathing became spasmatic. "Hi Malik" she said louder than intended.

He lifted his head from his book surprise to see her standing there with her tray in her hands. She had crept up on him and that usually didn't happen to him. An uncontrollable smile came to his face as he took in the contour of her budding body as he appeared to slightly become hypnotize staring into her mahogany brown doe like eyes. "Hey Misty" he finally said returning her stare. "What's up?"

"May I have a seat?" she requested slightly smiling.

"Sure, you brought your tray" he replied marking his page before closing the book.

"Thank you" she replied placing her tray down then peeking over at her girlfriends before taking her seat. "What is your street name?"

"What makes you think I have a street name?" he inquired shoving some lettuce into his mouth.

"Every person in the hood have a street name" she replied smiling. "What is yours?"

"Some people call me Lion" he replied shoving some sweet peppers into his mouth while returning her stare.

"Yeah, that's the name I heard" she revealed grinning. "Why did you come to my aid three yesterday?" she blurted out.

"I asked myself that same question" he replied slightly hardening his eyes while wiping his lips with a tissue.

"Easy, big boy" she replied giggling at the seriousness that suddenly engulfed his enchanting eyes. "I really wanted to thank you for what you did for me."

"Not necessary" he replied finishing his lunch. "Why do he constantly keep getting at you?"

"He likes what he see but I don't" she replied slightly hardening her eyes. "He's much darker than I am but you wouldn't know it by him calling me darky and midnight" she slightly snarled. "I told him repeatedly that I wasn't interested in him, but you know how guys can be."

"Some guys" he corrected her.

"Yeah, some guys" she replied slightly smiling. "Where do you live?"

"Flag House. What about you?"

"I live near Eastern Avenue at The Homes. How come nobody really know you?"

"Apparently, somebody does if you have my street name" he replied staring in her doe like eyes again. "Nobody knows me mainly because I usual stay in my lane" he replied watching two young ladies smiling over at him then wiggling their fingers.

"Wasn't you scare of Rhino?"

"Should I have been?" he asked staring at her curiously.

"He's so much bigger and taller than you."

"You know it's not the size of the dog" he replied with a coy smile.

"It's the fight up in him" she finish the quote grinning. "Where do you hang out?"

"Mainly at the Billie Holiday statue" he replied grinning.

"What do you do all the way over there?" she asked surprise by his answer.

"Read" he said lifting his book.

"Read?" she replied slightly giggling. "Did you mean what you said yesterday?"

"I mean most of the things I say but you have to be more specific" he said still admiring her eyes.

"So, we can be friends?" she asked with apprehension.

"I've been wanting to meet you since the third day of school" he confess slightly smiling.

"I've been wanting to meet you also" she revealed lightly giggling.

"With the introduction out of the way, I hope we do become friends."

"With the girls peeking at you more now because you beat down Rhino, I hope it doesn't interfere with our friendship" she stated staring deeply into his eyes as two young ladies were walking pass smiling in his direction.

"I didn't want or desire this spot light that I place on myself for getting out my lane" he slightly snarled.

"Yes, you did" she said smiling at another girl walking pass to get a closer look at him. "And I for one appreciate it tremendously" she shared ignoring the slight snarls of two girls walking pass.

"Well, I have to go" he suddenly announce gathering his debris and getting to his feet, but she was moving just as fast.

"Where are you headed?" she heard herself asking unconsciously.

He pause to stare in her eyes before answering. "To where the lies are buried" he said with a smirk.

"Where?" she asked openly confused.

"To where the lies are buried Misty" he repeated grinning. "The library, young lady" he replied with a coy.

"Cute" she admitted giggling as she followed him towards the trash receptacles.

"Later" he said dumping his trash and placing the tray on the cart then they went in separate directions.

As she rejoined her girlfriends, she couldn't contain the broad smile that had engulfed her face.

"Damn, Jamila" her girl stated as she reclaimed her seat.

"What Chocolate?" she asked staring at the swag in his walk as he walked out the cafeteria.

"Girl, you were drooling all over him" described Sweets giggling.

"I don't drool" she denounce her comment.

"I'll be damn" Monica counter. "If you didn't have that bib on, your saliva would be running down the front of your shirt" she said as her girls giggled at her expression.

"Yawl are tripping" she replied waving them off.

"Well, one thing for sure. A whole lot of bitches are peaking at his geekish ass now" Sweets said peeking at two girls staring at her while snickering.

"Let them" she replied catching the slight snarls of the two more girls walking pass. "I have the inside track with him."

"I hope you do something with it. Lion is a very handsome guy" Monica shared her opinion.

"He's that Monica and so much more with his sexy Asiatic like eyes" she giggle over at her.

As Lion casually walked towards the library, he had an unconscious smile on his face. After studying Misty face up close and personal, she is even more attractive than he thought. Her eyes almost caused him to blush as she stared into his eyes, but he don't do any damn blushing no matter what a girl may say. He's not saying that he wasn't on shaky grounds while interacting with her because he was. As he walked into the library, he acknowledge Ms. Robinson with his smile while proceeding towards the black literature department. He took his usual seat then reached inside his bookbag and pulled out the book he was reading called "ATM and J-Lo" then got comfortable. Before he started reading, he stared out the window for about ten minutes just taking in the scenery. As he started devouring the book again, he paused to reflect on the scenery that the author was creating when his peripheral vision caught a subtle movement. Lifting his head, he spotted Misty approaching and a perplex expression came to his face.

"Yeah, what's up?"

"What are you doing Saturday?" she asked staring down at him.

"Why?"

"House music is being played at the festival in Druid Hill Park."

"Na, not my scene" he replied returning her stare.

"Supposed I ask you to come just for me" she inquired with a slight smile.

"Don't" he replied returning her stare.

"What are you going to do Saturday?" she asked disappointed in his refusal to escort her.

"Not attending anything in the park" he replied with a slight smirk.

"What are you doing Lion?" she asked not liking the little smirk on his face

"It's not my scene Misty" he reiterated again trying to contain the hardness that usually reside in his eyes.

"I don't like the way this friendship is materializing" she confess slightly pouting.

"I'll be at the library for the first couple of hours reading or studying that SAT Book then I'll find a basketball court to hoop at and that's usually up at Chadwick" he shared as the explanation soothe her feelings.

"After you play ball, what are you going to do?"

"It all depends on if my big brother don't pick me up Friday after school. If he does, he'll keep me close until late Sunday afternoon."

"Is that how you spend your weekends?"

"I'm very content" he slightly smiled. "What do you do on the weekends?"

"Me?" she suddenly flash her radiant smile. "I hit the streets hard with my girls. We are all around the west side. From Park Heights to Edmondson Village, we are constantly on the move. By the time night fall, we are hanging at or near Shake and Bake. Do you skate?"

"I know how but I don't go to Shake and Bake."

"Where do you go? Out in Woodlawn" she inquired.

"I don't skate Misty. I just know how" he said slightly smiling at her expression, again. "I don't hang out Misty" he reiterated again.

"Nowhere?"

"Nowhere" he slightly smiled.

"So, you really are a geek."

"Sticks and stones" he replied grinning, and he could see that she didn't appreciate it. So, to infuriate her more, he said "I have less than twenty minutes before my next class."

"And you would like to spend it reading, huh?"

"Honestly, yeah" he admitted seeing her fury exploding her eyes.

"Well, I won't disturb you anymore" she said sarcastically.

"Thank you" he smiled at her as she suddenly turned mumbling something as she walked away. Her phat little ass was jiggling a little extra as she damn near stomp her feet through the floor. A coy smile consumed his face as she turned down the next available isle. For the next three years, he and Misty would become extremely close friends despite him not catering to her needs or petty desires. He was constantly checking her for certain prissy dispositions she tried to display especially when they were out together. One thing that he could not ignore was that every summer her body would change physically, and her appearance did also. The beauty that was once hidden from the eyes of others revealed itself. They were at Dru Hill Park swimming pool when he first saw her silhouette in a tan bikini, and she took his breath away. She openly blushed at his expression. Her breast were so firm and full looking that he wanted to cup one on his hand. From her smooth acme free deep mocha complexion to her sexy naval ring, she got when she turned fifteen. She had his full attention and admiration.

She also caught the attention of all the young drug dealers at the pool who were fishing for new prey and also those dealers from around their neighborhood. Her flaring hips and phat little ass wiggling like Jell-O had the dealers suddenly jockeying for position. Her smile was infectious and had everyone whispering words of admiration in her ears as she walked pass, but she could only see and hear Lion's alluring words. Although he didn't have the high fashionable clothes that the drug dealers possess, he was very attentive to her and intellectual. For some strange reason, she found those traits extremely sexy. He would tell her things when they met at the Billie Holiday statue that left her thinking and there is nothing more intriguing to her or any girl than a guy that could make them think. He didn't attend parties, hang on the corners or with a group of guys, if you wanted to locate him, go to the Billie Holiday statue first then one of the numerous libraries around the city especially the main library down-town on Cathedral Street.

There were a whole lot of young ladies vying for his attention over the next three years, but he never allow it to go to his head. He stayed humble. Although most made their intentions vividly clear, he was flatter but never tasted their forbidden fruit. Misty was the pendulum of his heart and the air that sustained him. When they would hang out together, he was always a gentleman even when she openly flirted with him sexually. The first time they kissed passionately was on her sixteenth birthday and they promise to lose their virginity with the other after graduating high school. Neither suspected they would never experience that bliss again. Who could have foretold him getting locked up for murder two weeks later and spending the next three years incarcerated?

So, he was truly taken by surprise when he was walking out of the library across from Dunbar High when SWAT would swoop down on him. Confused and unable to follow their instructions while staring at all the weapons pointing at him, they snatched his book bag off of him then slammed him viciously onto the concrete and searched him from head to toe twice. Being taken to the East Side Police precinct on Edison Highway, he had inquired numerous of times, why he was being detained, but he never got any response. Being black that privilege is instantly taken from you. Seeing he was being escorted to homicide, he was suddenly gripped by fear. Why homicide? He has never handled a gun in his life and damn sure haven't shot one or killed anybody. When the two white detectives walked in, they instantly became belligerent. Accusing him of shooting some guy up in Park Heights. He tried repeatedly to explain that he have never been to the Heights because like so many other east siders, trouble would follow them. The further he have ever venture on this side of town was to Mondawmin Mall or down town to buy some clothes. Occasionally, he would catch the speed line (subway) to Johns Hopkins Station to buy his favorite meal from out of Northeast Market on Monument Street. He never consider getting off at Upton Station to hang around Pennsylvania and North although he was very curious about both locations. Road Block took him to these spots often, but he wasn't permitted to go alone. So, the more these detectives called him a liar and a nigger. The more his snarl appeared until he gradually became silent. Nothing that came out of their mouths was coherent to him anymore. He shut down on them.

At his bail review, a Mr. Thomas from the law firm of Blackmon and Burns was there to represent him. He was hired by Road Block. Although he didn't possess a juvenile record and revealed that he was a straight A student, the judge gave him a no bail status because of the violence associated with the crime. As hard as Mr. Thomas fought for him, he didn't hide his discuss in the judge's decision especially when a white boy getting caught with a key of heroine was released on ten-thousand-dollar bond. After leaving the court room, he went straight to the prosecutor's office to retrieve the alleged evidence they had to connect him to the crime. What he witness as evidence was a bunch of bullshit circumstantial evidence and he voiced his opinion. Who are these alleged C. I's (Confidential Informants or snitches)? The prosecutor tried to discuss a plead offer, but he wasn't feeling it and he told them that Mr. Mohammad wouldn't be feeling it also. He assured them he would have the discussion with his client because he has to not because he wanted to. Lion couldn't understand how they could be asking him to take a plea of ten years for a murder he didn't commit. The bullshit was to perplex for him to get his level head around. The evidence they had could be attributed to any person that was black and he just so happen to be black.

When he walked into the court room on his trial date, he search the court room until his eyes connected with Road Block sitting in the back row. Monster was sitting right next to him glaring over at the many cops on the opposite side of the isle. Wearing a brown two-piece suit with his brown Stacy Adams shoes, he looked very professional but young. Only when the judge entered, did he and the others had to get to their feet. Only then did he see Misty and a small smile creased his lips as he took his seat. As he listen to the circumstantial evidence, his mind was on the physical evidence they needed to put into evidence, but none materialized. Who in the fuck is these two guys claiming to have seen him shooting the guy down at Garrison and Park Heights? Staring over at the white jurors, he couldn't but help wondering where were his peers? The ones that was supposed to be judging him. Where were they? The individuals he was staring over at was definitely not his peers and he doubted if they even lived in the city at all. The bullshit trial lasted two days and he was naturally found guilty then sentence to twenty-years for second degree murder. Why not first-degree murder?

As he was being escorted out the court room by correctional officers from B.C.D.C, he and Road Block held a long stare then slightly smiled at one another just before the door closed behind him. He knew Road Block will be all over those guys once they leave the court house. He was taken back to the holding cell then escorted back to the Old City Jail and place back on the juvenile section. Word of his conviction eventually made its way around the section, and nobody evaded his space or ask questions of him. He would remain there three months before a bed was finally available in one of the programs for juvenile offenders in Jessup.

The day he climbed into the bus to be taken out to Jessup was a bright sunny April morning. As he stared at the horizon, his mind was all over the place. Staring down inside the cars as they drove down 95 South, his eyes connected with an old black woman. They exchanged stares until the bus was taking their exit. In the distance, he saw the gray walls of the institution. Driving through the double steel gate, he stared up at a correctional officer holding an assault weapon staring down on them. Exiting the bus with the other criminals, he stared around at the strange unfamiliar environment. His eyes were taking in his confines until his name was called then escorted to the juvenile offenders building with seven other guys. Walking into the dormitory setting, he heard the usual slick things coming out of guys mouths, but he ignored them like he did when he was still on the streets. He found his bunk and sat upon it while he laid his bag down at his feet. He stared around at the place that would become his home. Occasionally he would catch somebody staring at him then whisper something funny to one of his partners, but they have the right to look and say wherever they choose, right? The Constitution states it, right? As with most things in a male dominated area or arenas, he was finally approached by the alpha male and three of his friends with intentions of intimidating him or with aspirations of extorting him, whichever. With his peers looking on at the routine they have witness numerous of times before, they stood or sat around waiting to see what the new guy would do. Road Block told him to never take flight but to fight. He moved with stealth speed and unleashed his control wrath upon them. He unmercifully dismantle them while ignoring their pleads for mercy. Breaking two of the guys arms while dislocating the alpha male's shoulder and breaking three fingers.

"Brother!"

A voice shouted at him causing him to cease his unmerciful attack. Turning, he stared into the eyes of a bronze complexion guy.

"I'm Mustafa (chosen one). Your case is extremely weak brother and could win it on appeal. So, don't create another charge here" he said returning his stare and watching his eyes gradually soften. "What do they call you on the streets?"

"Lion" he replied, releasing his bloody victim while returning his stare then turned and went back to his bunk. He grabbed the book he had been reading at B.C.D.C then laid back.

As the first-year crept pass, he gradually got acclimated to his unfamiliar environment and created a routine for himself. He would wake before the rising of the morning sun and do an hour of extensive exercises in the shower area before shadow boxing for six rounds. By the time the others started to stir, he would be completing his shower then waiting for breakfast. As soon as it was possible, he was off to the library. Although several guys were trying to get close to him, he wasn't being receptive. He has always been a loner and being incarcerated didn't mean he had to change who he was. He turned down every known gang approaching him about being recruited. He told them all he was already affiliated. The surprise look that came to their faces was priceless. When asked which gang he was affiliated? He corrected them saying Red, Black, and Green isn't a gang, but a statement. When one would step beyond requesting and start insisting, he would shut them down. "I came here alone, and I will survive here alone. A real man doesn't need backup to prove he's a man. A man stands alone" he told them all returning their glares or snarls. This didn't stop them from trying to recruit him and he honestly didn't mind. He did get in a lot of boxing and trying new combinations. The ass kicking's he administered to the right motherfuckers and his message to increase the peace eventually got him the tranquility he was seeking. All forms of recruitment cease including the Moslems. He walk as a male lion, alone.

While at Jessup, he acquired his GED on the first attempt and that wasn't a good image coming out of the hood. Hearing about his good fortune, individuals started approaching him about assisting them in acquiring their GED's including Mustafa. As in life and everything else, nothing is free especially while being incarcerated. His demand was very unorthodox to say the least for brothers coming out of the hood, but everybody that desire his assistance would have to oblige him. His request was simple. They would study and talk about the bible for an hour every day. He wasn't a religious type of guy, but neither was those he was going to assist. When he was asked why, a coy smile appeared on his lips. "We eat and drink to nourish our bodies so let's venture into the bible to see if it will nourish our souls." He was quick to say he was a spiritual person even before coming to Jessup.

As with most things, he had an initial question that he would ask them in the form of a proposition. "Brothers, I know yawl aren't interested in the bible and under constant duress on America's shores like we are as a black race. You must understand why we are being persecuted. I know I wanted to know why" he stared staring around into their harden eyes. "If someone can answer a simple question, I have a surprise for you" he shared with a coy smile.

"I for one don't like that smile" Mustafa replied grinning.

"Nor do I" cosigned Twin grinning too.

"All I want to know is who was Adam first wife?"

"Eve!" the majority replied confidently as he shook his head and walk away.

During some of their discussions, they found themselves in the library researching the things that he advocated especially after finding out about Lilith and why they would change her into a demon? Other things they read for instance was Deuteronomy 28:48-until he have destroyed you. Do you know of any other race that have been physically, mentally, and spiritually destroyed other than us or as enslaved as described in the bible? Or 28:49-as swift as the eagle flieth, a nation whose tongue thou shall not understand. What nation symbol is the eagle and whose tongue we did not understand? Even the brothers of Islam found themselves joining his spiritual journey, their conversations weren't about which is the true religion. The messiah Isa (Jesus) didn't advocate Christianity because Christianity didn't exist until 332 years after his death by the Roman Catholic Church. As far as Jesus is concern, he would tell them to read Hebrew 7:14. Although the Torah or Old Testament used the word "descendant" of Juda, contrasting words like offspring, rise from and other synonyms are used in later bibles like the King James version to dilute the strength of the original word. Descendent. The hour classes balloon to two hours especially when you see where the Garden of Eden actually existed and it's not on Afrika as told by our teachers and enslavers.

As far as his GED preparation classes, he had a ninety percent graduation rate. Those that failed on their first attempt acquired their GED's on their second attempt with ease after seeing where they were weak. Having private conversations with some of them, he constantly kept hearing the same words. Laws in America are bias and don't think Justice isn't peeking under that motherfucking veil that her white ass is wearing. The proof was revealed by individual cases and in some of the law books, it is proven. How can two men with the same charge have different outcomes especially when you are a person of color? How? How did he arrive where he was now confined? This was his introduction to wanting to know and understand why these bias standards or mysteries existed in law. This was when he started studying college courses on criminal law.

He don't remember when Mustafa, Twin and Two-Piece latch on to him, but they became like shadows. Four the hard way was a descriptive associated with them. If you saw three, the other one wasn't far behind. They spent the majority of their free time in the library reading and studying. They would print out old maps before the countries names were change and distribute them amongst those attending his study sessions. His three amigos got so used to going to the library with Lion that time has started elapsing rapidly especially after the first year. From the time God woke him up, he was enriching the lives of those that came into his circle. Those that came to be argumentative were instantly escorted out of their session and not permanented to attend ever again. Some had tried to get with Lion with their little clicks, but his click wasn't about drama, they turned it straight into a nightmare on them with Lion having the leading role.

Three years had suddenly zoom pass and he didn't realize it until his eighteenth birthday. He had kept his mind so distracted that he found himself lightly laughing. The letters and pictures from Misty was also a contributor for the lapse of time. He had taken her first letters and compare them to the ones she was writing to him now. An impish grin always crept across his lips, there was so much maturity in her words now. She would describe how his embrace would make her knees slightly buckle or how kissing him would ignite the ambers between her thighs. On her eighteenth birthday, she sent him two pictures standing very provocative in a two-piece bathing suit. His dick instantly became hard. He shared her picture with Mustafa, Two Piece and Twin, but the others would have to conjure the image they describe to them with their impish smiles. He was in the yard having one of his usual conversations with the brothers when CO Jefferson was heading in their direction. She had one of the sexiest walks among the female CO's for a woman in her early thirties.

"Lion" she address stopping in front of the group.

"Queen Jefferson" they chime together placing their hands over their hearts admiring her eyes.

"Kings" she replied trying in vain to contain her smile. Since Lion came in on the scene, men are actually starting to act like men and not niggers. She admired the young man for using his reputation in a positive way like creating his GED and study classes. Some of the most vicious and murderous motherfuckers was sitting around like men and discussing things instead of grabbing a knife or a gun to settle a simple disagreement. His imprint is very evident. Staff members and correctional officers included advocated keeping him until he was twenty-one then send him to an adult population. The Commissioner reviewed his record then forward his papers the very next day. He would remain until he was twenty-one. "Your lawyer is here?"

"That's strange" he smiled getting to his feet. They were the same height when he initially arrived, but now he was easily five inches taller and steadily growing. "Brothers, one love."

"One love Lion" they replied, admiring Officer's Jefferson's ass as she walked away. He could vaguely hear their moans and groans from the fellas as he fought to contain his snicker and eyes.

"You will get your chance to admire it too Lion" she shared nonchalantly while peeking over her shoulder at him. Her coy smile caused him to suddenly smile also. Walking up the metal steps, she seem to walk exceedingly slow, but he wasn't complaining. Her pants revealed the imprint of her flaring hips as the pantie line disappeared around her thighs. His only regret was they had to climb just one floor. "Did you enjoy?" she asked allowing her eyes to go towards his dick as a slight smile came to her lips. "Yeah, you was starting to enjoy it" she suddenly giggled causing his smile to become broader. "Right here" she stated opening the door revealing two men sitting inside.

"Come in, Malik" invited the black lawyer getting to his feet. "I'm Saada (Happiness) Hammonds from Justice 4 All" he shared shaking his hand. "Your case were mentioned by several of our former clients and what you have been doing the past three years during your incarceration? Very impressive, young man" he complimented offering him a seat then his eyes became profoundly serious. "So, my boss put a team of investigators on your case last year. We discovered that the prosecutor's office neglected to reveal certain things to your previous lawyer" he shared causing Lion to glare over at him. "Apparently, the officers on the case was working for a drug dealer in the Park Heights section of the city and for some strange reason wanted you securely tuck away."

"What?" he commented instantly snarling.

"Do you know why?" he inquired staring deep into his eyes for a lie.

"No, sir" he replied honestly returning his stare.

"Well, we have our suspicions but nothing to substantiate them" he shared slightly smiling. "Excuse the question, but is anybody in your family associated with the drug game?"

"My immediate family? No, sir" he lied, never averting his eyes. "Not the way you mean" he replied. "Have you talked or seen my mother?"

"Yes, we have" he admitted.

"Do she look like somebody benefitting from the drug game?" he asked not really expecting an answer.

"No, Malik" he replied solemnly. "You are her only child, huh?"

"Yes, sir" he replied slightly hardening his eyes. "What is this all about Mr. Hammonds?"

"Well, those two witnesses against you were charged with perjury last month" he informed him.

"Perjury?" he repeated staring at him then over at his associate. "Why?"

"That is the million-dollar question" he replied returning his stare.

"The reason why I'm here is because the prosecutor's office have an offer on the table for five-million dollars for your duress and false incarceration."

"Twenty or they could kiss my ass" he recited slightly snarling. "Or we can take this straight to the civil courts. I would love to express the dangers I've experience and witness while falsely incarcerated, especially about the three attempts on my life because I refuse to be gang affiliated" he included to the lie.

"I can only imagine the image" he replied solemnly. "I will get right back at you" he replied.

"You know where to find me" he said getting to his feet. "Enjoy your day sir and express my gratitude to your boss also."

"I will" he assured him shaking his hand then watching him being escorted out the room and down the hallway.

"Good news I hope" Officer Jefferson said staring up into his eyes.

"Better than good Queen" he smiled down into her grayish eyes causing her to blush as she usually did.

"Do you know you have a very provocative stare?" she asked leading him back to the metal stairs.

"I hope it's only at you. I wouldn't want to give these guys any false impressions" he smiled staring in her eyes as he walked down the steps first listening to her giggle.

"Well actually" she lightly giggled. "You give Officer Monica the same provocative stare" she shared grinning.

"I must learn to hide my desires better" he smiled looking back up at her as he open the door for her to exit.

"Don't it's very flattering Malik" she said softly while walking pass and lightly brushing his hand with her fingers as she continued towards her post.

He continued towards his partners sitting on the bleachers, but he didn't join their discussion. He sat further up deciphering what Mr. Hammonds had said to him. He was set up but why? Why would anybody need him tuck away? He instantly thought about Road Block, but he wasn't big time especially with the murder of his mentor and the double life sentenced to his partner. So, what part does he play in this bullshit? He's not in the game. His partners knew that something transpired with the lawyer but wouldn't find out until he was ready to share it. They have seen this intensity in his eyes before and it wasn't good for somebody. They didn't quite understand why they called this soft-spoken young man a lion until he first revealed his claws to Shot Gun and Tuffy. Medieval didn't have shit on him. Nothing.

Later that night, he gave his partners the eye then they congregated near the fire exit door.

"What's going on Lion?" inquired Two-Piece.

"I'm going home brothers" he blurted out staring in their eyes.

"What?" said Mustafa staring at him closely. "Something transpired with your case?"

"Besides the two guys being charged with lying under oath and the officers that arrested me are being indicted. Yeah, I know it's fucked up but I'm going home brothers" he slightly smiled.

"Congratulations Lion" Twin said suddenly smiling then giving him a hug. "You know you are going to be miss."

"I will be thinking about yawl too and don't doubt that. I have never had partners before and I'm glad I allowed yawl to enter my private world" he shared sincerely while staring intensely into their eyes individually.

"Well, I for one won't miss his workouts" Mustafa mention snickering.

"Nor will I" cosigned Two-Piece as they tapped knuckles laughing.

"They are trying to give me five million for my duress, but they are going to have to give me a hell of a lot more" he said with conviction in his voice and in those sometime menacing eyes, but all they could do was burst out laughing because they knew he meant every damn word.

They eventually settled for fifteen-million dollars three months later. He had gotten acclimated to his environment and staying those extras months only gave him time to organize his thoughts. After signing some papers, his release papers was in his hands seventy-two hours. Walking back towards his cell instead of the yard, his mind was all over the place, but he had three days to organize it. As he laid on his bunk, he started mapping out his initial plans. He wasn't going to let anyone know that he was coming home or the civil case he was awarded. He wanted to surprise Road Block and especially Misty. Although she had slowed down on her writing to him over a year ago, he didn't take it personally. He knew she had a boyfriend somewhere tuck away. She was just too damn cute and phat as shit to be single. All he wanted to do is see if they could reconnect. The final three days didn't go as slow as he had expected. He was woken to a sunny sky with his partners and closest friends spending the last moments of their time with him. Mustafa, Two Piece and Twin promise to continue what he initiated including increasing the peace amongst the brothers. He promise to get with them all as soon as he hit the streets. When the bewitching hour finally arrived, they escorted him to the main hallway then they exchanged hugs.

"One love brother's" he wish them, placing his hand over his heart while staring in their eyes individually.

"One love Lion" they returned shadowing his move.

He saw the sadness starting to creep into their eyes. For the last three years, they were constantly together like shadows. From playing chess or domino to playing spades, they were connected at the hip. He included them with the offer from the warden to remain until they were twenty-one. They thought he was bullshitting them until the paper work was place in their hands. They couldn't believe what he had done for them. So, at this disheartening moment, all he could do was just wink at them as the CO open the gate for him to pass through. He was escorted to the Commissioner's office to sign his release papers and accept an envelope left by the prosecutor's office. He took the envelop then folded it and place it in his back pocket. He had acuminated a little more than twelve-hundred dollars working privately with some OG's acquiring their GED's. He walked with the CO to a waiting van that will transport him back into Baltimore City. Observing the scenery heading back to the city, everything seems so strange. Although the ride only took forty minutes on 295N, it felt like hours. For him, he wasn't free until he step out of this damn van and sat in a hot tub of bubbling water. Driving through the city, a broad smile came to his face admiring the sway of the young ladies hips and how their asses appeared in their jeans. He was expecting to get release near the J.I Building on Madison Street, but he was released at the Royal Farms Arena. Right in the heart of the city. He stood there looking around like a tourist. He eventually walked down Liberty Street towards the Radisson Hotel. He entered the lobby and requested a room for three days at least ten floors up or higher. They accommodated him with one on the fifteenth floor with a balcony over-looking the Inner Harbor. Once in his room, he open the envelope and stared at the six zeros behind the fifteen then started smiling. He grabbed his electronic key then headed right back out the door for his first destination. Wells Fargo Bank at Baltimore and Calvert Street. It was almost ten o'clock when he walked in and handed the cashier his certified check from the Baltimore City Finance Department. The look on her face cause him to smile at her as she excused herself to briefly talk to her manger then returned.

"How would you like this, Mr. Mohammad?"

"I would like fifty thousand in cash and a five-million-dollar certified check made out to Shabazz Mohammad. He would hit Mustafa, Two Piece and Twins account with twenty-five-thousand dollars each. With them being partners in crime, they will be spending the next ten years incarcerated, but they were on a completely different path since meeting and getting acquainted to Lion. The rest of the money he wanted in a saving account. Forty minutes later, he was walking out wearing an impish grin. He caught a hack (illegal cab) to Audi of Owings Mills and cut him loose after paying him twenty dollars for the ride. Walking around the lot, his eyes came to rest upon a beautiful four door metallic gray Audi A7. When one of the sales persons finally came, he was sitting on a metal box staring at the office. Oh yeah, he had a slight attitude and wish he hadn't cut his ride loose or he would have told them to kiss his ass.

"How may I help you?" the late forty white sale persons asked staring at his attire.

"How much?" he asked flatly.

"This used model have."

"I didn't ask what it have, sir" he stop him in his presentation. "How much?"

He stared over at him slightly hardening his eyes before answering. "I can let this go for thirty-thousand."

"If I was paying cash?"

He stared at him again surprise by his statement. "Straight up cash. I'll let it go for twenty-three. Is that fair?"

"Yes, sir. You can take two-thousands for yourself and hook me up with a year of car insurance" he told him extending his ID to him. Fifteen minutes later with full insurance coverage, he was pulling off the lot grinning from ear to ear. The slight factory tint on the window was just enough. Cruising back down 695, he took the Woodlawn exit then turned left onto Security Blvd. He turned left onto Windsor Mill Road and pulled up on K&G's parking lot. Buy two get one suit free and just about everything else except their shoes. He drop about two thousand dollars before forcing himself to leave. He still haven't finish considering where he would be living. Before returning to his room, he drove to a hot weed spot on Pennsylvania Avenue he heard about while locked down. Sure enough, those boys was up by the basketball courts on Fulton Avenue. He brought himself an ounce then stop at the Red Fox Lounge to buy some top papers and a bottle of Parrot Bay coconut. The OG's was swearing by it. He drove down Pennsylvania Avenue to connect to Lexington Market and brought himself some sweet and sour chicken then went to his hotel. Parking in the underground garage, he grabbed as many clothes as he could then caught the elevator to his floor. He laid everything across the bed then shot back down to the garage to retrieve whatever he had left. After hanging everything up, he walked to the radio and turned into 88.9 Morgan State. The OG's he became acquainted with only listen to jazz and he acquired a love for it although he was only nineteen. He took that hot bubble bath while enjoying the many jazzes musician playing. He reemerged a half hour later and put on some fresh underwear and a pair of shorts. He enter the communal area then started rolling up several white boys (joints) then he took them to the balcony with his drink and took a seat. Although it was only one-thirty, he had accomplished a lot his first couple of hours on the street. Staring out at the Inner Harbor, he fired up his joint. He had got acquainted with marijuana while preparing the OG's for their GED test. The quality of this weed damn near choke him to death. His lungs still haven't gotten use to hitting it from his chest like the OG's, but it always got him high as a motherfucker. He sat for hours sipping on Parrot Bay and smoking joints staring out over at the Chesapeake Bay as the orange ball in the sky slowly dissipated.

He got to his feet and went inside around eighty-thirty. He strolled straight to the bathroom to take a shower. Fifteen minutes later, he emerged and walked into the bedroom. Standing in front of the closet and staring at the clothes, he finally decided to wear a two-piece gray casual set with a pair of soft bottom slip-on Johnston black shoes and a small black brim hat. Glancing at his Movado watch, it was already ten o'clock. A little smile came to his lips as he closed the balcony door then grabbed his key and a couple of joints before exiting the room. Standing inside the descending elevator, he stared at his image from the stainless-steel doors. Stepping out in the garage, he climbed into his car and starting up the engine. Lee Morgan's "Sidewinder" filled the interior as he placed the car in gear and pulled out of the parking spot. The first thing on his agenda tomorrow is going to Sound Stage to get himself some music.

He jump on 95 South then transfer over to 695W heading towards Reisterstown. Taking his exit, he proceeded up Reisterstown Road to Identity. Pulling up on the parking lot, he found a spot several rows from the door. He sat watching the door for an hour before a used Yukon pulled up on the lot. As he watch the SUV, the driver found a spot then the occupants started stepping out. As soon as Road Block stepped out of the back door with four other guys, a broad smile came to his face. He was wearing a suit that seem to be tailor to his massive frame. The guy walking next to him must be Monster. They did make an awesome pair. As they enter the club's door, he climbed out of his car and proceeded towards the front door. He paid the ten-dollar entry fee then stayed in the shadows. Road Block and his partners were to his left sitting in a small area conversing with some women. He took a position directly across from them at the bar, so they were in his line of sight. He watched two of his partners constantly snatching women to the dance floor. He caught Road

Block on several occasions staring around like he was looking or expecting somebody. They were there about two hours when he suddenly stood up again but looking agitated and looking around with his eyes harden. He was searching for something and that was evident. He scan the place twice before his eyes rested upon him, but he didn't react. He just kept staring intensely until Monster got to his feet also and joined him staring over at him. Lion raised his glass then smiled causing Road Block to methodically walk in his direction ignoring what Monster was saying to him as Lion got to his feet to meet him.

"Malik?" he called coming closer while his smile fully consumed his face. "What the fuck!"

"Hey, Big Brother" he greeted embracing one another tightly.

"When did you come home?" he asked extending his arms still in shock.

"Yesterday."

"Yesterday. Why didn't you reach out to me?"

"I had some business to take care of first" he replied returning his smile. "You must be Monster" he implied.

"Yeah" he replied engulfing his hand in his. "Welcome home."

"Thanks" he replied then focus back on Road Block. "Can we talk?"

"Hell, yeah" he replied putting his arm around his neck and leading him to another little area right of the front door and took a seat. "What's up?"

"You still grinding for Boogie?"

"Regretfully, yeah" he admitted slightly snarling.

"Be your own boss" he told him pulling out the certified check and extending it to him.

He took the check and stared at it then shock filled his eyes. "Are you serious? Where did you get this kind of money?" he asked still staring at all the zeros.

"When corruption incarcerate an innocent man, restitution has to be paid and they paid it" he informed him slightly smiling.

"What am I going to do with all this?" he asked unable to contain his smile.

"Do what you do?" he replied returning his stare.

"Damn, thanks little brother" he said looking over at Monster and waving him over. The first thing he showed him was the certified check and he stared over at Lion smiling from ear to ear.

"This is a connection for you down in Miami" he told him extending a slip of paper to him.

"I see you have been busy" he replied accepting the slip of paper grinning.

The remainder of the evening they talked and talked and talk. Not until the lights gradually came on did, they cease their conversation. He refused Road Block invitation to stay with him. He had other things that demanded his attention. Specifically, Misty.

The next morning around eleven o'clock he was cruising the streets again. A lot has changed in the city in three short years. He headed down Pratt Street until he connected to Broadway then turned right. As he drove over the cobblestone road, he turn the corner spotting Sound Stage and parked. He walked inside and acted like a child in a candy store. He brought well over two-hundred-dollars' worth of predominately jazz CD's. Returning to his car, he placed Clifford Brown's "In Paris" and four others jazz musicians inside the five-disc player with a navigational system then open his moonroof to allow the music to filter out as he pulled away from the curb jamming. As he drove back up Broadway, he turned left onto Monument Street and proceeded past Johns Hopkins Hospital. Northeast Market was pack with Hopkins workers and students going to lunch. As usual, hackers stood around outside gawking at the women and giving out shouts looking for their next customer. He turned unconsciously on

Collington Avenue then drove past his mother's new rented house then turned left onto Jefferson Street. At Patterson Park Avenue, he turned left heading up towards Biddle Street. As soon as he turn onto Biddle, he spotted Misty sitting on her steps with several guys and girls. He parked across the street from them to admire her. They initially stared at his car before allowing their short attention span to kick in. They forgot about him in less than two minutes forcing a slight grin to come to his face. They got right get back to doing what they were doing. Smoking blunts and sipping on alcohol. He sat for a moment watching her interaction. She appears to be hooked up with a mocha complexion guy since he was sitting between her open legs in a pair of spandex shorts. The car is what held everyone's attention not him. As he open the door and climbed out, he stared straight in to her eyes. Her reaction couldn't be contained staring across the street at him. She wasn't sure if she was having another one of her dreams or not. She had so many of them over the years concerning him. As he came across the street, she never got to her feet or show any true emotions except shock.

"Hey family" he greeted continuing to stare into her eyes.

"Hi, Malik" she greeted but still remained seated as the guy stared up at him.

"Can I have a word with you?"

"Sure" she replied. "Excuse me, baby" she address the guys still staring up at him, but he never returned the guy's cold stare. As she got to her feet, she could see how tall he has gotten. As they moved away from those trying to ear hustle, she asked. "When did you come home?"

"Yesterday" he replied slightly smiling. "Damn you look good."

"Thanks, Lion" she slightly blush then peek at her boyfriend glaring at them. "You look extremely good also. Are you staying with your mother?"

"Na, I'm at the Radisson by the Inner Harbor. When can I see you?"

"I don't know" she replied staring at the guy still staring at them. "I might can see you later tonight" she replied taking another peek at her boyfriend.

"Don't get caught up" he told her slipping his cell number to her.

She took the number then discretely tucked it away against her left thigh. "Is that your new car?"

"Na, my brother" he lied.

"I'll call you sometime tonight even if I can't get away."

"Okay" he replied. "You really do look extremely sexy Misty" he slightly smiled then turned and retraced his steps back to his car then climbed back inside. He started up the engine and pulled into traffic. He watched from his side-view mirror knowing that her boyfriend was going to scrutinized her.

As she went to reclaim her seat, she couldn't ignore how handsome he had become in three short years. Her immediate concern was Lamont. How will she answer the questions that she knew he would be seeking answers? Will she be honest and watch his jealousy raise its ugly head or lie?

"Who the fuck was that?" he snorted staring at the car pulling out its parking spot.

"Malik" she replied starting another corn roll.

"Malik?" he repeated reflecting. "You ex-boyfriend?"

"Yeah" she replied watching him turning the corner.

"I thought he was locked down" he mention peeking over his shoulder at her.

"So, did I."

"What the fuck does he want?" he inquire peeking back at her again.

"Just to say hello" she lied.

"Make sure that's all he wants" he snarled over his shoulder at her. "When in the fuck did, he get out?"

"Yesterday."

"What else did yawl discuss?"

"Nothing, baby" she lied.

"He wasn't trying to patch back up with you, was he?"

"No, Lamont. I told him I was involve with you" she lied again.

"I hope he don't create no drama over what he lost, or I'll crush his bullshit" he threaten staring in her eyes. "As long as he stay in his motherfucking lane, his ass is safe."

"He will" she replied trying to assure him. If he tried stepping to Lion with his thuggish bullshit, he will get embarrassed, but she had enough common sense not to mention it. As the sun gradually started descending, she kept peeking at her watch. Why haven't he left to go stand on the corner to make his money? He was usually gone by now but tonight; he was lingering around like he knew she had something that she wanted to do. She needed him to get back into his routine so she could reach out to Lion. There was a lot of things she needed to discuss with him, especially his intentions.

Lion didn't hear from her in two days and that wasn't cool when he consider the things, she wrote to him. She already broke one of their promises. He knew she wasn't a virgin anymore and there was no doubting that fact. As develop as she had become physically, no way she could keep the promise she made, or could she? "Na" he had to admit to himself lightly snickering. When she finally did call him, they had a long extensive conversation. Yes, she still cared for him. No, she lost her virginity over two years ago. When he suddenly asked her to leave Baltimore with him to points unknown, he didn't like her hesitation or the evasiveness she suddenly displayed. As hard as he tried to convince her that they would be good, he never mention the settlement money. He needed her to come willingly and face the uncertainties with him not because of the allure of his money. She said, she needed time to consider his proposition, but he knew the answer by her hesitation. A week later she called to give him her answer. An answer that he already knew but wanted to hear the words filter pass her lips. She was going to stay in Baltimore with Lamont shattering his heart but not his dreams. He simply replied okay then hung up after saying goodnight. He got with Road Block a few days later and shared his plans of going down South but he didn't reveal that it was going to be the Black Mecca, Atlanta.

He packed his car up with his little possessions three days later then jumped on 95 heading South about eleven o'clock that night then transfer over to I-85. The ten-and-a-half-hour drive was completed in a little over nine hours. He really need to slow down, but his pimp demanded to be open up and he open her up. He caught the morning traffic when he entered Atlanta and got a room at the West Peachtree Hotel. He brought a newspaper to check who were renting rooms by the week. He located one near Nassau and Ted Turner Drive for one-fifty a week with free wi-fi. Searching the papers realtor section for two straight days and the internet, he finally found what he was looking for. A true diamond in the rough. He called the realtor to arrange a tour. They agreed to meet the following morning at the location he informed the realtor. He arrived in a quaint section of town called Florida Heights for a foreclosure home.

Standing on the side walk, there was a lot of potential and financial benefits for the weather battered house especially with the rebuilding going on in the area. The house was a sore sight to the eyes for the home owners and developers who were trying to transform the community. Home owners would rotate cutting the grass in the front while neglecting the massive backyard. He purchase the almost four thousand square feet abandon house for three-hundred-seventy-five thousand dollars cash after negotiations. Houses in the community was going for the high seven-hundred thousand to low eight-hundred thousand. The remodeling company the realtor hooked him up with guaranteed him that the house could easily be completed in eight weeks to his specification if not earlier.

The two-hundred-fifty thousand dollars remodeling was given a check and they got to work the very next day after the house was inspected. The remodeling money will include everything he needed to transform this house into his home including a new roof, inground swimming pool, the furniture, stainless steel appliances and dark ebony oak wood floor throughout except in the basement. The basement will have a thick light laminated floor.

While they were doing their thing, he register with Morehouse University. Accepted after passing their entrance exam, he paid his tuition and decided to test his hand in the duality that existed in law. Two weeks before school was to commence, his home was completed. Accepting the keys, he walked slowly through-out the now four-bedroom house with four bathrooms. He sacrifice one bedroom to expand his on suite and create a beautiful walk-in closet to get dress inside with a full-length mirror. With the construction of the master bedroom balcony and Olympic style pool, the house is the most luxurious in the community and was recently appraised for nine-fifty thousand dollars which caused an impish smile to come to his face. Later that night, he sat on his balcony and stared up at the star filled summer night. At that very moment, a sense of tranquility consumed him, and his mind ran back to Misty. He was wondering what she was doing and thinking?

At that very moment, Misty was sitting inside Melba's Place on Greenmount Avenue on ladies night when Mint Condition's "Nothing Left To Say" filter through the speakers causing her to unconsciously pause as Lion suddenly came to her mind. Once she told him that she couldn't accept his invitation to leave town together, he never asked why and that some-what surprised her. She knew her reply broke his heart, but she also knew that he was a strong person and would eventually rebound. What she didn't expect was that all form of communication with him would suddenly cease. Granted, Lamont didn't really have shit going on for a guy that was twenty-five. Still living in the basement of his mother house and with her other three siblings, the little bit of money he obtain is from working a corner a couple of hours a day for a guy and not a legitimate job then getting with her when darkness fell. Smoking blunts and drinking liquor is all he is bringing to the table. Compared to Lion, he is an ugly duckling. How he acquired her virginity is still a mystery to her. She had tried to convince him to acquire his GED after reading how Lion formed his class while incarcerated, but he wasn't being receptive. He constantly kept trying to insist that with his criminal record a GED wouldn't amount to nothing or guarantee him a job. The more he talked, and she listen, the more she slowly understood that he wasn't looking towards the future or planning for one. Whenever she mention her aspirations, he never showed any genuine interest or try to assure her that it was possible like Lion constantly reinforced in her like when she almost quit school after his incarceration.

When she tried reaching out to Lion three months later, his cell phone was no longer activated. Shock had engulfed her. Did he really leave town? She found herself searching the libraries on the west side including the main library down town, but her searches went in vain. When she spoke to people that knew him, most admitted that they didn't even know that he was home. If he really did leave, where did he go? Did he ask another woman to go with him? If he did, who? If she were to ask Monster about his location, all he will do is snarl at her with his menacing eyes. When he had asked, why she didn't leave town with him especially claiming to be so in love with him? She didn't have an answer for him but when he continuously caught her with Lamont, he put it together and wasn't very flatter by her decision. He called Lamont a worthless piece of shit and other unflattering words. Since getting her ass chew out, she took account of her life, and she wasn't very please. If she had left with Lion, she knew he would have done everything possible to enrich her life, but she choose to stay in Baltimore to an uncertain future.

A week after Lion slip away in the middle of the night or early morning hours; Road Block was formulating what he needed to accomplish. He had to acquire four houses to be his stash houses after figuring out how to split the east side into four zones. He already knew who his four lieutenants will be. He just haven't pulled their coats yet. After establishing which guys will be their sergeants in arm, he place his plans into action. After cashing the certified check, Road Block placed three million dollars into the over-sized black briefcase and exit the bank with Monster. They climbed into his late model Toyota then proceeded to their next destination. They took MLK Boulevard and connected to 295S towards Thurgood Marshall International. He found a parking spot in the underground over-night parking garage then exit and proceeded towards the main terminal. Once inside, they headed straight to the ticket counter to purchase their first-class one-way tickets to Miami. This will be the first time that either of them have flown inside a plane. As they sat in their seats, they felt the turbines thrusting the plane forward then gradually elevating. Leveling off, they quietly discussed their plans for a fourth time and every angle was covered.

When they landed at Concourse G in Miami, the two immaculately dress massive men had all eyes following them as they casually walked through the terminal. They went straight to Hertz Rental to acquire a Cadillac Escalade XL that resemble the ones that Lion admire. They climbed inside then enter the address that was text to him into the navigational system. Exiting the terminal ground, Road Block jump on 195E then connected to 95S. The navigational system had him pulling up on the parking lot of a place called Syndicate Wynwood located on NW 5th Avenue. Reading the name of the place had both men smiling at one another before they step out of the SUV. With Monster clutching the briefcase, they enter the quaint club and approached the dark skin Cuban woman.

"Good afternoon, I'm here to see Mr. Santiago" he stated admiring her dark eyes and smooth acme free complexion.

"Your name" she inquired admiring his mysterious eyes.

"Road Block."

"Road Block?" she repeated suddenly smiling up at the massive teddy bear. "Yes, you are handsome" she complimented picking up the telephone and having a brief conversation before returning it to its cradle. "You can go right in. Mr. Santiago is sitting towards the far right."

"Thank you" he slightly smiled down at her tipping his hat before turning and following her instructions. As he turned the slight corner, he spotted Mr. Santiago sitting in a booth smoking a Cuba cigar with two bodyguards standing next to him. He was in his early fifties and dress in a white silk Versace suite with a white Fedora. "Mr. Santiago?"

"You are certainly a road block" he replied smiling while getting to his feet to shake his hand. "Have a seat young man" he offer reclaiming his seat.

"Thank you" he said unfastening his suit jacket before taking his seat.

"Would you like something to drink?"

"No, sir but thank you anyway" he said returning his stare.

"Do you know why I gave you this meeting?"

"No, sir."

"I wanted to meet the big brother of the guy that protected and took my son under his wings while incarcerated" he revealed staring in his eyes. "You didn't know how Lion got this connection huh?"

"No, sir" he replied surprise by the information.

"Well, he did and wasn't looking for nothing in return. He started mentoring him and others" he shared. "My son surprised the hell out of me by getting his GED in the class that your brother started. You didn't know that either, huh?" he said with a coy smile.

"No, sir" he admitted honestly slightly grinning.

"My son is now completing his first year at Florida State studying business. He has aspirations of managing one of my clubs" he shared proudly while smiling. "Where is Lion? I want to thank him personally."

"He left the city over a week ago and I haven't heard a word from him yet."

"You will" he assured him. "My son informed me that Lion spoke of you almost every day. You are in the game as a street soldier but with greater aspirations."

"Yes, sir. The streets of Baltimore is prime for a takeover. There isn't anything out there that have fools drooling over and I'm looking for a good connection."

"I'm the right connection" he replied returning his stare. "How much are you looking to spend?"

"What are you charging for a key?"

"For you, eleven-five a key. How many do you want?"

Road Block didn't answer right away as his eyes averted his eyes as he calculated then a faint smile came to his face as he returned his eyes to Mr. Santiago. "I would love to buy three-thousand keys, but I'm short. I only brought three-million dollars with me" he revealed.

"Three-million" he repeated causing his eyes to focus on the briefcase then back at Road Block. "You can get that three-thousand keys" he assured him.

"Thank you" he replied openly smiling.

"I can get that to you within the hour."

"There isn't a rush. We will be waiting until the sun goes down to make our trip back up" he informed him.

"Good" he replied slightly smiling while pulling out a card and extending it to him. "Go to the Hotel Victoria and give that card to the receptionist. One of my men will contact you at your room around seven o'clock, alright?"

"Yes, sir. I would like to pay you now. I'm unarmed in your city and can't protect my money" he admitted slightly smiling.

"No problem" he said, and Monster extended the briefcase to the bodyguard standing across from him. "If I were to kill you and take your money, Lion will come huh?" he asked with a slight smirk.

"As sure as I am there is a God" he assured him slightly smiling.

"Yeah, I heard that he would" he admitted returning his smile. "I like your honesty Road Block. Hopefully, we will do a lot of business together."

"We will, sir" he assured him getting to his feet then shaking his hand.

In two short years, Road Block formed the East Side Boyz and locked down the entire east side. With the bodies that his street soldiers stretched out, the message was sent out loud and clear. Motherfuckers from outside of the east side can try their hands but his soldiers were brutal and unmerciful after giving them a warning. If you weren't connected with the East Side Boyz, you really need to keep your business off of their turf.

After Lion sophomore year, he sent a round trip ticket to Road Block by FedEx with a telephone number. Upon receiving his airline ticket, Road Block called the number and they spoke for about twenty minutes before ending their conversation. Three days later, he was standing inside the Hartsfield-Jackson International staring at the people exiting the plane. Road Block eventually materialized, and a broad smile came to his face. They embraced one another tightly then headed towards the conveyor belt to retrieve his suitcases then headed out the main terminal door to his car.

"You still driving her?" he asked placing his suitcases in the trunk then closing it.

"She runs great" he told him as they climbed inside.

"A little tight wouldn't you say" he stated struggling to fasten his seat belt.

"Only for you" he replied pulling away from the curb. He connected to Rt.20 and took that to 285S into Florida Heights. He was cruising along

Ralph Abernathy Freeway and Road Block's head was on a swivel admiring the cornbread and beans asses of the southern women. Pulling up in front of his house, he stared over at his younger brother.

"Whoa! All this is yours?" he asked smiling at the massive size as they climbed out and started heading towards the front door.

"You are welcome to come live with me" he invited inserting his key then pushing open the front door. "Place your suitcase at the door and make yourself at home" he told him leading him into the family room where a poster size picture of him and Road Block at Patterson Park when he was about twelve.

"Damn" he burst out laughing. "Look at you."

"Me? Look at yourself" he counter. "Jerri juice, really Sha?" he teased taking a seat. "Those keys are yours" he informed him.

"Thanks" he smiled picking them up then attaching them to his key chain. "Where is the vehicle this Cadillac key go to?"

"I have an Escalade XL in the garage" he informed him. "You are going to need wheels to get around."

"Where am I going?" he asked taking a seat.

"While I'm in classes, you are going to want and get out. Trust me, women are going to flock to you like bees to honey when they hear your accent" he replied lighting up a joint laughing.

By the second day, he came home from class to find Road Block entertaining two extremely attractive Bertha Butts sisters. He made his presence known but he kept it moving towards the basement where he usually study. Although Road Block was there for only a week, he was knocking bitches off like he was an aphrodisiac. He actually had the audacity to have two women swimming naked and sleeping with him one night. You would have thought he was a celebrity when they went to the jazz clubs that he frequent. Southern women didn't admire just his massive size, but the immaculate style of dress for a man his size. Days after he had

left, Lion's house telephone kept ringing off the hook by women looking
for him. He had told them repeatedly that he had returned home yet now,
they were ringing his doorbell. When he talked to him the proceeding
weekend and informed him that women were requesting his presence, he
told him he would be returning to his private little smorgasbord in about
a month and he did. You could pencil him in for once a month like it was
an appointment.

Mya was the one that knocked the rest of the ladies out of the block.
With her mocha complexion and radiant smile, she kept Road Block
laughing and in check. She had graduated from Savanna State with a
degree in finance and more importantly, she didn't have any children.
When they went out to the jazz clubs together, he watched his brother being
very attentive to her and her desires. She brought out that rare essence of
him that few have ever witness. He was truly smitten by her and there was
no doubting that for Lion. The night before he was to return to Baltimore,
he pulled Lion up.

"Are you busy?" he asked coming into the family room and staring
down at him.

"Na, what's up?" he asked putting his book aside and staring up into
his eyes.

"I think I'm in love with Mya" he blurted out flopping down into his
chair and staring over at him.

"And what is wrong with that?" he asked with a coy smile.

"I can't be falling in love."

"Why?"

"Because of what I'm involved in Malik. She would be a liability."

"You mean somebody that people could use against you?"

"Exactly" he admitted honestly slightly hardening his eyes.

"My invitation is still on the table for you" he reiterated. "Move down
here permanently with me and get out the game."

"Meeting Mya have caused me to reconsider your invitation but I'm just starting to make some real money Malik. Maybe after a couple of years if she and I are still flowing."

"If you keep breaking her back, she just might turn up pregnant and that will force your hand" he replied snickering.

"Don't jink me man, damn" he said knocking on the wooden coffee table laughing. "She doesn't like me using condoms and sometimes I do appease her, but I'm going to be safe."

"How do you do that?"

"What?" he asked slightly confused.

"Be safe when you appease her sometimes" he replied with a coy smile.

"I guess I'm not" he replied grinning. "I did tell her that she will be the mother of my children one day if she stay close."

"Well, she can't get much closer than leaving her toothbrush after just three nights" he mention snickering.

"Oh, you spotted it huh?" he burst out laughing. "How is things with you and Akilah (bright)."

"She is desiring more than I'm willing to give her right now."

"And what is that?"

"To be exclusive but that wasn't the original deal and I'm not going to concede to her wish" he shared with conviction.

"Well, if the contract was original written and agreed upon, changing the format for any reason is a bleach of contract" he replied chuckling.

He had met Akilah during the summer classes he was taking in his fresh man year. With the credits that he had acuminated during his incarceration, he was taking the next phrase after his introduction into law. Although she was a year ahead of him over at Spelman, they kept bumping into one another at the law library or she would spot him in the black literature department reading. She would hit the little clubs surrounding their campus that cater to their needs, but he was always M.I.A. Even when the crazy Q's were throwing their parties, he was still absent.

She was cruising up the 900 block of Piedmont Avenue listening to DMX's "What Do You Want" when her peripheral vision caught the image of Lion walking inside the Kat Club. One of many jazz spots. Although she was heading to Sutra Lounge to hook up with her girlfriends, she found herself hooking a U-turn and pulled into a vacant parking spot down the street. She grabbed her cross-body bag then step out of her lip stick red Tesla S and proceeded up the street after securing it. Entering through the front door, she was pleasantly surprised to know there was no cover charge. As she enter the quaint environment, she was surprised to see the place fashionably furnish and filled almost to compacity. She had drove this route so many times and never paid the place any attention. As she stood right of the door scanning the place, she eventually spotted him sitting in a semi-secluded table sipping on a glass of white wine and reading. She was glad that he wasn't there to meet someone. A coy smile suddenly came to her lips as she walked towards the bar to order herself a glass of Moscato. As she waited on her drink, she stared over at him. Wearing a light weight gray pin-stripe Armani suit, he appeared even more handsome to her, or it might be the effects from the cocaine that she had snorted. After paying for her drink, she proceeded towards him ignoring the provocative slurs from the men she was walking pass.

"Hello" her sultry voice greeted him.

Breaking his concentration, Lion was surprised that someone was able to walk up on him as she did, again. His eyes slowly raised while taking in the contour of her body. Wearing a pair of blue hipster jeans that revealed her slightly muscular abs with her birthstone were being displayed under a playboy mid-range T-shirt, her honey complexion seem to glisten is the diminish light. With no form of make-up, her medium lips wore just lip gloss. Her grayish eyes caused him to suddenly smile. "Hi, Akilah."

A look of surprise engulfed her eyes. "You know my name?"

"Apparently and the meaning" he included smiling up at her. "Are you going to take a seat or were you just passing by?"

"I'll take a seat" she replied taking a seat across from him while watching him closing the book and placing it in an empty chair next to him.

"What are you doing visiting my world?" he asked staring in her eyes.

"What do you mean?" she asked staring at him perplex.

"This isn't the hip-hop scene" he replied grinning. "What brought you inside?"

"You" she found herself admitting while returning his stare. "I spotted you walking inside as I drove pass."

"You need to keep your eyes on the road, young lady" he suggested grinning.

"What is your name?"

"I'm Malik" he replied lifting his glass to her.

"I've seen you around. Where do you go to school?"

"Morehouse."

"How do you know me?" she inquired taking a sip from her drink.

"I don't" he replied. "I spotted you on several dates and caught your name one night" he revealed.

"Life should be experience and enjoyed" she explained returning his stare.

"There is nothing wrong with exploring your options" he replied grinning.

"I hope not" she replied with a coy smile. "Where are you from?"

"Baltimore."

"Baltimore? What are you doing down here?"

"Attending school" he replied with a coy smile.

"So, you live with your parents?"

"Na and I'm single" he included before the question was asked.

Three months later, she mention that he never invited her over to his perceived apartment. He told her that he will eventually. His hesitation caused her to start peeking at him and this caused him to privately smile to himself. She openly accused him of hiding something from her. He tried to convince him that he wasn't in the habit of throwing his home address to people including a beautiful woman. She even had the audacity to insinuate, not accuse, that he was married and had children hidden away somewhere. Her words seem to cut like a knife that he instinctively harden his eyes. "If I were married or was blessed to have children, I would never deny them especially just to crawl between some women thigh." He stress that he was a much better man than that and thought she knew it also. This implication or form of questioning was initiated by her girls, but she was the one that has to deal with the aftermath. She notice how he has subtly taken a step back and it was her fault. Why did she have to challenge the things that he said and shared? He was cruising pass Spelman Book store when she spotted him as she was talking to some friends. When he blew his horn and pulled over, an impish smile came to her face. She haven't seen or heard from him in over two weeks since he checked her again in a jazz club one night for her sarcastic disposition.

"Hey, Mr. Secretive" she greeted him in front of her associates.

"What's up?" he replied returning her stare. "Hi family" he greeted the others.

"Family" they chime in return.

"Are you busy?"

"Why?" she asked returning his stare.

"I have told you about your unflattering sarcasm" he reminded her. "Are you busy?"

"Not really" she replied softly.

"I want to show you something. Where is your car parked?"

"Over there" she pointed.

"Hop in and follow me."

"Why don't you just drive me?"

"Because if you start that sarcasm, you need a way home. Besides, I'm not your designated chauffeur" he told her causing her friends to snicker and giggle.

"I'll holla at yawl later" she said opening the door and stepping inside.

He drop her off at her car then she followed him up the ramp to I-20. Once in the third lane, she reach inside her purse and pulled out a canister that held her cocaine and took two snorts. She was fully relaxed by the time they transfer over to 85N. As the words of Xscape's singing "Do U Want To" reached her ears, she heard herself lightly giggle at the way Malik always checked her when she tried to get out of her lane using her prissy disposition as he describe it and he didn't care who was around or didn't like it. While the other guys that were vying for her attention and affection including him, those guys would endure her antics but not Malik and he showed that by easily staying away from her. He had left her at numerous occasions when she started regressing around him. On those occasions, she actually felt embarrassment. He was definitely a rare man and not smitten by her beauty. She hadn't realized that they had left the highway until they had gotten caught by a red light then she looked around. As she focus on the area, she couldn't help but admire the luxurious homes with their manicured lawn. Following him up a long narrow drive way that eventually revealed a gorgeous house, she step out of her car and approached him still admiring the house.

"This is a beautiful home" she compliment gripping his fingers as they approached the front door. "Who live here?"

"I do" he replied inserting his key then pushing the door open for her to enter first and closing it behind himself.

"You do" she stated looking over her shoulder at him astounded as he walked pass leading the way towards the family room. "This is fabulous."

"Thank you" replied heading towards the kitchen. "Make yourself at home. Would you like a glass of Moscato?"

"Yes, please" she replied walking around the first floor admiring his Afrikan sculptures and masks. "How old were you there?" she asked smiling up at the post size picture.

"Twelve."

"Who is that with you?"

"My brother Shabazz."

"Does he live here with you?"

"No, I live here alone as I told you Akilah" he reminded her.

"I thought you lived in an apartment" she admitted.

"Nothing wrong with assuming" he said returning with a bottle of Moscato and two glasses then taking a seat on the sofa. After he filled both glasses, he reach inside his wooden box and pulled out three white boys (joints) then lighting one.

The scent floating on the air caused her to turn around and walked methodically back towards him. "I didn't know you smoke weed."

"How would you?" he asked extending one of the glasses to her. "Do you want one?" he asked with an impish smile.

"No, thank you" she replied searching inside her purse. "I only fuck with the brothers" she shared pulling out a blunt smiling. "So, I see why you are so secretive about your personal life."

"It didn't have anything to do with a wifey or children" he reiterated. "This is my place of tranquility and it's going to remain that way."

"I am sorry that I said that because I know you are a better man than that."

"I constantly tell you to have your brain in gear before your mouth starts to run, young lady" he reminded her.

"I know" she replied solemnly while slightly shaking her head. "So, this is why you haven't press up on me?" she inquired pulling from her blunt.

"No, it isn't" he corrected her. "I honestly have decided if I wanted to have a sexual relationship with you" he confessed.

"What?" she stated shock by his words.

"You have a lot of bullshit with you Akilah. You are a beautiful young lady but somebody in your past have harden you."

"No, they haven't" she denounced his opinion and observation.

"I'm glad that this is just my opinion" he slightly grinned. "I see how other guys endure your antics because of your outward beauty, but I'm not them."

"No, you aren't Malik."

"Although you said that you weren't looking for any obligations and I appreciate your honesty, but I'm still contemplating about making love to you."

"Don't contemplate too long" she counter hardening her eyes while returning his stare.

"Who can truly miss something or someone that they never had or experience Akilah?" he asked returning her stare but not her slightly harden eyes.

That was over a year ago when he revealed just one of his whole cards to her, he still remained very secretive about his personal life and past especially when she ask about his first girlfriend. On the night of the Dirty South Tour with Little Jon being the main guest, she slipped away from her associates and crept over to his house slightly intoxicated at one o'clock in the morning. Knowing he left a key under a specific flower pot, she let herself in and quietly climbed his steps disrobing. She could hear the faint sounds of jazz filtering out his ajar bedroom door. When she push the door open with her clothes in her arms except her thongs, his ears perk up and an impish smile consumed his face as she dropped her clothes then walked seductively towards him. He took her on a sexual journey through a universe that she didn't know existed. It was on one of their sexapades that she said she loved him, a word she swore wouldn't escape her lips to another man no matter how she actually felt, but she had in her erotic state of mind. He rationalized that when he didn't reciprocate the same emotional admiration that things once again started regressing with her and that sarcasm that he thought she had check reemerged, again. The first time he step away from her was for about three weeks. The second time it was for two months. She knew that her next strike would have him giving her back her resume and placing walking papers in her hand then retrieving another one from the many vying young ladies. One thing she did come to understand about him was that he wasn't threatening her with ending their affair, he was promising her and eventually it did.

Graduating from Morehouse in three years with honor because he didn't have a personal life. Road Block and Monster came down to celebrate and party with him. He invited several friends that he had acquired over the years to celebrate with him. Seeing his house for the first time, they were blown away. They never suspected that he had it going on like he did, but they now understood why he kept his hand so close to his chest. Single, no baby momma drama and handsome as a motherfucker. If women knew the cards that he held, they would have tried to play their hands. He had several exclusive law firms vying for him after completing his internship and passing the bar exam. With his life in order, he felt like nothing could go wrong, but life will have many more surprises for him.

With the gradual rising of the morning sun, he walked over to his closet and pulled out five suits. He will wear his light gray Armani for his flight home. After placing his suits in the garment bag, he grabbed several pairs of under garments and his hygienics products then placed them in a large leather bag. When he unintentionally grabbed two pairs of jeans and his Tim's, he knew he was getting ready for some dirty shit. Taking a quick shower, he stared at his reflection in the full-length mirror as he dried his body. Standing six-foot five, his well develop body was sculpture. With less than five per-cent body fat, his two-hundred-twenty-five pounds looked good on him. He slipped into a pair of Joe Boxers and a wife beater. Putting on his silk pajama's pants, he walked out of his bedroom into the dark hall way then descended the steps. The dark dense wood floors never gave away his position as he moved towards the family room. Instinctively grabbing the remote, he press the on button and Dizzy Gillespie trumpet filled the room. He walked into the kitchen to retrieve several pieces of fruit before taking a seat on the couch. He stared up at the picture over the fireplace of them when he got out of jail and taken at Identity. They both possess broad smiles. Something that neither did frequently. He allowed his mind to reflect as he stared up at the picture.

Although fifteen years younger, his brother was always looking out for him especially after finding out he wasn't alone in this world. He loved his big brother role and displayed it by the things he did. Lion never had any fashionable clothes but that changed instantly. Road Block spent well over a thousand dollars on getting him clean up. Everything he learned about the streets, he learned from his brother especially how to defend himself. Standing on the corners were a no-no. Standing six-foot-eight and weighing two-hundred seventy pounds, he didn't go against what his brother insisted. If he told him to step off, he would and without any sly looks or mutter words. When he was boxed in by three guys trying to take his money when he was twelve at Upton Station, Road Block never stepped in. He watched with the crowd how his younger brother would react. He reacted viciously. Just like a Lion. The nick name stuck, and he lived up to it every time somebody got out of their lane on him. Never initiating anything but his intellectual disposition had many fools misreading him. He ripped off a lot of heads until his name started being whisper in the streets from the grapevine.

At seven-thirty, a cab pulled up in front of his home and blew its horn. Securing the front door and setting the alarm system, he placed his suitcase in the trunk then climbed into the back seat. The ride to the airport took twenty-five minutes. He paid the fare then retrieved his suitcase. Walking through the terminal, he was used to women and strangers staring up at him standing six-foot five. With his eyes hidden by his Hugo Boss sunglasses, he would stare back at them. He retrieved his first-class ticket then proceeded to gate twelve for his flight. As he stood in line with the other passengers, he stared out at the plane that would deliver him to his destination. The morning sun wasn't over the trees yet, but the sky was clear, and the temperature was slowly rising. Finally boarding, he found his window seat then settle in listening to his music. He open the book he had brought to divert his attention, but that didn't work. Memories of his past kept creeping into his mind. The only time he thought about his mother briefly was on Mother's Day. That was the only reminder that he had a mother. He actually couldn't remember her birthday. She had abandoned him lovingly, financially, and emotionally by the time he was eight years old. He couldn't contribute it to his father's incarceration but for her love for crack and heroine. When he was accused of murder, she never came to his trial, but he somewhat expected it. Malik had actually pleaded for her to come visit him during his first year of incarceration, but she chose her addiction over him, and he never requested that she come again. So, when he did get released, going inside to visit her at her roach infested house never entered his mind. Do you know how it feels to hate the person that gave you, life? Well, he did. Only through time and maturity did he soften his stance but not necessarily his heart. The non-stop flight should have him landing at Thurgood Marshall Airport by eleven o'clock. It appeared, just as he was starting to get into the book, the plane started descending then touched down. He was almost home.

Walking through the terminal with his bags, the clock had eleven-fifteen.

He was trying to decide if he wanted to catch a cab or the train into the city. He eventually decided on keeping his money. He brought a day pass then caught the train. If visitors only knew how to get into Baltimore, cab operators would be wasting their time at the airport. As a child, he used to play hooky from school sometimes and ride the train and trolley from one end of the line to the next while studying his school work. He knew when the train stopped at Cherry Hill all kinds of characters would board and they didn't let him down. Most were coming from the drug clinic getting their morning blast before heading to Lexington Market. One of the hottest drug spots in the city to acquire the drug of your choice except Sundays only because it was closed. He always got a big laugh watching the white folks react to the effects of methadone. Hilarious.

When the train stopped at Camden yards, he suddenly grabbed his bags then exited. Heading towards the Hilton at the Inner Harbor, he entered the plush lobby and proceeded towards the receptionist.

"May I help you?" the honey complexion receptionist asked wearing a beautiful smile.

"Yes, Ms. Jackson" he replied staring at her name tag then into her light brown eyes. "Do you have any suites over-looking the Inner Harbor?"

"I'm sure we can accommodate you, sir" she said checking her monitor. "I have room fifteen-thirty available."

"I'll take it. Thank you."

"May I have your driver's license, please?"

He reached into his breast pocket to bring out his bill fold then extended his license and credit card to her.

"Thank you, Mr. Mohammad" she replied. "You have well-manicured hands" she said checking him out and his wedding finger. "Atlanta, huh? I've always wanted to visit the Black Mecca."

"It's a lovely city" he replied watching her entering his name into her computer. A subtle scent of her perfume consumed his nostrils.

"I hope to get down there one day" she shared peeking up at him.

"You should" he said. "I'm sure you would love it."

"If the scenery is anything like what I'm looking at, I'm sure I will" she openly flirted smiling while extending his license and credit card back to him then turning to retrieve his electronic key card. The slightly snugging pants revealed her panties line and just how phat her petite ass was. "Are you here on business or pleasure if you don't mind me asking?" she inquired extending his card back to him.

"Business" he replied accepting the cards and replacing them in is breast pocket.

"Not too much, I hope" she smiled.

"Only time will tell" he replied grabbing his bags. "Enjoy your day Ms. Jackson."

"My first name is Khatiti."

"Khatiti?" he repeated as a smile crept upon his face. "Sweet little thing, huh?"

"Yes, I am" she replied slightly blushing that he knew the meaning of her name.

"I'll holla, T.T" he slightly grinned then headed towards the elevator. He could feel her eyes running up and down the contour of his body. Pressing the button of the elevator, the door open then he stepped inside. Looking out, she was still peeking at him. Their eyes connected then shared a smile just as the door closed.

"Damn, he's fine" she said to herself grinning.

"Who?" her girlfriend asked coming from the back office staring around.

"Malik Mohammad" she replied with a coy smile.

Entering the suite, he placed his suits in the walk-in closet then took his hygienic material into the on suite and place his items on a face towel. He pulled out his other toothbrush canister that held his joints. He took one out then proceeded into the living room. Turning on the music, he tuned into Morgan State's WEEA to listen to some jazz. He open the balcony door then stepped out and took in the scenery before taking a seat. He lit the joint then pulled from it slowly. Over-looking the Inner Harbor, the city was just starting to wake up. While those that had employment have been up for hours, panhandlers were claiming their corners for the day to become a nuance while others were just walking the streets to fill their empty day. He had a lot to do this morning. His first mission is to claim his brother's body from the morgue then make funeral arrangements before heading to Woodlawn to get him a head stone. He would take care of all these things today. Tomorrow, he would get with the detectives to see how their investigation was going and then seek his retribution.

It was almost two o'clock when he finally left the hotel, he jumped in one of the many cab drivers parked out front and gave the address to where he wanted to be taken. Twenty minutes later, he was arriving at the Baltimore City Chief Medical Examiner Department. Stepping out of the cab, he stared at the sterile looking building. He took a deep breath then ascended the steps. Walking through the front door, he approached the information desk.

"May I help you?" an old white woman inquired staring up at him.

"Yes ma'am, I'm here to claim Shabazz Mohammad body" he replied solemnly.

She pulled out a clip board repeating his name several times as she scanned down it. "Yes, we have him" she replied staring up at him. "May I have some form of Identification."

"Yes ma'am" he replied extending his driver's license to her.

"Thank you, Mr. Mohammad. Oh, are yawl related?"

"Yes ma'am, he's my older brother."

"Sorry for your lost."

"Thank you."

"Take that elevator down to the basement" she pointed.

"Yes, ma'am" he replied accepting his I.D then proceeding towards the elevator and took it to the basement. He followed the signs to where he had to go then paused before lightly tapping on the door.

"Come in" a man's voice requested.

Opening the door, he stepped inside staring at the middle age white guy with a white coat eating lunch.

"Mr. Mohammad?"

"Yes sir."

"Will you follow me please?" he said getting to his feet and covering his food with a napkin then leading the way through a set of double doors. The temperature dropped tremendously as they walked down the hallway. Entering another door, the smell of chlorine consumed his nostrils. With his clipboard in hand, they walked pass several stainless-steel drawers before he finally stop. Pulling out the draw, he uncovered the head of the person on the table. "Is this Shabazz Mohammad?"

"Yes sir" he replied staring down at his brother's lifeless face especially the bullet wound to his head.

"Do you need a minute?"

"Yes sir" he replied never averting his eyes.

"Take as much time as you need."

"Thank you" he replied watching him walking towards a little desk by the door. He pulled the cover down to his waist to inspect his body. There were several bullet wounds on his body but the fatale one was a single head shot. Only then, did tears flow from his eyes unconsciously. Not because of his sorrow, na It was because of his steadily growing anger; he fear the lion that has laid dormant for so many years that was starting to stir.

He remember the last time Lion had raised his head. He was attending college during the summer months after completing his freshman year. He was heading towards the student's parking lot when he notice a young lady with a flat tire. Leaning against her white Lexus in her acid wash jeans and sculpture abs, he offer his assistance.

"You're not worry about messing up your clothes?" she asked slightly smiling.

"The cleaners can do their job" he informed her starting to roll up his sleeves.

"No, wait a minute" she insisted standing erect. "My boyfriend said he was on his way."

"That's good" he replied starting on his other sleeve. "Hopefully, he'll get here before I'm done. Where is your spare?" he asked staring into her brown eyes. Her dark complexion reminded him of Misty and made him unconsciously smile.

"You have a very impish smile" she mention studying him grinning.

"Admiring your complexion, excuse me. Where is that spare?"

"In the trunk" she mention watching him retrieving it and then open his trunk to get his hydraulic jack. As he place the spare tire next to him on the ground, he jack the car up slightly then loosen the bolts. "I hear an accent. Where are you from?"

"Baltimore" he replied cranking the car completely up then pulling the flat off.

"I've seen you around" she admitted.

"Sorry I can't say the same" he replied staring up at her.

"I'm Natasha."

"Malik" he replied slightly grinning then grabbing the tire and placing it on the rim.

"I see you spend a lot of time in the library."

"How? Do you?" he asked putting the bolts back on.

"I have a tendency to procrastinate" she admitted lightly giggling. "I haven't seen you at none of the parties on campus."

"I don't dance" he replied tightening the bolts.

"You don't dance" she giggled again.

"Na, I don't" he answer staring up at her grinning.

"Well, the Q's are having a party this Saturday. If you're not busy, I hope you come through."

"Time will tell" he replied jacking the car down then grabbing the flat and placing it in the trunk for her then returning his jack. "Well Natasha, it's been a pleasure" he smiled grabbing his bookbag then continuing on his way while rubbing his hand on some tissues.

"Malik! Do you need a ride!?"

"Na, I'm okay!" he shouted over his shoulder continuing on his journey.

"A guy that don't dance" she found herself saying as he disappeared around the corner. She waited an additional half hour for her boyfriend before starting up her car and pulling off.

From his obscure position in his car, Lion sat watching her. When she suddenly pulled off, he lightly chuckled. He wouldn't want to be her boyfriend. How could he neglect such a beautiful young woman? The answer suddenly came to him, and it made him smile even wider. Just as he started up his engine, a white Saleem pulled up and the driver got out looking around. High yellow pretty boy type. Who the fuck was he looking for? Her car wasn't there so what was he looking for? He watched him pull out his cell phone then climb back in his car and pull off. He place his car in gear then pulled away from the curb accelerator.

With no classes on Friday, he found himself back in the law library taking notes and quotes for three hours while listening to his jazz through his blue tooth. After organizing his notes and marking certain points on his presentation, he place the books back on their shelves and place his notebook back into his leather bookbag then got to his feet. He was exiting when he stumble upon Natasha with a couple of her girlfriends.

"Hey Malik" she greeted warmly.

"What's up Natasha? Queens" he address placing his hand over his heart.

"Hello" they chime back checking him out from head to toe.

"Well, are you coming to the party?"

"I still haven't made up my mind yet" he admitted admiring the sun shining through the light sundress she was wearing with no slip.

"You will have a blast" she insisted smiling up at him.

"Come, Malik" her light skin girlfriend cosigned staring up into his eyes. She was definitely stepping on her girl's feet.

"No promises" he replied returning her stare grinning. "Sorry but I really have an appointment to keep."

"Where do you live?" inquired Natasha staring over at him.

"Not too far from campus" he surrendered. "Got to go ladies. Nice meeting yawl" he said turning and walking away.

"Mmmmm, who is that guy Natasha?"

"Malik, Sweets. He is the guy I told yawl about that changed that damn flat for me."

"You never mention how attractive he was?"

"Is he?" she suddenly giggled admiring the swag in his walk.

"Well, I like what I see Dee-Dee."

"Who don't?" she responded. "Is he seeing anyone Natasha?"

"Not that I'm aware of" she replied wishing they wouldn't gawk all over him.

"Where is he from, Atlanta?" inquired Sweets.

"Na, he's from out of Baltimore."

"You don't know where he live off campus?" Dee-Dee asked.

"Na, I just meet the guy, damn" she admitted grinning.

"Well, I hope he come to the party tomorrow night" Sweets shared.

"So, do I" confessed Dee-Dee with an impish grin.

As they proceeded towards the gym, Natasha couldn't believe she was actually getting jealous over all the questions like she knew the damn answers. Granted, he was handsome as a motherfucker, but that's no reason to drool all over him. From what she gather from those that somewhat knew him, he stayed to himself. Never seen in any of the pubs surrounding the campus or the many clubs around the city. He seem to disappear after leaving his classes and resurfacing the following morning. Always dress casual but Tim's and Rock Ports were worn during in-climate weather. He's not an introvert but he didn't extend himself socially either. Exactly, where do he live? Does he have a girlfriend as Sweets asked? The only way she was going to acquire those answers and anymore is to talk to him directly. Hopefully, he will come to the party.

Saturday night, he was sitting on his balcony star gazing when he suddenly got the urged to hang out. He check his watch and it had eleven o'clock. He had more than enough time to catch a set at St. James Live or Blind Willie's. Two of the jazz clubs he frequent every weekend. As he pulled out a blue three button Versace, he suddenly paused, and a coy smile creased his lips. He place the suit back and grabbed a black pair of baggy jeans. He pulled out his black and white Jordan's with a white, short-sleeve shirt asking, "Do you know who you are?" He grabbed his black New York fitted baseball hat then departed his room. Descending his steps, he turned off most of the lights and set the alarm system before stepping outside. He climbed into his car and headed up I-75 towards 675. Cruising down Ralph D. Abernathy Freeway, he turned left slowing down tremendously onto Joseph E. Lowery Blvd. admiring all the young ladies. There was no mistaken they were fucked up or where they were headed. Nearing Atlanta Student Movement Blvd, he searched for a parking spot. Finding one several blocks away; he made his way towards the sound of the music with the crowd. He stared at the white Saleem, and that same coy smile came back to his lips. It was midnight and people were still filtering in as groups.

Walking into the frat house, the usual scents associated with Q's having an enjoyable time was present. The DJ was banging out the latest sounds as the dance floor were everywhere. No specific spot. Guys had girls bending over touching their toes while doing the Martin Lawrence on that ass. He grabbed two miniature bottles of Moscato and made his rounds. There were several people there he was acquainted from his classes and others from just hanging out. You could tell by the expression that they were surprised to see him there and dress the way he was. As they got better acquainted, two hours had elapse. He was constantly asked to dance but he declined every one of them. He just continued to socialize. Hearing the first notes of "This House Is Not A Home" he heard.

"May I have this dance?" a soft sultry voice asked.

Turning, he stared up and a slight smile came to his lips. "What's up Natasha?"

"You heard me" she replied reaching for his fingers. "Can I have this dance?"

"My pleasure" he replied. "Excuse me Kings and Queens" he told those he was talking to and allowing her to direct him to the dance floor. Facing her, he open his arms to feel her melting into his embrace.

"I've been watching you Malik" she shared staring up at him with a coy smile. "A lot of young ladies are discussing you" she revealed still smiling. "I had to come see who they were talking about. You know I was surprised to see it was you. It took me a minute to figure out after watching numerous of ladies getting disappointed, you only like to slow dance, huh?"

"I'm guilty."

"Yes, you are" she smiled. "How long have you been here?"

Checking his watch, "Wow, its two o'clock already. A little over two hours" he shared surprise by the time.

"You have some place to be tomorrow?"

"Na."

"Oh, I thought you was about to get up out of here."

"Na, I've been enjoying myself."

"Do you have a girlfriend here or back in Baltimore?"

"Na, I'm single."

"Why?"

"Because I can't afford a girlfriend" he stated causing her to burst out laughing.

"You're funny" she smiled. "We aren't that expensive."

"Yes, yawl are and time consuming" he included causing her to giggle again.

All the while they was dancing and flirting, they were being watched. As she ran her hand up his back again, he felt her hand stop and her body suddenly become a little tense.

"Who's this?" a guy's voice asked slightly slurring his words.

"Hey, Johnathan" she address facing him. "This is Malik. The guy I told you that changed my flat tire for me" she explained.

"You seem to be a little friendly with someone you just met" he stated staring down at her.

"Excuse me" Lion said starting to leave.

"No, we aren't doing anything" she said insisting that he stay. "We were just dancing Johnathan" she stated in a slightly stern voice.

"Rubbing your hands up and down his back is just dancing!?" he asked staring coldly at Lion.

"Excuse me" Lion said again starting to walk away.

"Where in the fuck do you think you're going?" he asked impeding his movement.

They were actually the same height and weight class. An uncontrollable smile crept across his lips. "Excuse me" he said trying to step around him, but he impeded his movement again. "Okay, tough guy. Let's do this. Either move or I'll move you."

"Move me motherfucker!" he requested shoving him.

The beat down came quick, but Lion still didn't know why he threw the guy out the damn front room bay window afterward especially since he walked out through the front door.

"Mr. Mohammad!?"

"Yes" he replied coming out of his daydream. He turned with a slight snarl on his lips and face the guy then stared back down at Shabazz. "Who did this to you, Sha and why? I will find out who and they will definitely pay. I promise you" he said to himself pulling the sheet back over his head then turning and walking towards the man.

The coroner got to his feet then extended the clipboard to him. "I need your signature, please." As he signed the paper work, the man couldn't help staring at him. He remember seeing this guy face somewhere, but he just couldn't remember where? He wasn't a professional athlete, but he knew he recognized him. "Thank you" he said retrieving the paper work then giving him a copy along with the death certificate. "You can retrieve his personal belonging from the police station on Erdman Avenue. Sorry for your lost, Mr. Mohammad."

"Thank you, sir" he replied.

"Do you know which funeral parlor will be collecting him?"

"None, cremate him and I'll pick up the remains Wednesday."

"As you wish, sir."

"Thank you" he slightly smiled then retraced his steps. He had initiated this conversation with Road Block years ago. He finally made him understand that the body is just a containment for the essence of who we are, the soul, the illumination of God that is placed in us. Without this containment center, we wouldn't be able to recognize one another from the illumination. God claims the important essence of us. So, why go and pay thousands of dollars and possibly going into debt to bury a containment center into another containment? This practice is a European thing. Culturally, this was not our practice but one we foolishly adopted. As the scriptures states, from the earth we were created and to the earth we must return. Stop being exploited during a most vulnerable time for a family to appease a foolish European ideology.

He don't remember taking the elevator back up or walking out the main entrance. He stood on the corner to get his focus. He was alternating his plans. He waved down a hack then proceeded to the Eastern Precinct off of Edison Highway. He gave the driver ten dollars then walked through the main entrance to the information desk.

"May I help you?" a middle age black woman asked.

"Yes ma'am, I was told I could retrieve my brother's personal belonging from here."

"The person name?"

"Shabazz Mohammad."

"Yes, we received a call that you might be heading this way. Detective Ron Johnson would like to speak to you. Will you have a seat and I'll contact him for you."

"Yes ma'am" he replied turning and taking a seat. Twenty minutes pass and no detective. Patience has never been his best quality. He suddenly got to his feet to leave.

"Mr. Mohammad! Mr. Mohammad!" she called to him.

He stopped and turned to face her. "Yes ma'am."

"The detectives really would like to talk to you."

"Excuse me ma'am, but I'm here to retain my brother's property and nothing else. Talking to five-o is not on my agenda today or no day. When they're more professional, I'll get back with them" he told her hardening is eyes. "Will you allow me to retrieve my brother's personal- property or not, ma'am?"

"The detectives would really like to talk to you" she reiterated ignoring his question.

"No, huh and that's a shame" he stated staring at her coldly then turning to walk out. He was just about to clear the outer door when he heard his name being called.

"Mr. Mohammad!" the detective shouted walking briskly towards him. "Sorry for the delay. May I ask you a couple of questions?"

"No, I'm here to retrieve my brother's personal possession."

"It won't take you long?"

"Not interested, Detective. Where is his property?"

"Down stairs, will you follow me?"

"I won't get lost" he replied slightly hardening his eyes at him. "Just tell me where I need to go."

"I'll escort you. I'm not too busy" he insisted taking the lead. He pushed the elevator button then stepped inside. "I've seen your face some place" he mentions trying to remember where he saw him. When the elevator door open, they was standing in front of the property room. "Hey Mack, what's up old timer?"

"Well, well, well" he smiled at him. "Look at what the cat done dragged in. How have you been Jackson?"

"I'm alright" he replied shaking his hand vigorously.

"Release the property of Shabazz Mohammad to his brother."

"No problem give me a minute please" he said staring him in his eyes then turning to perform his duty.

"Can you tell me anything about your brother?"

"Oh, you're going to try and have an interview anyway, huh?" he stared over at him shaking his head. "Na, I really didn't know my brother. We weren't close" he lied looking for the property officer.

"We're at a lost as to what happen to your brother" he began fishing. "He has no criminal record not even a parking ticket" he said staring into his eyes.

"And?"

"And I found it extremely puzzling. Why would he have a weapon on him?"

"Living in Baltimore and you're wondering why?" he slightly chuckled. "Really" he replied shaking his head then looking for the evidence officer again.

"So, you're advocating…"

"Sir, I'm not advocating nothing detective" he replied with a stern voice checking him then added. "If anything, common sense tells everybody to strap when walking these violent and psychotic streets. With the corrupt history of five-o in the city, who is the real criminals?" he asked staring into his eyes.

"You live in Baltimore?"

"No, I'm in Atlanta."

"What do you do?"

"Sell drugs" he replied sarcastically returning his stare.

"We're just trying to make sense out of this, Mr. Mohammad. Six people were killed, and one seriously injured."

"How do you asking me about my profession has anything to do with my brother's murder or your investigation?" he asked staring at him coldly. "How?" he asked but no response. "What did the injured person say?"

"Nothing, yet. He's heavily sedated from his gun wounds. Once he's able to talk, we'll have an interview with him."

"That's good, I hope something positive comes out of it."

"What was your brother occupation?"

"Minding his business, I suppose" he replied returning his stare.

"Whatever it might have been it was serious for so many people attempting to touch him."

"Or his size intimidated them" he counter watching the property officer returning.

"Here you go, young man" he said placing an envelope through the metal window. "I need your signature right there" he said pointing and getting his signature. "Thank you" he replied giving him a carbon copy.

"Thank you, sir" he said taking the property. "Enjoy your day" he wished him, starting to turn. "Enjoy your day also, Detective" he said pressing the elevator button then stepping inside. He exited the building then stood on the sidewalk looking around. He eventually waved down another hack then headed out towards the Gwynn Oaks section of town. He asked the driver to wait for him while he went inside to take care of his business. Ten minutes later, he was exiting with a recipe for the urn then climb back into the hack. Drop me off at Lexington Market" he told him. Driving past Mondawmin Mall, a coy smile crept across his lips remembering the things he got away with, with Misty. Cruising down Pennsylvania Avenue, it was nice to know that Shake and Bake, the roller rink was still open. The statue of Billie Holiday still stand strong counter corner to the renowned Royal Theater at Moser Street. He used to sit at her monument for hours just reading. At Lexington Market, the scene had gotten worst. The addicts were becoming younger and younger. He paid for the hack then tried walking into the market without some drug dealers whispering what product they were selling. Finally walking inside, he walked around surveying several stalls before finding one that looked safe enough to eat from. He decided on two crab cakes and a supreme salad with four large bottles of water. He grabbed several old newspapers before leaving to get the reporters view and opinion of the murders that occurred. He nodded and smile at T.T as he headed towards the elevators.

Entering his room, he took his meal and the newspaper out on the balcony. With jazz playing in the background, he slightly snarled at the stories, but several things were consistent. According to police reports and the investigator for the Sun Paper, all of the deceased lived in Cherry Hill and had extensive criminal records which includes distribution of drugs and illegal weapon possession. Of course, five-o went into Cherry Hill trying to reconnect with old snitches, but nothing was on the grapevine and understandable. Who was crazy enough to boast about the murder especially of Road Block?

"The two other victims especially Shabazz Mohammad didn't have a criminal record at all. Diki (Warrior) Carter did do three years at Hagerstown Correctional Facility for his alleged part in a carjacking but been clean since coming home almost ten years ago. Both were being highly recruited for football coming from out of Dunbar High. Detectives are speculating it was as usual a drug deal gone wrong, but this investigator don't accept their speculation. Where is the evidence to suggest such a claim? An estimated one hundred casing were recovered from the crime scene, experience tells this investigator reporter that this was not a drug deal gone wrong but an orchestrated assassination. Why is the question that needs to be considered not speculations considering the two demised didn't possess an excessive criminal records or anything that consisted with drug dealing? Detectives are still wondering as though they were naïve as to why two seemingly law-abiding citizen had powder residue on their hands and their palm prints on separate weapons. Even this reporter can answer that question. Because its' easier to get a gun on the streets of Baltimore to protect yourself than to find employment. There are also some vicious predators out there trying to get paid. While the police do their investigation, this reporter will be doing his."

A coy smile creased his lips. He grabbed the bag with his brother's possession and tore it open. His placed the contents on the table before him. A wallet containing his driver's license, a bank card, a picture of them in Atlanta's Black Museum and a set of car keys belonging to his metallic gray Escalade. The driver's license had a Columbia address. As he stared at it, he knew his mission wasn't completed today as he had hoped. He had to locate his brother's vehicle somewhere near the 5th Regiment Armory. The newspaper said the assassination took place near Dolphin and McCulloh

Street near the McCulloh Homes. So, he would start there. He grabbed his trash then discarded it in the receptacle. Grabbing his hat, he was out the door again. He caught a cab in front of the lobby to Dolphin and Druid Hill. Walking down Dolphin Street, he crossed the street. His brother would have walked on the opposite side. As he slowed his pace, he stared at the ruminants of blood. He took sight of the crossfire lanes. He walked another ten feet before stepping into the street. More blood than before. Walking down the middle of the street, blood spatters were everywhere. Crossing to the other side, indentations of where bullets struck the wall could be seen. Continuing, he came to a small street leading to a court. He press the lock button on the keys and listen but nothing. He continued further then press the lock button again and got a response. He walked into the court and there it was. Lightly tinted windows and dirty as hell. Residents were sitting outside escaping the smothering heat inside of their homes. They watch him closely as he pressed the vehicle button to allow him access inside. They had been watching the abandon SUV for three days with aspirations steadily growing. Several people had taken a closer look inside, but nobody broke into it because any of their neighbors would snitch if the right person came asking.

He sat there for a moment before starting up the engine and Sonny Clark's "Cool Struttin" filled the interior. He open the moon roof to allow his music to escape through the moonroof then placed the Columbia address in the navigational system. After adjusting the mirrors, he pulled out of the parking spot. He jumped on Martin Luther King Blvd. from Druid Hill Avenue then jumped on 395S then transfer over to 295 S. He reached his destination in a half hour. A black 750 Beamer was parked on his parking pad. So, he parked on the street. The traditional ranch style home is exactly like something his brother would buy. Everything on one floor. Climbing the steps at his home wasn't something that Road Block enjoyed. He sat staring at the house after he turned off the engine, his brother's neighbor stepped outside of her house as he stepped out the car.

"Shabazz is that you?" the woman asked softly while coming closer.

"No, it's his brother" he replied coming around the car.

"Malik" she replied smiling at him then it slowly dissipated. "So, it's true" she said rejected. "I was hoping that the news got it twisted especially after seeing his SUV pulling up. Shit!" she vented allowing her tears to suddenly flow freely. "Excuse me, I'm Charmaine" she introduced herself while wiping her eyes then shaking his hand. "Your brother was a blessing no matter what he might have been about. If not for him, I don't know what me and my three children would have done after my worthless ass husband abandon us," she revealed slightly hardening her eyes then they suddenly became soft. "Your brother stepped in three years ago and brought this house then signed it over to me. Did you hear me?" she asked flashing a beautiful smile. "He just gave it to me, Malik" she shared as her eyes suddenly became watery again. "How many men you know would do that and not ask for something in return? How many do you know Malik?" she asked with conviction as tears flowed from her eyes again. "Your brother was a beautiful man and he spoke very highly of you all the time" she smiled. "He always came back and shared his experience with you, but he never revealed where you lived. I loved your brother. If you need anything, anything at all just ask. You also have my condolence" she slightly smiled heading back towards her home crying.

He proceeded to the front door. Opening it, he stepped inside then closed the door and leaned against it. From his position, he took in the scene. A large poster size picture of them when he was about fourteen-years old was over the fireplace. He wore a pair of jeans, Tim's and a button-down brown shirt with a Cleveland Brown fitted hat while Sha had on a two-piece walking set with a medium brim hat. Their broad smiles revealed they had shared a genuine laugh. The light gray walls complimented the ebony color floors extending throughout the house. He kneel to pick up the mail that has been acuminating and placed them on the small table to the left of him. He slowly inspected the first floor, the addition instead of a garage created a beautiful family room which bought instant value to the house. He still had his parking pad, right? Descending the steps to the basement, everything was almost the same as his house. The heavy bag, speed bag, jump ropes and gloves was towards the far left. Another stereo set was situated in front of two over-sized love seats and a couch that had to be specially ordered. The thing was massive. Exactly right for a three hundred plus pound man and his partner. A light thick laminated floor extended throughout with a bar containing six chairs. Retracing his route, he inspected all three bedrooms especially the master bedroom with its on suite and walk-in closet. A picture of them when he graduated college was next to his flat screen television. He remember that week very vividly.

He had sent a round trip ticket for him initially to a mutual friends house. To inform him of who sent it, he used a code that only he would recognize. He could only image the look that probably came to his face. He arrived on time at Hartsfield-Jackson International. Coming off the airplane, he was standing there wearing a broad smile when their eyes met.

"Big Brother" he greeted opening his arms.

"Little Brother" he replied scooping him up into his massive arms while laughing. Placing him back on the floor, he stared into his eyes again. "You look like you're doing okay" he shared admiring his black Armani suit.

"I'm good" he assured him grinning. "Let's grabbed your bags and get out of here" he told him leading him toward the baggage claims department. Grabbing his two suit cases, he led him back towards his car. Pressing the trunk button, they placed his bags inside. Climbing inside, he started up the engine and Wynton Marsalis filter through the Bose speaker as they drove up the ramp to Rt.285. They drove in relatively quiet as Road Block took in the green scenery.

"So, why did I have to come down on a Thursday?"

"Because I'm graduating from Morehouse tomorrow" he smiled at him.

"Morehouse? Are you serious?"

"Yup, fifth in my class."

"A book worm huh?" he slightly chuckled. "I'm proud of you boy."

"So am I" he replied taking the off the ramp then proceeding towards Northside Drive. After an assortment of turns, he slowed his speed.

"Did you move?"

"Yeah, I couldn't refuse the latest offer for one point two million" he shared grinning.

"I know you don't live around here?" he stated staring at the tree line street and manicured lawns.

"I have the best house on the block again" he boasted pulling up on his parking pad.

"Damn!" he declared admiring the massive home. "All this is you?" he asked stepping out and closing the door behind himself. He retrieved his suitcases from the trunk then follow Lion towards the front door.

"The place was an eye sore before the renovations" he told him inserting his key then pushing the door open.

Stepping inside, Road Block stared up at the tall ceiling with recess lighting. The dark wood floors extending throughout with African artifacts situated in certain areas on the first floor. This brought a smile to his lips. Placing his bag at his feet, he methodically walked over to a poster size picture of him and Lion on his sixteenth birthday. They were chilling inside Dru Hill Park watching the girls at the swimming pool in their very seductive bathing suits. The expression on their faces indicated that they were staring at something that definitely had their attention. The impish smiles on their faces indicated it. They sat up talking and laughing until almost four o'clock in the morning. The next morning around eleven o'clock he was strolling across the stage to receive his diploma. He had gotten a friend to take a picture of them and he also introduced him to Natasha. She also told him about how he threw her ex-boyfriend out of a window causing Road Block to burst out laughing. Lion showed him just how bad most shooter were on the streets when he placed his Glock .40 in Road Blocks hand. From fifteen yards away, he was piss poor and he laugh his ass off. Once he educated him about the fundamentals of equal height, equal light, he improved tremendously especially from fifteen yards away. His range at twenty-five would improve. At lease, he's now hitting the target.

He extinguish the basement lights then walked back towards the living room. He grabbed the remote and turned on the music. Miles Davis and John Coltrane "Round About Midnight" filled the quietness. He sat on the couch contemplating his next moves. He don't remember falling asleep. The morning sun creeping through the window is what woke him. Glancing at his watch, nine-forty-five. Extremely late by his standards. He washed his face then applied some Palmer's coconut butter to his face. He grabbed the keys then walked out the door. As he headed up 95N, he took the 365-S ramp to M.L.K Blvd then turned left onto Pennsylvania Avenue. He stopped at the top where it connect at Fulton Avenue and pulled onto J.H. Brown Funeral Home parking lot. Why do all funeral homes smell alike? He rented the main hall for the memorial. Although his brother would have feed them, he wasn't his brother. His business was completed in a half hour including the flower arrangements. He got a call that he could retrieved his brother's remains and went directly to collect it then shot right back to the funeral home. Next stop, the black owned bank near the Inner Harbor. Walking inside, he approached one of the middle-aged black workers.

"May I assist you?" she asked staring at his attire slightly smiling.

"Yes ma'am, my brother was murdered a couple of days ago and I'm here to close out his accounts."

"I'm sorry for your lost" she said staring into his eyes.

"Thank you" he replied slightly grinning.

"I need his death certificate and your I.D please" she requested. He pulls out his driver's license and the death certificate then extended both to her. She hit a couple of keys then study the screen. "He has a security code" she informed him with a strange expression.

"I'm not surprise" he smiled.

"Do you know his pass word?"

"Give me the hint" he requested.

"In what land was the garden of eve?"

"Afro-asiatic" he replied nonchalantly slightly smiling.

Entering his answer, she stared at the screen peculiar as she gain access, but he knew why? She assumed like so many others without doing her own research. She pulled up his account then stared over at him perplex. "Just a moment please" she requested getting to her feet then going into a supervisor office. They spoke briefly before they both returned.

"Mr. Mohammad, I'm Mr. Jamaal (he is beauty) Temple" an exquisitely dress early fiftyish man slightly smiling introduce himself while shaking his hand. "Will you follow me please" he requested taking the lead towards his office. "I was devastated over the demise of your brother. When I heard what happen to Road Block, I actually felt like grabbing a gun" he stated adamantly with conviction in his eyes and in his words. Using his nickname, he revealed that he had a close relationship with his brother beyond business. "Have a seat please" he offered as he went to a private floor safe. He retrieved a yellow envelope then extended it to him. "I was told to give this to you and nobody else. Come, let me escort you to his safety deposit box" he said leading the way towards a lower level where an armed guard was station on the outside of some iron bars.

"Good afternoon, Mr. Temple" he greeted with a genuine smile.

"Good afternoon, Ralph" he replied returning his smile while using his key to enter then escorted him to the deposit boxes and claiming his.

He took him to a small office. "When you're finish, we can complete our business upstairs."

"Yes sir" he replied as he turned and walked away. He closed the door and surveyed the room for cameras before opening the steel canister. Inside, several diamond studded watches like Rolex and BVLGARI but there was some with names he never heard like Hublot and Frack Muller. There were also several wrist bracelets by designers like David Yurman and Versace Medusa plus about fifty-thousand-dollars in cash. Opening a leather folder, he found a ten-million-dollar life insurance policy and the deeds to several homes in the city including his own home. There was a flash drive that definitely perked his interest. Lifting the tray, a light chuckled escape him then an impish grin crossed his lips. A black Glock .40 with four eighteen round clips fully loaded. There were also two envelopes. One said open immediately while the other had leisure on it. Opening it, the message was simple. "If you're reading this, I was murder, but you don't have to look no further than the game. I love you." His breathing became shallow while his heart rate slightly picked up as his anger slowly build. His suspicion was correct, and he would find out who? He grabbed the black trash bag in the trash can then place the contents inside except the Glock and twenty-thousand-dollars. He placed the Glock in the small of his back and the money in his breast pocket then returned to Mr. Temple's office.

"So, how do you want your transaction?"

"You can transfer it to this account except fifty thousand dollars" he said extending his saving account routing number to him. "I want to keep an account open in my name and this is for you" he said placing the money under a folder.

"That's not necessary, Malik" he said shaking his head.

"You know it's not polite to refuse a gift" he mention slightly grinning.

"Your brother assisted this bank a hell of a lot over the years and apparently his good nature rubbed off on you. Thanks, Malik" he said getting to his feet to shake his hand. "Enjoy your day."

"You too Jamaal" he smiled then turned to exit. His business was completed in thirty minutes. He walked back out-side then returned to his suite to shower and change his clothes. He gather his belongings then checked the room twice before closing the door behind himself. Taking the elevator to the lobby, he approached the receptionist desk.

"You're leaving us already" Ms. Jackson asked unable to hide her displeasure.

"Yes, I am T.T" he replied placing the electronic key and his credit card on the counter top.

"Are you heading back to Atlanta if I'm not being too inquisitive" she asked with a coy smile while preparing his receipt.

"Na, I'll be in the city for a while."

"I hope we run into one another."

"Who knows" he smiled at her. "This city isn't as big as people thinks."

"Those of us who haven't been anywhere would contradict that statement" she slightly grinned handing him back is credit card.

"True that" he admitted. "I hope you enjoy your day" he wish her as he gather his leather bag.

"Enjoy yours as well" she replied watching him heading back towards the elevator. He must be driving somebody's car. As she watched the elevator door closing, she wonder would she ever see him again.

At Garrison and Park Heights, Ice was sitting in his Infinity monitoring one of his corners. He's been having trouble with this location. He should be making a hell of a lot more than he was. As he watch their operation, one thing he didn't like almost instantly was the mule and his money stood too close together. He don't mind losing his drugs or any of them but not his damn money too. They were also paying too much attention to the street wise flirting young ladies pressing up on them. Women aren't anything but a damn distraction when you should be looking out for five-o. Just as he was about to address them, he notice Sunshine pulling up behind him in his white Escalade. Getting out, he approached the passenger side door then climbed inside.

"What's happening Ice?" he asked getting comfortable.

"Not too much, what's up with you?" he asked wondering why he was in his territory.

"Road Block's Escalade been seen driving through the city" he informed him staring at him observing his corner boys.

"What?" he asked grabbing his attention from the corner. "Are you sure?"

"I haven't seen it myself, but the source of the information is good" he assured him returning his stare.

"So, Lion's in town huh?" he stated with a slight snarl then returned his eyes to the corner boys.

"Byrd said he would return" he reminded him. "They're having a memorial for him on Saturday according to social media. Are we going?"

"We all have to show our faces!" he snapped staring at him like he had asked an asinine question. "I hope that little nigger bounce after this shit is over."

"I doubt it" he replied. "According to Byrd."

"Fuck Byrd!" he snapped hardening his eyes at him.

"You can say what you want, but I'm listening to him. He think Lion isn't going anywhere until he gets some answers."

"That little nigger won't get shit from the streets, nothing. Only five-o can provide him answers but those answers won't lead him to us."

"I hope not" he admitted lighting up a cigarette then pulling from it. "You know when you do scandalous shit, you can't leave any loose ends."

"Loose ends" he repeated staring back at him with harden eyes.

"What? You mean my people in Cherry Hill. Those motherfuckers know how to keep their mouths close" he told him with a slight snarl.

"Considering their reputation as snitches when the heat gets hot, that doesn't bother you?"

"Snitches? Bullshit! My people won't say shit!"

"Man, you need to get into the streets more" he slightly smiled. "When you have a high profiled case concerning a B.G.F snitching to the Feds to save his bitch ass. Your contractor is not even in the game, what do you think a motherfucker in the game gonna do when he's under pressure?"

"Keep their motherfucking mouth closed if they know better" he claimed.

"When I'm conducting my business around Philly and Camden, Jersey, I don't lay claim to Baltimore."

"Well, I would" he stated flatly.

"Do so and those cities would treat you like the black plague" he informed him.

"Man fuck them!" he countered staring at him. "As far as Lion is concern, there's no way he can find out about us. No, motherfucking way."

"You're ready to bet our lives on it?" he asked staring him in his eyes before opening the door then stepping out. He came to a conclusion walking back to his car. Ice was a stupid motherfucker. Byrd knows this kid and place the warning sign on the table. Byrd never gets excited but excusing Lion as just another guy infuriated him with Ice. If Lion gets the slightest scent of blood, he will become a manhunter as Byrd described to him privately one night before the actual hit. His eyes held a conviction and apprehension he rarely seen in his eyes. Granted, he too was down for the take-over, but the mentioning of this guy name Lion had him wondering was it worth it?

The day he laid his brother to rest was a usually cool day for July. As he sat up in the balcony observing so many of his brother's friends and business associates, he knew those responsible for this day were among the on-lookers. As groups of women came in crying, a sadness suddenly filled his heart. His brother was a usually generous person when it came to women. Those women were crying had just lost a damn good friend and provider. If they weren't on drugs, he would assist them as much as he dared. He had paid for twenty young ladies to attend nursing school and they all graduated. Assisting a woman in getting her children school clothes, paying the rent once or electric bill twice was nothing to him. If you didn't try to play him, he could be the man he was. While most drug dealers thought he had lost his got damn mind, his humanity wouldn't allow him the luxury of enjoying the wealth he had acuminated without sharing it. He knew he was also one of the cancers that was engulfing their city and his community. Something he was very aware of while making some form of restitution.

Scanning the room, he finally found his mother. The heroin and crack had taken its toll on her. Her body appeared frail, but she always kept her hair up. Still slightly attractive despite her addiction, she sat in the front being consoled by some guy. Although he knew he had to say something to her, he didn't know what? She hadn't fulfilled her role as a mother or parent so why should he fulfill his role as a son? The only connection he had with her was biological and nothing else. Scanning the room further, his eyes rested on a group of guys sitting in the middle towards the left side. Their attire left no doubt about their position and the men sitting behind them as bodyguards confirmed his suspicion. Studying each one of them closely, he slowly recognized one. Although older and much heavier from living the good life, he could still recognize Byrd. He used to be close friends with his brother back in the day. He crept behind his brother's back to fuck a girl that he knew Sha was feeling and she knew it. That one discretion was enough for Sha to sever their friendship. Introducing her to cocaine mixed with heroin, she gradually occurred a slight habit.

He rode her curves a few times then drop her like a bad habit for another quest. Realizing how much she had fucked up, she tried in vain to amend her deception and indiscretion, but Sha cut her completely off and Byrd damn sure didn't give a damn about her one way or the other. Two years later, she was a full-blown addict turning tricks on Pennsylvania Avenue for thirty dollars. Watching him closely, he was discretely searching for someone, and Lion knew who?

As the memorial began, the words the preacher recited didn't bring peace to his heart or soul. The only man he absolutely loved was in an urn while those responsible were still breathing and more than likely, attending this memorial. His attention went back to Byrd. The light skin guy to his right was whispering something to the guy at his right. The expressions that engulfed their faces was intense. Whatever they were discussion made Byrd react whispering something to them before straightening up with a look of discuss on his face. The displayed cause Lion's intuition to start twitching. Hearing his mother voice disrupted his train of thought.

"I am Malik's mother and that's all I am. Malik is Shabazz's little brother. I had an opportunity to step up for Shabazz when his mother O.D and their father went to prison, but I didn't" she confess slightly lowering her head. "I put my addiction before either of them. And I'm not proud to admit it. No, Shabazz wasn't an angle but none of us are. If you think you are, you're a damn liar. Although I would see Sha occasionally around the city, he always extended himself to me even though he knew what I was going to do with the money he gave me. His generosity is well known and what kept me from tricking to support my habit. I know his brother did this for him, but I haven't seen my only child in almost thirteen years. I abandon him when he was incarcerated for a crime he didn't commit. He's extremely close because I can feel his presence" she shared embracing herself while staring around the room. "All I can request is that he acknowledge me before he disappears again. If those responsible for murdering Shabazz is here, restitution will be required" she said, revealing as menacing stare. "I pray that the law catch you first. No, that is a lie because I want the streets to get you. If the streets extracts its form of justice, you would have prayed that five-o had gotten their hands on your scandalous asses first" she told them with malice in her eyes. "If not, you will see why they call my son Lion" she informed them staring out at them with menacing eyes before she slowly descended the steps and reclaimed her seat.

Lion stared back at the light skin guy. Her words seems to have slightly shaken him. His head was now on a swivel looking around until the guy he was arguing with said something to him causing him to settle the fuck down. He clasp his hands together then slightly lowered his head trying to gain control. What his estrange mother said was true. Pray that five-o or the streets extract restitution, because he knew deep down inside, he was about to regress and transform into some ungodly medieval motherfucker. As the sermon gradually came to an ending and the last prayer were being quoted, everybody got to their feet and lowered their heads as Road Block's remains were cuddle in his mother's arms except Byrd and his associates. They were scanning the room again. Not until they started filing out and looking up into the balcony did, Byrd finally notice him. Dress completely in black with his eyes hidden by a pair of Oakley sunglasses was Lion staring down upon them. Although none of them remembered him but Byrd, why should they? Most people outside of the East Side didn't know Road Block even had a little brother including some that knew Sha all of their lives. As the others looked in the direction that Byrd was looking, there were no mistake who the stranger was. From his position, they knew he had witness everything that had transpired down below including Sunshine incident with Ice Pick. Just as a lion would survey for prey, he was surveying for his. Byrd tipped his hat to him slightly smiling and he removed his sunglasses to reveal his eyes and acknowledged him by tipping his hat also as he led the group out. He put his sunglasses back on then took a deep breath. His eyes went back to his mother and the people giving her their condolences. A slight coy smile came to his face as he shook his head. He suddenly turned and descended the balcony steps then position himself to watch Byrd and his entourage. He wanted to make a mental note which car they were driving especially the light skin guy.

"Malik? Malik?" his mother's voice caused him to avert his eyes from Byrd and placed them on her. "Oh my God, it is you!" she said walking towards him smiling as he removed his sunglasses causing her to stop in her track and her smile slowly dissipate because of the intensity in his eyes.

"Mother" he replied nonchalantly while peeking at the guy escorting her.

"How have you been baby?" she asked wanting to reach out and touch him but knew she didn't deserve that privilege. She couldn't even remember the last time she even hugged her only child.

"I'm doing just fine under the circumstances."

"Will you ride to the grave site with me, please?"

He paused for a moment before responding. He stared out into the parking lot at Byrd and his associates before staring back into her eyes. He could see her desperation. "Under one condition."

"Sure, what is it baby?" she asked slightly smiling.

"No conversations."

"What?" she replied, a little surprise by the demand.

"You heard me, Mother. Can you do that?"

"Yes Malik, I won't say a word. I promise" she said staring into his eyes.

"Is he serious baby?" the guy asked staring over at him with a slight smirk on his face.

Before he knew what was happening, his ability to freely breathe was suddenly gone as fear engulfed his eyes. With both of his hands-on Lion's arm, Lion had wrapped his finger around his throat then pulled his victim to him and whisper. "Stay the fuck out of my lane or get wreck you leeching, motherfucker" he warned the guy staring into his eyes before releasing his vice like grip and allowing him to breathe again.

"Didn't I tell you to watch what you say and to stay in your damn lane! This is family business, not your business" she hiss at him while staring at him coldly. "He is not Sha!" she told him then turned and headed out the door with the guy still gasping and a girlfriend close in tow. She open the door of the limo then stepped inside leaving the door open for him.

Lion put his shades on then proceeded out the door and stared over at Byrd before climbing into the limo. Sha's grave site was in the Gwynn Oaks Cemetery. This is the spot where he used to take him to feed the geese when he was about ten. He was so surprised to see wild geese so close to the city and astounded by their natural size especially the aggressive males when protecting their family. They all can be a little aggressive when free food was being surrendered. When several came at him trying to intimidate him to drop his bag of bread crumbs, he reacted like a lion causing some of them to take flight and others scurrying away. As he sat there eating the bread crumbs in front of them, Sha was laughing his ass of. When he had asked him, if they were in the hood do you think you would still see them? He naturally burst out laughing at the absurd question before answering. No way, they would be somebody's dinner. The thought made him slightly grin then focus on those in the limo before returning his eyes to the view outside. The guy had track marks on the back of his left hand revealing that he shot the vein out further up his arm. Abscess must have occurred, or he would still be hitting in the traditional places. His attire reassured him that he was nothing but a leech. Who would hire a frail, ass junky? The woman was guilty by association and that was all he needed to know. The ride there seems quicker than anticipated. He allowed her to pour his ashes into the hole that was provided saying, "From the earth we were created and to the earth we must return." The urn will return to Atlanta with him. While everyone return to their vehicles and head back to the funeral parlor for something to eat that someone sprung for, because he damn sure didn't, he will stay behind to cry over his brother. This will now be the place he could come to meditate on his mentor and brother instead of laughing with him and building more memories.

Once he gained controlled, his eyes had become harden again and his mind took on a more sinister side. The same mind-set it took to set up four corrupt drug enforcement cops in a criminal case. His mind was filtering through the things he knew and speculated. All the assailants were from out of Cherry Hill and if there were survivors, that's where they will be unless someone decides to get rid of loose ends. A smart motherfucker would. Living in Cherry Hill, they will eventually flash what they earned. Either by buying new clothes and jewelry or investing coming out with a package of their own. A new used car is the usual give away. Either scenarios will shine a spotlight on them, and he'll be right there to drag them into the darkness for some privacy. He need to get his clutches on just one of them and he'll gladly surrender everything he knows including their social security number before still getting a bullet to the back of the head although most likely, he want the guy to see it coming.

When he finally arrived back at the funeral parlor, he greeted several people he haven't seen since he was sixteen.

"Excuse me, Lion" a stranger pardon himself. "My name is Bunkie, brother. Let me holla at you for a moment" he requested getting a little distance from those he was talking to. "I could have very easily shared with everyone what your brother did for me, but it's not their motherfucking business" he express with a slight snarl. "Road Block was a straight up G and I'm not talking about a gangster either. The biggest heart I know for someone in the game with his status. When I caught a nickel while working for him, he took diligent care of my wife and two children. How many motherfuckers in the game would do that?" he asked hardening his eyes as his voice revealed his emotions. "I've squared up since coming home but

I still got connections in the streets. Since your brother and Monster got assassinated, yeah, I said assassinated, the streets are noticeably quiet and that's extremely unusual. If you need me for anything, anything" he stress staring in his eyes. "Call me" he said extending his number to him. "You need somebody to watch your back Lion. Call me anytime day or night, brother" he stress slightly frowning while staring intensively in his eyes.

"Thanks brother" he said shaking his hand. "I do need back up."

"Not anymore" he said suddenly turning then walking out the door.

He stood there watching Bunkie walking across the parking lot towards Pennsylvania Avenue.

"Lion, it's been too many years" a voice said to him causing him to turn around.

"Hey Byrd" he replied shaking his hand. The years haven't appeared to touch his health for a forty-something guy. He appears to still work out lightly which said a lot to him. He remember watching him and Road Block boxing back in the day. He was nice with his hands, but Road Block was slick with his. He used to admire how Road would kiss a guy's glove as it missed its target then dig up in their asses. Slick shit, and with his size and power, he was putting people to sleep regularly. Only those that wasn't smart enough to comp a deuce would taste his power.

"So, how have you been?"

"I been okay."

"It's fucked up what happen to my man, Sha" he said staring in his eyes. "We think it's some niggers from out of town because the streets are very quiet."

"Na, too many rounds" he replied dismissing his suggestion. "Try again" he offered returning his stare.

"Too many rounds, what do you mean?"

"Every paper that I've read estimated that there were approximately a hundred to a hundred and fifty rounds being discharged. Does that sound like motherfuckers from out of town trying to get paid?" he asked returning his stare.

"Na, it doesn't" he had to admit. Out of towners would never discharge that many rounds for a simple stick-up or hit.

"Is there any stick-up crew in Baltimore that's known for carrying two AK's?" he asked staring deep into his eyes.

"Two AK's?" he replied surprise by the information.

"Yeah, Byrd" he replied staring in his eyes. "Does that sound like a stick-up crew?"

"Na, there's no stick-up crew packing like that" he had to admit.

"I didn't think so either" he replied slightly grinning.

"What do you think?"

"Not a robbery, that's for sure" he told him. "I'm puzzle as to why? Did he ever infiltrate somebody turf?"

"Na, Sha don't get down like that" he stress returning his stare.

"Yeah, I know" he cosigned slightly snarling.

"What did five-o say?"

"Who said I talked to them?" he asked staring in his eyes and watching how he reacted to the question then suddenly smiling and watching how relaxed he suddenly became. "Same bullshit as usual. Drug deal gone wrong" he said nonchalantly not surrendering any more information.

"Sha don't have a rap sheet" he mention.

"Yeah, I know that but who am I to dispute the professionals and those with the word integrity on the side of their vehicles?" he asked with a slight smirk.

"Where are you living now?"

"On America's soil" was all he surrendered.

"Alright" he slightly smiled. "If you need anything, call me" he said extending a card to him.

"Sure will" he told him peeking over his shoulder at his entourage watching him closely especially the light skin guy.

"Stay cool Lion."

"You too Byrd" he told him watching his entourage following him out the door. He caught all their eyes directly except the high yellow guy. His eyes remained very evasive. The stare from one guy had him peeking on him closely.

"Man, that little nigger isn't shit" Ice Pick chuckled as they walked towards their car.

"You're dumb enough to stagger right into his trap" counter Byrd. "You didn't hear what he said? Assassination not robbery. He's far from dumb Ice no matter how slick you think you are. If you continue to play your hand, you're going to become a bleep on his radar and that won't be healthy for your body."

"Boy, you're tripping" he counter waving him off while laughing and nudging Bash.

"You're not hearing me. You dumb motherfucker" he suddenly smiled at him instead of glaring. "If I knew you was an asshole, I would have never gotten into business with you."

"Fuck you Byrd!"

"Na, fuck you!" he stated stepping forward towards one another ignoring the spectators, but Bash stepped in between them.

"Chill, yawl!" Bash insisted staring at both men. "Yawl got motherfuckers peeking at yawl" he slightly snarled at them. "You know five-o is set-up somewhere taking pictures and snooping. So, chill" he urged them.

"Bash, we got loose ends" Byrd reminded him.

"Meek or his boys won't say shit! The twenty G's they received guarantee that" he tried to assure him returning his glare.

"Are you willing to bet our lives on twenty G's? Well, I'm not" he told him staring into his eyes with a slight snarl on his lips.

"Leave Meeks alone, he's family. If he's touch, shit is going to get real crazy in the streets up around Edmondson Avenue" he warned him.

"Is that a threat motherfucker?"

"Na, men don't make threats, You know that. I'm making a promise" he assured him returning his cold stare.

"You and I are going to have a very private conversation after this shit is over" Byrd informed him grinning slightly. He was going to beat the living shit out of him this time and dare his bitch ass to reach for a gun. He will have immense pleasure in blowing his ass away.

What the group didn't know was Lion watched the whole scenario unfold and the almost eruption of violence. A coy smile came to his lips as a faint smell of fear was on the air. He watched as sides were being formed. Whatever caused the argument must have been serious. Only a nigger's life being in jeopardy would cause a disruption at a funeral. "They know something" he silently whisper to himself. He needed to get to Cherry Hill.

"Hi Lion" a soft voice spoke to him.

He turned to see the mature face of his first love. Her ebony complexion was still smooth with locs that extended down to her shoulder blades and that radiant smile. "Misty?"

"You remember" she smiled giving him a hug. Damn he felt good and smelt just as exotic as his eyes have always appeared to her. "It's really good seeing you, again" she said releasing him. "Damn, you got tall" she giggled.

"Just a little" he replied. "Damn woman, I see that you've been blessed" he complimented her admiring the contour of her body especially those slightly flaring hips.

"Thank you" she replied slightly blushing. "When did you get into town?"

"Monday."

"Was you going to call me?"

"Eventually" he assured her. "I had to contend with all this first."

"His home coming was beautiful" she told him staring out into the parking lot. "What's up with those fools?"

"I only know Byrd and vaguely remember the one he called Ice. I'm assuming they must be the other biggest distributors in the city."

"Yes, they are" she assured him. "I might not be in the streets now, but I know who's running them. Byrd has been beefing with Ice Pick for years then shit took a serious turn when Ice Pick cousin got caught up in Edmondson Village three years ago trying to hit one of Byrd's lieutenants and drove themselves straight into a dead-end street. Big dummies" she lightly chuckled. "Bodies were getting stretch-out from one end of the west side to the other as homicide detectives were working overtime trying to get a handle on it. And while all this was materializing, the East Side Boyz was watching like vultures. Ready to pick their bones. If Road Block didn't mediate to increase the peace, the Feds was just about ready to crash the city, and nobody wants those trigger-happy book worm looking fools around. Only persons that would have still been making money would have been your brother and Sunshine."

"Sunshine is the light skin guy, huh?" he asked still staring out at them.

"Yeah."

"Why just those two?"

"Your brother kept his men feed and they were very loyal to him. Sunshine inherited his position from his older brother. He still have another dime to do for trafficking up in New York. Everything was already set for him. All he had to do was keep the books straight. If any corner came up short, he had soldiers to deal with such things."

"So, he's not a true grinder huh?"

"Not the way you mean it, he never stood on no corners or bust that tool" she informed him lightly chuckled. "The guy walking with Ice is Bash. An extremely dangerous guy. Make no mistake, he doesn't have a problem in banging that tool."

"Is he Ice's bodyguard?"

"I don't know what he does but he's always close to Ice when they are on the streets" she informed him as they watched their vehicles pulling off the lot. He was trying to make a mental note of each vehicle. "So, what are your plans?"

"Getting my brother's business in order."

"What, you're not staying?"

"I have a life some-place else Misty" he replied.

"But, what about Road?" she asked staring at him puzzled.

"Five-o is on it" he replied returning her stare.

"What?" she asked surprised by his statements. "Five-o? They are a motherfucking joke. So, you are just going to leave, huh?" she asked with harden eyes.

"Listen" he told her in a slightly stern voice and hardening eyes catching her completely off guard. "What-ever intentions I might have you don't need to know them or concern yourself, alright?" he stated staring into her eyes.

"Okay, Lion" she replied in a soft meek voice. She had forgotten just that quickly who she was talking to and paid the price by getting her sensitive feelings hurt.

"Tell me about Bunkie."

"Bunkie? You know Bunkie?"

"I'm asking you a simple question" he replied ignoring her question.

"One of many who is obligated to your brother and an elite street soldier" she informed him. "If he's offering his services, take it" she advised him slightly hardening her eyes. "Take it Lion."

"I'll keep it in mind."

"So," she slightly sigh. "What are your plans for this evening?"

"Chilling at my brother's house" he shared.

"I hope you're not thinking about selling it. Property should always stay in the family. Do you have any children?" she asked staring at him.

"Not yet, what about you?"

"Na" she replied. "Too many bullshitting men in Baltimore. The good ones that aren't already taken would rather play the field than have a monogamist relationship and sometimes, I don't blame them with all the bullshit some women bring to the table. I do not have intentions of joining the ranks of single parenthood, but I remember what you wrote while incarcerated. Babies are life yearning to be born. Men seem to run away from their responsibilities or is it us?" she shared slightly grinning. "Are you seeing anybody romantically?"

"I was dating a young woman for two years. She was constantly in my ears about having a child together and I told her repeatedly that I was cool with that. All I asked is that she be a little more patient while I finish school and get a job. Well, she couldn't wait and bounce."

"She left you because of that?"

"Na" he suddenly chuckled causing her to stare at him with a smirk.

"I didn't think that would be a reason to drop somebody" she replied. "So, what really happen Lion?"

"I caught her on the bathroom floor with her legs up trying to insert my sperm out of a condom" he shared slightly smiling.

"Are you for real?" she asked astonished. "Scandalous bitch" she said shaking her head smiling.

"Yeah, kind of fucked me up also. Excuse my language" he apologized.

"I wonder how long she was doing that?"

"Exactly what I was wondering" he admitted unable to contain his laughter. "After that, I couldn't trust her. She had that child she desired a couple of years ago by a drug dealer. He's now doing ten years on a manslaughter charge."

"Whoa, she got what she wanted but at a price" she replied. "Are you going to break bread with your mother?"

"Na, there are so many other things I can do than break bread with her."

"No matter what's she about Lion, she still gave you, life" she said. "Since you're going to be just chilling, give me a call around eight so we can do something."

"I think I can do that" he said then added. "Don't break your date."

"I won't. There is nobody that holds my heart" she smiled stepping closer and kissing him on the cheek. "Holla at you later" she said pushing open the door then stepping out. She walked to her gray Toyota feeling his eyes on her then climbed inside. Starting up the engine and opening the moon roof, X-scape's "Who Can I Run To" filter out the car as she drove pass waving then blowing him a kiss.

What she said did have some merits. His mother could have aborted him but instead she decided to give life its opportunity thus him life while placing her life in danger during the process. From what he heard growing up and the few pictures of them, she did stop sniffing dope while she was pregnant. She contributes his laid back and quiet disposition to the effects of her smoking marijuana. She did at least consider his health during his incubation even if she didn't consider her own once he was born. She eagerly went back to her familiar lifestyle. Will he ever humble himself to her, maybe but not now, and definitely not today?

Sitting across the street, the Detectives working the case were puzzled and searching for a reason. Shabazz didn't fit the characteristic of a drug dealer, especially a high-profile dealer. The watch he wore was valued at two-hundred dollars with no other jewelry. He had a hundred dollars in his pocket and no credit cards. Highly recruited as an offensive tackle while at Dunbar High, he spent two years at L.S.U building his resume with two straight college all-stars nominations until he blew his knee out in his junior year. Through all his physical therapy, the knee wouldn't retain strength and his prominent career was over. Although he graduated with a degree in psychology, he didn't possess a job and only had three hundred dollars in his savings account. According to everything they could find out about him from their C. I's (confidential informants or snitches), he was a model citizen.

They sat across the street of the funeral parlor observing those that visited. They had shot over four rolls of film taking pictures of all those attending the memorial. Seeing some of the biggest and mid-level drug dealers in the city congregating at one place was unusual, unless it was a party. There is no evidence to substantiate Shabazz was a drug dealer or affiliated and you sure can't fought a person for who they know, right? Yet, although they stated that it was a drug deal that went wrong, nobody actually brought it especially an investigative reporter from the Sun Newspaper. Na, this didn't have shit to do with drugs or a robbery. This was undeniably an assassination, and they needed to know why? Observing Ice and Byrd getting into a slight disagreement, they took several pictures capturing their expressions. Pure anger and hatred was in their eyes.

Around six o'clock that evening, Lion was sitting in front of Road Block's computer. The pass word he choose to gain entrance was one he knew the answer from the hint. Placing the flash drive in a USB port, he brought up his brother's entire enterprise. Names with position including telephone numbers, stash houses with the count of cocaine and heroin, who owes him and how much. He will be collecting every single dollar. He wrote everyone's name down and their telephone numbers. He still had some decision to make but he'll decide them as he goes along. His connection in Miami was also included. He had a well prolific system in place and his low profile is why five-o never got wind of him. He will call Bunkie later tonight to see if he would ride shot gun with him tomorrow. A little after eight o'clock his cell rang.

"Hey, what's up?"

"I'm calling to say I have to break our date."

"Is everything alright?"

"Yeah" she sigh. "I got some personal business I need to take care of. Can I call you tomorrow?"

"Sure."

"Who the fuck is that you're talking to!?" a man's voice in the background asked.

"Who in the hell are you talking to like that Lamont!?" she snapped back. "I got to go. I'm sorry" she said abruptly ending their brief conversation.

Nine o'clock that night, he reached out to Bunkie. He was eager to assist him in any way he needed. Besides riding shotgun for the collection, he might include him in another adventure but that can wait. They will hook up at Collington and Jefferson Street on the east side. He did tell him to strap up, but word on the streets, he is always strap even when he's taking a shit. He called all seven of his main distributors informing them that he will be heading their way tomorrow at noon. All he could now do was hope that none of his brother's friends and associates don't try to short change him. The count according to his brother has to match or he would have to regress to a person he once was, regrettably.

It was a little pass midnight when exhaustion overwhelm him, he fell asleep laughing at Martin's dumb ass. The morning sun creeping through the window is what stirred him woke. Peeking at the clock, it was nine-thirty. "Damn" he smiled. Usually, he would get up and work out for about two hours but not today, he went straight to take his morning shower. He got dressed in a gray Versace with a Chinese collar light gray silk shirt and a gray Fedora hat then went next door to asked Charmaine if she could drop him off on Rt.40. She said she could. It was about eleven o'clock when he pulled up on a Chrysler parking lot. Thanking her, he walked over to inspect several used 300 before being amazed by a metallic-gray 300 with a sunroof. He was admiring the interior and the navigational system with a five-disc CD holder. He straighten up seeing a sales person approaching.

"Good morning, sir. How may I assist you?"

"I'm interested in this. If I pay straight cash, how much?" he asked the middle age white guy staring in his greenish eyes.

Inspecting his attire, he quoted. "Eighteen."

"Write it up, please" he said extending his license to him and an envelope with twenty-two thousand dollars inside. "Keep the change after the full coverage insurance is taken out" he told him.

"Yes, sir. Thank you" he replied heading back inside to do the paper work.

He was pulling off the lot twenty minutes later heading East on Rt.40. As he drove down Edmondson Avenue, people were waiting on bus stops to be taken down town. Getting caught by a red light at N. Alton Avenue, those standing on the corner and crossing in front of him were all staring inside the car at him. "Na, this isn't happening" he said to himself checking his watch. He had an hour and half before he was to hook up with Bunkie. Driving down Edmondson Avenue, he took the Hilton Parkway exit to get over towards B.C.C.C on Liberty Road. Down the street near the Liberty Car Wash was Grace window tinting spot. A half hour after arriving he was pulling off the lot. The tint was exactly what he needed. He drove down Liberty Road towards Mondawmin Mall. He took it down to North Avenue then turned left proceeding down to I-83 S then exiting at Fallsway to Monument Street. When he turned right on Collington Avenue, he cross McElderry Street then slowly, pulled up on the corner of Jefferson. Bunkie was already there. He pulled up next to him lowering the driver's window so he could see who was driving.

"What's up Lion" he greeted walking over then climbing inside and fastening his seat belt.

"What's up?" he replied, tapping knuckles then pulling away from the curb. "First stop is at Milton and Patterson Park. God help anyone who thinks this is a joke" he informed him turning left onto Patterson Park then proceeded up. As he drove pass the first stash house, two guys were on the porch watching his car closely. The tinted windows prevented them from seeing inside. As he hooked a U-turn and parked across from them, one of the guys pulled out his cell and had a quick conversation.

"May I help you?" the other guys asked.

"I'm here to see Chaka. Tell him Lion is here."

"You're Lion" the guy asked surprised but staring at him. He didn't fit the stories he had heard about him. This guy was immaculately dress from head to toe. "He's expecting you" he said tapping on the door three times then stepping aside.

"Thank you" he replied hearing a two by four being slipped from its metal brackets.

As the door swung open, a guy cradling a Remington 870 shotgun invited them in and to follow him as a second guy re-secured the door. Very few furniture, just the necessities.

"Lion!" greeted Chaka getting to his feet and giving him a hug. "You still look the same" he commented extending his arms and smiling at him.

"I see you're eating well" he smiled at the once skinny man.

"Yeah, living right and a good woman can do that" he said rubbing his stomach smiling. "You know why I didn't make the memorial, right?"

"Yeah, I got the run down.

"Good, we're still trying to put this shit together" he shared hardening his eyes. "Let's handle this business first" he said pulling out a doctor's bag filled with about three hundred G's and his book. He had an additional three keys of coke ready to be cook and another four keys of dope ready to be cut.

As he scrutinized his book, he returned his eyes to him. "Good count" he told him. "Everything else is yours including what's on the streets."

"What?" he asked shock. "Are you sure, Lion?"

"Everybody got to keep eating, man. Road Block might be gone but not his responsibilities."

"Yeah, but."

"No buts man" he smiled at him then suddenly getting to his feet. "Just don't share what I'm doing with the other houses."

"Na man, our business is our business" he assured him.

"Somebody is plotting Chaka, but they didn't take me into account and that's a motherfucking mistake. Nobody is crashing the East Side Boyz, nobody" he shared with conviction. "Man, it's nice seeing you. I'll hit you up before I leave town."

"You better" he said opening his arms for another hug. "Holla at me man."

"I will" he assured him grabbing the bag then following the guy out the door and placing it in the trunk. He did the same thing with every stash house he went to. The last one was on Eager and Greenmount near the Latrobe Homes. They parked on Eager Street then walked up the one-way street. Sitting out front of the house was two guys in their early thirties; they were nodding and not from lack of sleep. He and Bunkie peeked at one another then shook their heads. They didn't feel them or notice them until they were damn near upon them. If they had been the stick-up boys or worst, five-o, they would have caught them sleeping.

"Whoa! Whoa! Whoa!" the older of the two guys said getting to his feet. "What's up fellas?" he asked taking on a tough guy disposition.

"I'm here to see Rocky?"

"Who the fuck are you looking all GQ and shit?" he chuckled staring down at his partner cradling a saw-off in his lap then down at Lion.

"Somebody you really don't want to know" he replied casually while returning his stare.

"Say what little nigger?" he snarled coming down the steps.

That was the extent of his aggression, Lion grabbed him so fast that he didn't have time to react. Slamming his head into the guy's face then lifting him like he was a child and slammed him on the hood of a parked car knocking the wind out of him. He slam three vicious straight right into his face. All the fight he thought he had in him disappeared as Lion's Glock 40 pressed firmly against his cheek. His partner stood revealing the saw-off, but never made a move except to peek at the .45 Bunkie was clutching in his hand. "Where's Rocky?"

"In the house" the other guy responded.

"Go tell him I'm here."

"Lion, right? Road Block's little brother."

"Yeah."

"He's inside waiting on you."

"Lead the way" he motion with his hand then slapped the semi-unconscious guy across the face with the butt of weapon then releasing him as he slid off the hood head first and slamming his face into the sidewalk. He place his weapon back in the small of his back. After the guy tapped the code, another two by four could be heard sliding from the L-brackets.

"This is Lion" he announced then stepping aside for them to enter.

"What the fuck happen to Big Tony?" the guy at the door asked seeing him getting off the ground bloody.

"Being disrespectful as usual" he replied nonchalantly returning to his post on the porch.

"Maybe he'll learn something" he said securing the door. "Follow me" he requested leading them towards the kitchen.

"Lion, glad to finally meet you" Rocky said leaning back in his chair like he ran shit like Tony Montana. He didn't show him no form of respect as far as shaking his hand or getting to his feet. "Sorry to meet you under these circumstances."

"No doubt" he replied returning his stare. "Is everything in order?"

"Business man like your brother, huh?" he asked flashing a two-dollar smile. He reached down next to him and pulled out a leather bag then placed it on the table. "Two-seventy-five."

"Two-seventy-five" he repeated. "You must have five keys inside that bag hiding someplace" he said staring over at him.

"Five keys? What are you talking about?" he asked leaning forward.

"According to my brother's records, your math is way off. Unless you produce those five keys, things could get very awkward" he told him returning his stare.

"Wait a motherfucking minute" he said getting to his feet. "What are you implying?"

"Nothing yet unless those five keys don't show up" he warned him pulling out his Glock then resting it against his thigh. "If Road were alive, you wouldn't dare try to short him. If you're under the assumption that just because he's not here, you don't have anything to worry about. You are gravely mistaken. So, where in the fuck are those keys?" he asked staring at him with a slight snarl while chambering a round.

"Easy man, easy! I got them!" he finally admitted lightly laughing but Lion wasn't laughing. "Jake, go get them."

The guy standing behind him departed heading towards the basement. He descended the steps returning quickly with the five keys. He placed them on the table.

POW! The forty-caliber slug ripped through his right shoulder shattering his collar bone. "That's for trying to play me" he told him as he stumble backward against the wall staring over at him in shock. His crew never made a move. Two of them actually had smirks on their faces. They were hoping someone would put a hot one in his dumb ass for all the stealing he was doing. Road Block was paying them good. But this scandalous motherfucker always kept dipping, playing on Road Block's good nature. Well, Lion wasn't Road Block apparently. "Jack, those five keys are yawls. The money coming in from the streets is also yawls. I did the same thing with every other stash house, but asshole here is the only one that step out of his lane. If you give his scandalous ass one single dollar, I'll be piss and you wouldn't like that" he told him staring into his eyes. "Do you understand me?

"Yeah, Lion" he replied slightly smiling.

"He's out in the cold and anybody that doesn't like it can join him. I know yawl need to keep eating so I'm not going to cut yawl off. I'm feeding yawl, but not that bitch ass whimpering nigger over there" he said pointing his Glock at Rock while staring at him coldly. "You are running this now not him. He's cut the fuck off and if you have a problem with that Rock, I really do hope you look me up" he invited him snarling over at him. "Let's bounce Bunkie." They turned and left the premises. Walking out onto the porch, he shot Big Tony a cold stare, but he averted his eyes. Climbing into the car, he asked "Where do you live?"

"Goodnow Apartments."

He drove down Moravia Road towards Herring Park getting better acquainted with him. He pulled up into his complex. "This is for you" you said extending five twenty-thousand stacks to him.

"Whoa man, that's too much."

"It's not enough" he told him. "Don't go too far. I going to need you and soon."

"I'm right here for you" he assured him stuffing the money in his jacket then stepping out. Lion could see the smile on his face from the rear-view mirror.

One thing about the streets and especially that grapevine, word gets out fast. The incident with Lion was already making news two hours later.

"Hey Byrd, I'm sorry to disturb you but did you hear what happen to Rocky?" Sunshine asked.

"Which Rocky?"

"East Side Rocky" he replied. "He worked for Road Block."

"Man, I haven't heard anything since coming home last night. What's up?"

"Lion bust a cap in his ass for trying to short him five keys. He also broke a guy's jaw with the butt of his Glock for talking slick."

"Yeah, that sounds like Lion" he lightly chuckled sitting up on the couch.

"Man, I've been thinking about what you said to Ice Pick because I told him the same thing. Loose ends can get motherfuckers unnecessarily killed."

"Not can, will" he corrected him swinging his feet to the floor. "What Lion is doing now is nothing? If he gets his hands-on Meek or any of the other guys, they are gonna snitch. Trust me. I don't know what's going on between Ice and Meeks but there is something. If he's threatening to spill blood in the streets over this guy, he's someone important to him."

"Yeah, I concluded that myself" he admitted. "But I'm still not liking his decision."

"Nor am I, but all we can do is hope that this stupid motherfucker know what he's doing."

"He don't" replied Sunshine. "I don't want Lion coming after me man. I saw something in his eyes that made me extremely uncomfortable."

"What you saw was revenge and make no mistake about it? I witness it too. If he finds out we are responsible for his brother's death, no amount of money or pleading will ease his retribution. Ice can continue to take him for a joke but Sunshine, I'm telling you, he's the most dangerous motherfucker in the state of Maryland right now and pray he doesn't get our scent."

"Man, I got to go" he sigh. "I'll holla at you later."

"Just chill man, you will know when he's getting close" he informed him.

"How?"

"One of us will be dead" he replied lightly snickering while ending their conversation.

On Friday afternoon, Lion re-entered the Hilton to find T.T attending to her business. As she surrendered the electronic key to a guest, their eyes connected, and a broad smile came to her face. "Enjoy your stay sir" she wish the gentleman then focused back on him. "Hey, Malik."

"What's up young lady?" he asked admiring her eyes and full lips.

"I thought you probably left town by now, but it's nice seeing you" she openly admitted still smiling.

"I'm delighted to hear that because you have been running through my mind also. Are you free to listen to some jazz and a light dinner?"

"You mean tonight?"

"Unless, you have plans. We can try to connect tomorrow."

"Na, we can hook up tonight" she informed him. "What time are you suggesting?"

"What's good for you?"

"I get off at six, but I can be ready by eight" she replied.

"Na, you're rushing" he suddenly smile. "We can try nine or later if necessary."

"Nine would be so much better" she admitted lightly giggling.

"Here's my number" he said extending it to her. "Give me a call when you're almost dress and we'll decide if you want to drive your own car or drive with me."

"I live in Gwynn Oaks" she informed him.

"And?" he replied.

"If it's not out of your way, you can pick me up" she replied grinning.

"And I gladly will" he told her extending his cell number. "Holla at me" he told her suddenly departing.

She watched him walking through the main lobby doors and a smile crept across her lips. "Damn, he has a sexy walk."

"Who in the hell was that handsome guy, T.T?" her girlfriend asked shaking her head.

"I don't know him, but I'm having dinner with him tonight" she shared sticking her tongue out at her then smiling.

"You don't know him but you're having dinner with him and tonight" she reiterated. "You?" she said then burst out giggling.

"Yeah, me" she replied trying to contain her smile. "Didn't you tell me I needed to get out more?"

"Yeah, but where did you meet him?"

"Right here a little over a week ago" she shared.

"See if there's any more at home like him" she said.

"I doubt it, but I'll ask" she replied returning her smile. She stared back at the door then smiled again. For over a week, she thought he had gone back to Atlanta and forgotten all about her then he walks through the main entrance wearing that mysterious smile he possesses. Where have he been the past week? What was he doing? These were the same signifying questions that dissolved her previous relationships. Asking inappropriate questions, like she was not a wifey.

Around nine o'clock, dress in a gray three-button Versace, Lion was climbing the steps to T. T's house on Gwynn Oaks. He lightly tapped on the door then waited. Seconds later, the door swung open, and an impish grin consumed his face admiring her attire. She had a white stretch form fitting dress that hit her just above her knees.

"Your uniform don't do you any justice" he complimented still wearing that impish smile.

"Thank you" she replied slightly blushing from the desire that had suddenly engulfed his eyes.

"Excuse me from staring."

"I'm comfortable" she replied. "Do you wish to come in or bounce?"

"I would love to come inside but I'm really hungry."

"Okay, let me grab my purse and I'll be right with you."

"Take your time" he told her as she turned leaving the door ajar. He stood on the porch admiring the trees on her block and the quietness. It took him almost three months to get comfortable with the quietness that his community provided, but once he did, he genuinely appreciated the quietness and tranquility.

"I'm ready" she announced making her presence known while securing the front door. As they descended the steps, she stared at what he was driving. "Is this yours?" she asked staring at the Chrysler 300.

"Yes, I decided to drive back to Atlanta" he replied opening the door for her then closing it once she was seated. He walked around and climbed inside then started up the engine. Donny Hathaway's "The Ghetto Live" filled the interior as he pulled away from the curb then hooked a U-turn.

"Where are you taking me tonight?" she asked fastening her seatbelt.

"A jazz spot down town on Charles Street called the Café" he informed her turning right on Liberty Road and took that back into the city. As they converse, he found himself peeking at certain corners as he drove pass especially North and Pennsylvania Avenue. Drug trafficking was still being openly displayed while vacant police cruisers sat yards away. I guess things will never change until people do or the police do their job. When he arrived at Baltimore Street, he turned left then proceeded towards Charles Street and turning left. He was fortunate to find a parking spot two blocks away. They climbed out together then proceeded towards the club. He paid their entry fees then stood in the vestibule scanning the spot. He located a nice table sitting on the far-left side. He unconsciously gripped her fingers then directed her towards the table. Once they were seated, a waitress approach them.

"Good evening" the mocha complexion young lady greeted them smiling. "How can I assist yawl."

"I personally don't need a menu" he informed her. "I would like your catfish with a large salad."

"Do yawl sell crab cakes?"

"Yes, ma'am. Large or jumbo."

"Large and a salad also" she informed her.

"Would yawl like a drink while your meal are being prepared?"

"Yes, please. I'll have a glass of Moscato."

"I'll take a glass of Parrot Bay coconut if you have it."

"We have it. I'll be right back with yawl drinks" she said turning and disappearing again.

"I don't recognize any of the black musicians on the walls" she admitted staring at a picture of a young Ella Fitzgerald.

"Sure, you do" he counter staring around. "Who is that?" he pointed.

"That's Billie."

"See, you do know at least one" he replied smiling as their drinks arrived. "Thank you."

"You're welcome" the waitress replied then got low again.

"So, you're not married?" she mention taking a sip from her glass.

"Na, not yet" he replied knocking on wood.

"Is it like that?" she asked smiling at him.

"No, not really. I picked up that bad habit whenever a woman speak about marriage" he admitted openly smiling.

"Do you have any children?"

"God haven't blessed me with any yet" he replied taking a sip from his glass.

"No baby momma drama?"

"Nope and never will" he replied with confidence.

"You sound very confident" she mention.

"I'm confident that the woman that will bring forth my roots will be a friend and remain a friend no matter which paths we take in our lives together or separately."

"I like that" she admitted. Too many of her girlfriends have found out too late that the man that they loved wasn't worthy of their love or wasn't mature enough to deal with her independence. "What do you do Malik?"

"I'm a lawyer" he replied catching her completely off guard as he pulled out one of his black business cards with gold lettering and extending it to her.

"A lawyer?" she repeated accepting his card and staring at it. "I would have never guest" she admitted smiling.

"Most people wouldn't" he cosigned grinning.

"How long have you been a lawyer?"

"Almost six years."

"You look too young to have completed law school. You look like you just graduated high school."

"I don't look that young. Damn, T.T" he replied causing her to burst out giggling.

"Sorry but you do" she replied adamantly still giggling.

He found himself reaching out to her three times a week to enjoy her company and informative conversations including how she had imploded her last two relationships. There were an insecurity that existed in her subconsciousness concerning her looks especially her deep mocha complexion and this caused her to scrutinize the men in her previous life. She needed to know why they wouldn't compliment the way she dress or wear her hair? They never complimented the perfumes that she wore, but Malik wasn't them. He would whisper in her ears how intoxicating her perfume smell mixing with her biochemistry or the alluring way he would stare at her just before they went out together. Referring to her as a Venus Flytrap caused her to openly blush and giggle like a school girl.

For her, Malik was the therapy that she needed so desperately. Someone who freely express his emotions while not trying to seduce her sexually but intellectually with hints of aspirations. Yeah, he was the type of man that she needed in her life, and she knew this after just one week of interacting with him. With his stern exterior expressions and mysterious eyes, you would never know how funny he could be. He actually made her almost piss herself when he told her of the incident at the Q's party. Whatever routine that she had before meeting Malik; he blew it apart. They spoke every day for about an hour after she got home and got relaxed.

While he was exploring T.T, Misty was blowing his cell up. He would have quick conversations with her, but that was usually it. When he didn't see T.T but wanted to get out of the routine he was creating, he would appease her occasionally. Although her conversations usually took on the same theme, why can't we patch up Lion? He would keep her at arm's length and shut down all conversations concerning what they had in the past or rekindling anything but their friendship. Eventually or reluctantly, she finally had to accept the obvious. She had made the decision to stay in Baltimore and be with Lamont. Her opportunity to be with him on his unknown journey had pass. She had decided to take a separate road. A road that didn't include him or his love.

Ice was sitting on his balcony in Catonsville sipping on a glass of Ciro while considering everything that have transpired in the last two weeks. He thought that Lion would have completed all his brother's affairs by now then take his black ass back to where ever he came. Instead, he's been reconnecting with Misty and some other sexy little thing. Both young ladies have been seen at several jazz spots around the city especially the mystery woman. Although everyone thinks that he's just enjoying himself, he's been caught twice trying to get into Johns Hopkins, but five-o's presence deter him and that wasn't cool. If he gets his hands on that ass hole Turtle, that illiterate motherfucker will put Meeks on blast. He didn't know who finance the hit, but Meek recruited him and that would be more than enough information for Lion. The last thing he wanted to do was take Meeks out. How would he explain to the mother of his three daughters that murdering their uncle and his wife little brother was for self-preservation? If a choice have to be made and it just might, Meek will definitely lose.

His whole plan is being slowly torn apart. When Lion caught Rocky trying to play him, he bust a cap in his ass without any hesitation according to those who witness it. Instead of shutting down the stash houses and collecting the money, he's keeping them feed. "What dumb ass motherfucker gives away keys?" he asked.

"Someone smart enough to know that someone is plotting against his brother's territory and the only way to prevent it is to keep shit flowing as they were" Bash told him returning his stare. "We can't touch those boys now especially those hustling around the Dome on Biddle Street or C&J."

That move alone, fucked up his whole plans, but he wasn't going to admit it. Cruising through certain sets, all their main spots were still jumping with motherfuckers on high alert and stepping to them would be twice as hard. Almost suicidal. With the prospect of employment with a new distributor gone, he knew his shit had just imploded. Lion made those motherfuckers obligated to him because of his generosity. Cunny motherfucker. Another disturbing thing is, who is riding shotgun with him? Bunkie of all people. How does he know Lion enough to back him up? Road Block, he answer his own question. After almost seven years staying clear of the streets after trying to be recruited by so many distributors except Road Block, he had finally picked up his beloved Magnum .45, again? Shit has become extremely serious, and he finally realized that Lion was a legitimate threat, but he won't admit it to Byrd, yet. The ringing of his cell phone broke his line of thought.

"Yeah, what's up Bash?"

"He's in Cherry Hill."

"Who?"

"Lion."

"Lion!" he stated getting to his feet. "What?"

"And he's not alone. Bunkie is riding shotgun."

"Fuck!"

"Exactly, do you think he's looking for your boy?"

"He's not sight-seeing that's for damn sure" he replied shaking his head. "Fuck!"

"What do you want me to do?"

"Nothing!" he stress. "I got to reach out to Meeks and put him on point. The last thing I need is for that fool to step to Lion."

"That would be a massive mistake."

"Yeah, but that knucklehead motherfucker still might step. Fuck! I got to go Bash. I'll holla at you later" he said ending their conversation. Shit! Shit! Shit! Why didn't Lion just bounce? He has well over two million dollars in cash from his stash houses. More than enough to live comfortably. He focus back on his phone and call Meeks.

"Hey brother-in-law" he chuckled. "What's happening?" he asked with a slur.

"Meeks?"

"Yeah, motherfucker. You don't know who you're calling" he asked snickering.

"What the fuck is wrong with you?" he asked hearing that junkie slur.

"Who the fuck is this?"

"Ice motherfucker! Are you high!?"

"What the fuck is it to you!? I'm a full-grown man!" he snapped back.

"There's been rumors about you fucking with "Boy," but I refused to listen. If I knew you were fucking with heroin, I would have never fucked with your dumb ass."

"I'm not fucking with no boy" he lied while unconsciously sniffling.

"Don't try to bullshit me! I sell the shit for a living motherfucker!" he reminded him shaking his head. How in the fuck did he set up a job with a motherfuckin' junkie?

"Man, what the fuck you want? I got people waiting on me" he asked changing the conversation.

"I should have never fucked with you."

"The motherfuckin' job got handle, didn't it? So, fuck what you think I'm doing?"

"Listen, fuck that shit. I need you and your boys to get low."

"Get low! Why?"

"The guy you hit little brother is cruising your set right now."

"Fuck that little nigger!"

"No! I need you to listen to me and get low."

"I got product out on these streets. I'm not leaving my shit in their hands."

"Your product will be the least of your problems if Lion gets his claws in you" he warned him.

"Fuck Lion! I thought you said he wouldn't be a problem."

"Well, I underestimated the kid, and I don't need you to do the same."

"Well, I'm not going anywhere without my money" he stated adamantly slightly smiling at the scheme forming in his mind.

Hearing that junky slur and the I don't give a fuck attitude pissed Ice off. This motherfucker don't understand the severity of the situation. In his dope-Fein mind, fuck the world and everybody in it. He wasn't about to lose everything he built because of some junkies tombstone mentality. "How much you need to get you and your boys out of town?" he heard himself foolishly asking.

"Um, I would say ten G's each could keep us out of town for at least two or three months."

"Let's hook up Saturday around ten o'clock."

"Shit, we can do that" he replied with enthusiasm. He couldn't hide his greed even if his life depended on it and it was. "Meet me at the community center."

"I'll be there" he said ending their conversation.

Meeks burst out laughing after hanging up. If that motherfucker thinks I'm leaving town, he done bump his motherfucking head. Putting an additional forty G's in his hands for them to get out of town, he's a bigger fool than he thought. He burst out laughing again.

In the meanwhile, Lion and Bunkie were cruising through the streets of Cherry Hill around noon. They were just turning the corner onto Cherryland Road when Bunkie stared intensively at a group of guys.

"Pull over Lion" he insisted keeping his eyes fixed on a guy. Before the car came to a complete stop, he open the door then leap out. At a quick pace, he was closing in on his target. After parking, Lion was bringing up the rear. Small groups of people watched as the scenario unfolded. "Yo, Duce!" he called. Just as the guy was turning to see who was calling him, a vicious right knocked him to the ground. The three guys standing next to him leaped the fuck out of their skins almost.

"What the fuck!" he said dazed from the blow. As he shielded his eyes from the sun as they slowly cleared and focus, he stared up and fear instantly entered them. "Bunkie!"

"Yeah nigger, get the fuck up!" he replied snarling down at him.

"Why, so you can knock me back down?" he asked staring up at him.

"Unless you want to taste my Tim's, you better get your bitch ass up" he warned him glaring down at him.

Reluctantly and struggling to get to his feet, he stood erect on wobbling knees. "Let me explain."

"I don't want to a word filtering through your lying ass mouth" he told him staring at him threateningly. "Come with me" he order snatching him by his collar to get some distance from the ear hustling motherfuckers standing around. He took him into a near-by court yard then slam him violently against the concrete wall.

"Okay, what do you want?" he asked staring at up at him then over to the stranger.

"Who suddenly got money out here in the past two weeks?"

"What?" he asked confused by the question.

"You heard me bitch!" he stated slapping him viciously across the face. "Who suddenly got money out here?"

"Meeks and a couple of his friend suddenly came across some money" he blurted out staring up in his eyes. "They put a package out last week."

"Where can I find this guy Meeks?"

"This time of the day he's probably watching his little crew hitting up his customers near the library on Cherry Hill Road."

"I know where the damn library is located. What does this Meeks character look like?"

"He's about five-eight, dark complexion and on the chubby side. He has a slight scar running down from his right eye."

"Do you have the money you owe me?"

"I only have thirty dollars on me."

"Kick it out and I'll be out this way next week to collect the balance. You hear me?"

"Yeah Bunkie" he replied extending the money to him.

"If you try to get low and I find you without my money" he stated suddenly slapping the shit out of him with his .45 causing a nasty gash in his right eyebrow. "I'm going to bust a cap in your scandalous ass especially if you try to get low. Now, get the fuck out of my face" he instructed watching him walking away and being cared for by his associates standing at the entrance of the court yard. "Let's bounce Lion."

"What the fuck was that about?" he slightly grinned over at him.

"That thieving, lying motherfucker stole my commissary" he shared as they climbed back into the car.

"How long ago was that?" he asked still grinning.

"Eight years ago," he shared trying to contain his grin.

"Eight years ago?" he repeated unable to contain his chuckle.

"It's the principle of the thing, man" he replied trying to contain his smile.

"So, I see" he continued to snicker. "Which way?" he asked pulling away from the curb.

"Hook a U-turn" he replied. "Cherry Hill Road will come up in front of you" he told him.

Five minutes later, they were pulling in near the Dollar Store and parking near the liquor store, but on the last lane. From their position, they could see everything. The small area was jumping with activity since it was the first of the month. After taking care of the rent and electric bill, most parents would put a little food in the house for their children. Fresh things like sneakers, clothes or under wear weren't brought or consider. They could use that money to spurge on their drug of choice especially if it had a kick to it. Every junky that shots heroin is searching for that very elusive first high effect, but never finding it.

They sat there for almost two hours before Meeks showed up driving a later model Altima with temporary tags. Dress in a fresh pair of Jordan's and fake gold jewelry, he pose like he just hit the lottery. The light skin motherfucker with him was unable to conceal his addiction but was looking just as fresh. They watched them pass their drugs to some teenagers then step back watching them distributing their narcotics for about an hour before leaving the area after having a quick conversation with them. Lion made mental notes of both men walk and small habits like the light skin guy chain smoking. Both guys appeared to be in their mid to later thirties with a noticeable addiction. He started up his car then left the area.

"So, do you want to snatch him up tomorrow?"

"I would love to Bunkie, but I have a date. We can do this Saturday" he replied peeking over at him slightly smiling.

"T.T again?"

"Oh, yeah" he openly smiled.

It was almost ten o'clock when Ice and Bash crept into Cherry Hill under the cover of darkness, he had the additional forty G's with him, but he had no intentions of putting it in the hands of a junky. His intentions are to get his ass in the car and take him on a short ride to put a bullet in his head then dump his body in the Patapsco River. The one person he knew he could trust for the job was Bash. They had met at Baltimore City Detention Center. Both were on N section. He was trying to beat drug charges while Bash was fighting an attempted murder charge. They both love playing chess and this was how they eventually connected. During the six months that they shared a cell, a lot of conversing and plans were made. After the corruption charges against the police department highly decorated Nextel Boys, both of their cases had to be dismissed. Just like in playing chess, Bash never did have a lot of conversation. So, you never knew what he was thinking. So, mentioning that Meeks needed to be taken out. He simply said, "About time."

When they pulled up on Cherry Hill Road where the community center was, the place was packed. "What the fuck?" he said slowing down.

"Look" Bash pointed at a sign staple to a tree. Cherry Hill 5th Reunion.

"That slick motherfucker" he replied hardening his eyes.

"How you want to play it?"

"We damn sure can't snatch his ass up like we intended. Damn" Ice said looking at the massive crowd.

"Maybe, we still might convince him to jump into the back seat" mention Bash.

"We can try but he's not that dumb especially if he thinks his life is in danger" he said going to the corner then hooking a U-turn. As he slowly came back up the block, Meek's spotted his big sister's lip stick red Caddy. He stepped out thinking it was her. As the passenger's window lowered, he looked inside. "Get in."

Apprehension instantly gripped him staring at a known murderer in Bash. He might live in Cherry Hill, but he knew who the hit men were in Baltimore, and he was staring at one of the most notorious. "Na, I'm cool right here" he said staring at Bash then over at Ice. "Where is it?"

"On the back floor, get it" he insisted unlocking the back door.

"Na, you can pass it out to me" he replied slightly smiling at him. If he had reached his head inside, a single shot to the head was guaranteed before snatching his lifeless body inside then closing the door and pulling away.

"Boy reach inside and grab it" he insisted hardening his eyes at him, but the ploy didn't work.

"Na, pass it out" he reiterated returning his stare while slightly snarling then peeking back at Bash menacing eyes.

"Grab that for him" he told Bash realizing his ploy wasn't working. "I need yawl on that Amtrak before Monday" he told him staring at him as Bash pass him the envelope.

"We'll be on the train late tomorrow" he told him accepting the envelop.

"Don't fuck me Meeks!" he warned him staring in his intoxicated eyes. "I need yawl gone."

"We will, damn" he smiled stuffing the envelope under his shirt. He had no intentions on leaving town or splitting this money with his recruits. Neither option was happening, and he was dumb as a motherfucker if he thought he would.

"Don't fuck me!" he reiterated staring in his cloudy eyes.

"We're family man" he chuckled. "We're gone. I'll hit Cookie up later telling her I got some business to take care of out of town."

"Call her tonight" he told him.

"I will" he replied still grinning. "Have a good night gentleman" he wished them suddenly walking away with a smirk on his face. As the car pulled off and turned the corner, he burst out laughing. "Suckers!"

"What's up Meeks?" one of his partners in crime asked staring at him grinning.

"April Fool's Day" he replied then burst out laughing again.

As they drove up Cherry Hill Road, Bash stared over at him. "You do know you made a bad move, right?"

"What are you talking about?" he asked taking a peek over at him.

"Do you really think that his junky ass is going to leave town?"

"He better."

"You need to have a back-up plan because that fool, isn't going anywhere" he voiced his opinion.

"If he don't, a sudden drive by shooting will occurred" he threaten hardening his eyes. He might have initially assumed that he fuck with that heroin but seeing him for himself, he was definitely fucking with it. Whether he was shooting or snorting it, both were bad for business.

Parked in the shadows, Lion watched the whole scenario unfold. Peeking at the Caddy as it drove pass surrender no information as to who was driving it except the monogram license plates saying Cookie. They watched as Meeks slapped his friends five before heading up the street.

"I'm going to post up near his hooptie" Lion said pulling away from the curb with his lights still out then turned the corner before illuminating his way. He parked one court over from where they spotted his car then got out and posted up.

Spotting the sudden emergence of a car's headlights, Meek instinctively cut through one of the court yards. Was it Ice double backing? He didn't know if it was coincidental or not, but he was going to play it safe. He had just conned a dummy out of forty G's, and he wanted to enjoy the fruits of his labor. Walking around with forty G's wasn't smart, especially in Cherry Hill. Spotting his car, he slightly relaxed as a smile crept across his lips. Staring around, the area appeared vacant except for the lights from the back of some of the residents windows. He inserted his key then pulled the door open illuminating the interior but as he started to climb inside, a motion to his left was caught in his peripheral vision grabbing his full attention. A dark shadowy figure materialized in front of him from out of nowhere. Before he could reach under his seat to recover his nine-millimeter, the lights suddenly went out.

Around midnight, Byrd got a call from the last person he ever thought would be calling him.

"Yeah, what's up Ice?" he asked nonchalantly while smoking a blunt.

"Man, I think I fucked up."

"Nothing unusual" he replied with sarcasm while lightly snickering.

"Now is not the time to be sarcastic Byrd!" he snap revealing it was serious.

"Oaky, what happen now?"

"I left Cherry Hill about three hours ago talking to Meeks dumb ass. I told him I needed him and his three partners to get out of town until I contacted him. I gave that motherfucker an additional forty G's to catch the first train smoking by Monday."

"Hold up! Hold up!" he insisted unable to contain his chuckle. "You gave Meeks more money. Man, he must think you're his personal ATM" he burst out laughing. "That fool isn't going anywhere and he damn sure isn't going to share that money with his boys. He'll throw their asses under a bus before he does that."

"That would be detrimental to his health and ours."

"Ours? How?" Byrd asked.

"I didn't mean it like that."

"Alright but watch your words" he warned him.

"I will but listen Byrd, that's not the worst thing" he said pausing.

"Don't hesitate now, kick it out. What else is there?"

"Lion drives around in a 300, right?"

"Yeah, he parked Sha's shit somewhere" he replied apprehensively. "Why?"

"I'm almost certain I saw him posted up in the shadows out in Cherry Hill."

"What!?" he stated louder than intended leaning forward. "Are you sure?"

"Damn, near" he replied.

"Have you gotten in touch with Meeks?"

"Na, his phone been turned off."

"What!? Don't say that" he replied getting to his feet. "Man, that's not good. Fuck! That's not good at all" he stated rubbing his manicured facial hairs.

"If I find out that his ass is still in town after tomorrow, I'll personally bust a cap in his lying conniving ass."

"Tomorrow?" he lightly chuckled. "If that was Lion you saw, he wasn't in Cherry Hill sightseeing and tomorrow will be too late Ice."

"Don't say that Byrd."

"Get your head around this, motherfucker. Meeks cell is off for one reason and one reason only. With it turned off, it eliminate it from being track. Lion has your boy Ice and I'm willing to bet whatever you want to bet?"

"Don't go there Byrd" he insisted revealing his nervousness.

"How much? We can bet turfs" he reiterated. "He's snitching right now if Lion have him and I'm positive that he does."

"I got to go" he suddenly said. "I need to try his cell again."

"Go right ahead, but it's a waste of time. He's in the clutches of Lion and that's a got damn shame" he said ending their conversation.

If Lion has his clutches in him, he will extract the answers he needed. Sooner or later, he will be coming for them. He tried repeatedly to contact Meeks, but his cell went straight to voice mail. He decided to call Cookie.

"Hey, what's up baby?"

"Have you heard from Meeks?"

"Not since Wednesday, is anything wrong?" she asked hearing the anxiety in his voice.

"Na, he was supposed to introduce me to somebody tonight, but he haven't called me" he lied.

"Sorry sweetheart but I haven't heard from him either. Is there anything you want me to tell him if he calls?"

"Yeah, tell him I said to give me a shout."

"Sure, will" she replied hanging up.

He sat there with his cell in his hand. Please don't let Lions have his claws in him. Please, he found himself pleading. Meeks has always been a punk ass motherfucker, but he was the only person he could hire for the job. Anybody else might have ties to the Eastside Boyz and that would have brought the wrath of Road Block and Monster straight to his front door. He had to find him or have another meeting concerning putting a substantial contract out on Lion.

In the basement of a vacant house on Chester Street, Meeks was just waking up with a splitting headache.

"Damn" he said reaching up and touching the spot where his head was hurting. His fingers returned with his blood on them. "What the fuck!?" he said staring at the two strangers in front of him. He didn't recognize either one of them but the shit he did over the years, he wouldn't have recognized them anyway. He looked down at his feet and realizing the chair he was sitting on had industrial plastic under it. "What's this about fellas?"

"Now before you get on the defense or deny any involvement, you have to ask yourself one simple question. Is this a stick-up? Is it, Meek?" he asked with a slight smile while staring in his eyes.

"No" he replied returning his stare then peeking over at Bunkie.

"Exactly" he suddenly smiled at him, but the smile didn't ease his fear. "If this were a simple robbery, we had you and could have cut you lose. Now, don't get it twisted" he allowed his eyes to become slightly harden as he pulled up a chair and took a seat in front of him. "This money is now ours and we really do appreciate it" he slightly smiled over at him then it quickly dissipated. "Now, let's get down to business. We aren't here coincidentally. We even know your name Meeks. I know you peeked that" he slightly smiled again then it quickly dissipated also. "So, please don't try to bullshit me. I don't possess particularly good patience" he warned him staring in his eyes. "Who hired you three weeks ago for a contract hit on my brother Road Block?"

"Hired me?" he repeated then peeked at Bunkie then back at Lion.

"Now if you're going to repeat every question that I ask with a question, you will be testing my patience and I must warn you; I get irritated very quickly when dealing with people who claim to be tough but really is naïve" he warned him as his eyes slowly became menacing. "Now, I'm going to ask you again. Who hired you for the contract three weeks ago?" he inquired again while staring him in his eyes.

"Contract? I don't know shit about any damn contract" he lied, and his eyes confirmed his lie.

"Do you really think you sitting in front of me is a case of mistaken identity?"

"Yeah man, that's actually what it is" he tried to convince him while peeking over at Bunkie who was slightly shaking his head at him grinning.

"You do, huh?" Lion asked bringing his eyes back on him.

"Yeah, because I didn't murder anybody" he said with conviction, but his eyes always gave him away.

"I am personally so happy you're taking this path" Bunkie suddenly smiled as he reached down and lifted a black leather doctor's bag that Meeks hadn't seen then extended it to Lion.

The clanging of metals inside as he sat it on a table next to him had Meeks eyes focused on the bag and perk Bunkie interest. Lion pulled out some electrical tape first then a ping hammer, a cross chisel hammer, a pair of wire cutter, a pair of shears, long nose pliers and a butane tank. "To coagulate the blood of any sever fingers if it comes to that" he informed Meeks as Bunkie had a smirk on his face. He was getting ready to get medieval on his ass. Lion slipped his hands into a pair of metal implanted gloves with the fingers exposed.

"Be a soldier Meeks" urged Bunkie slightly smiling. "Don't start acting like some little bitch now. You are supposed to be a cold and heartless assassin, right?" he chuckled.

"Fellas, yawl got the wrong guy!" he insisted ignoring Bunkie's statement as his tears started to flow freely.

"You could only wish I got this wrong" Lion said slamming a right hook against his jaw causing him to fall from the chair.

"Aaahhhh, shit!" he declared spitting blood from his mouth as Bunkie assisted him back into the chair.

"Yeah, you took that like a champ" Bunkie teased him snickering while patting him on the head.

"Who hired you?" Lion asked again while staring in his eyes.

"Man, you got the wrong guy" he persisted, and Lion's lack of patience revealed its ugly head. He beat the living shit out of him, literally. He actually shitted in his pants. With the stench of his bows around them, Lion place him back into the chair. His jaw was definitely broken, his bottom lip was split open, and his left eye was closing rapidly. After removing his shoes, his legs and hands was secured to the chair.

"Wait, wait" he insisted watching Lion.

"Who hired you?" Lion asked grabbing the ping hammer and staring in his eyes. "Who?" he asked suddenly slamming the hammer down on his right big toes when no response came.

"Aaggghhh, shit!"

"Who paid you Meeks?" he asked again in a calm voice and no response again.

"Aaggghhh, shit motherfucker!" he cried out again as his tears ran down his face. "Wait a minute. Wait a motherfucking minute!" he pleaded.

"Who paid you?" Lion insisted ignoring his pleads and with his hesitation; the ping hammer came down six straight times. Four times on his toes and twice on his knuckles before he finally surrendered.

"You have the wrong person!" he insisted watching his grabbing a cross chisel hammer.

"Who hired you, Meeks?" he asked as he saw his defiance in his eyes even with his snotty nose mixing with his tears. He wanted to be defiant. His defiance and hesitation brought the wrath out of lion as he swung the hammer forcefully under his knee cap then lifted slightly.

"Got damn motherfucker! Stop! Stop!" he pleaded from the agonizing pain. "Ice! Ice Pick hired me" he confessed crying from the excruciating pain from the apparent dismantle toes and broken knuckles, too.

"Was that him in that Caddy tonight?"

"Yeah, he was driving my sister's car" he replied sweating and exhausted from the beating.

"Did Sunshine and Byrd have a hand in this shit too?"

"All of them did including Bash crazy ass from what I heard."

"Bash? Who the fuck is Bash?"

"Oh, I know who he is" commented Bunkie suddenly snarling. "He's someone who makes money on my side of the tracks. Very psychotic" he shared. He remember how prison had changed him into the monster that he was. Tutu had allegedly rape him and he vowed payback. CO's was forced to isolate him from general population because of the attempts on Tutu life. After doing his three years, he was like a vulture on its perch. He waited patiently for Tutu to get out. He was dead less than twelve hours once he hit the streets with a dildo ram up his ass.

"What's your boys name you supposed to split the money with?" Lion asked staring down into his rapidly closing eyes.

"I was the last one" he lied spitting out more blood from his mouth. Before he could inhale, Lion snatch him by his nappy hair then brought the lit butane and started frying the left side of his face until he scream and begged for mercy.

"Mercy comes later" he told him with a slight snarl. "Who are they Meeks!?" he asked again with menacing eyes while staring into his frighten swollen eyes.

"Dino, Snoop and T-Bone" he snitch surrendering to the pain.

"I'm so disappointed in you" Bunkie said shaking his head while Lion picked up the black leather bag. He stared over at Lion with an unusual expression on his face. The look was one of admiration. He have done some devious shit in his day, but the medieval shit Lion did make him appear as an amateur. He didn't know what was in the black bag until it was open. Was these the tools of his profession? Who else carries such unsuspecting torture weapons? When they said he was nothing like Road Block, he now understood. Although both are gracious, he displayed that by keeping his brothers stash houses open and putting those who plotted the assassination in a no-win situation to take over the east side. Nobody, and I mean nobody, from out of the eastside would comfortably make any type of money being under constant duress from those seeking vengeance for Road Block. Damn good smart move.

"I want to thank you for your assistance" he said starting to return his tools back to his leather bag. "I guarantee you your friends won't be far behind. Is there anything you want to say before we go?" Lion asked chambering a round.

"I'm sorry brother" he replied looking up at him through battered and swollen eyes.

"I don't have a brother anymore, remember?" he asked slightly snarling.

"He said we wouldn't hear you coming" he shared spitting out a mouth filled with blood.

"What?" he asked, staring at him unusual.

"He said you would come" he shared looking up at him. "It was only business, man."

"It might have been business for you, but it's personal for me" he told him raising his hand and squeezing off a round. The force from the .40 caliber Glock hitting him in the forehead caused part of his cranium and brain particles to splatter out on the wall behind him. They laid him on the thick plastic then rolled him up in it. Lion picked up his single casing then sprayed bleach on the wall with ammonia. Exiting the vacant house from the back door, they walked out of the rat-infested alley and placed his lifeless body in the trunk. They drove him back towards Cherry Hill staying on Waterview Avenue. At Middle Branch Park, they discarded his body in the Patapsco River. Lion hooked a U-turned and headed back towards Bunkie house. Pulling up in front, he reached in the back and brought the leather bag forward.

"Don't say shit" he insisted extending the forty G's to him. They exchanged stares briefly before he accepted it shaking his head then climbed out.

Over the next two days they snatched up the final three assassins. All three of their bodies were eventually pulled from the river also at various locations. With their connections to Cherry Hill and criminal background, their deaths were not look upon as just coincidental especially by their community or homicide detectives. In their community, they were all known for associating with Meeks. Snoop and T-Bone were his secret get high partners. Everybody had wonder how they all suddenly came upon their money. Their deaths brought speculations that they did something again except this time, it's coming back to bite them in their asses. Homicide detectives was wondering if they were associated with the remaining witness, Turtle. He could shine light on the whole thing. Those who knew Turtle in Cherry Hill knew he was a participant in whatever transpired and definitely had information.

"Ron, what do you think is going on?" his young partner asked watching them strapping the body to the gurney.

"Shitty, I'm confused as hell, but these three bodies are connected, and I have no doubt about that" he replied.

"Connected?" he asked staring over at him. "To what?"

"I think it has everything to do with Shabazz's murder" Ron shared peeking over at him. "Either somebody is getting rid of loose ends, or somebody is extraction restitution."

"If that is true, only Jamaal can confirm it. He'll be in the hospital another three weeks unless he gets spook and signs himself out."

"If he does that, he's only confirming my suspicion and setting himself up to be murder."

"He's too dumb to realize that" Shitty lightly chuckled. "We need a search warrant for these guys homes and hope it turns up something. If any weapons are recovered that matches the ballistic from those casing we recovered, we'll have them but who is getting paybacks? His brother?"

"Na" he responded reaching inside his drawer and bringing out a magazine then thumbing through it. He had wondered why the face and name of Malik Mohammad sound so familiar to him. When he ran his name in the data base, his history revealed itself. The Baltimore Sun ran an entire page on him. A straight A student and highly sort after basketball player coming from out of Dunbar High. He aspired to be a civil servant.

A profession most black males never aspire to become. One afternoon, he was arrested for murdering a known drug dealer while injuring another in Park Heights. The arresting officers alleged he saw him throwing an object while running from the crime scene. Convicted off the testimony of two CI's (snitches) and bullshit circumstantial evidence, he maintained his innocence throughout the trial. Even when the prosecutor tried to give him a plea bargain of ten-years, he threw it back in their faces. He would rather be railroad than to admit to a crime he didn't commit. When he was sentence to twenty-five years to life, he never batted an eye. Have you ever heard of such bullshit? A first-time offender and they tried to give him life, but the jurors decided on second degree murder. After three years in Jessup, the Nextel Boys collapse."

"You are telling me he got caught up by those scandalous motherfuckers?" he asked snarling over the revelation.

"Yeah, the two CI's retracted their statements after they were sure the Nextel Boys were securely locked down and gave incriminating evidence against them. Malik won his release on appeal and earned himself a substantial settlement."

"How old was he when he went to jail?"

"Just sixteen" he replied showing him the article he was searching for. "Here we are" he said extending the magazine to him.

"Well, I'll be damn" he said smiling at the picture. "He's a lawyer."

"According to the article, a damn good one too. He's being prep for a vice-president position at the age of twenty-eight" he found himself laughing. "He has won several high-profile cases against Atlanta Police Department for violating citizens civil rights and extracting illegal information through illegal means. Prominent black law firms have been reaching out to him for years including the prestigious firm of Justice 4 All up in New Jersey."

"I'm fucking impress and that's hard to do" Shitty admitted smiling.

"So am I" he admitted. "I don't have him involved in this mess."

"We need to get those search warrants Ron and see what it will reveal if anything."

"I'll get right on it" he said picking up the phone to call the prosecutor's office to speak to his girl Charmaine.

The whole city was talking about the quadruple homicides in Cherry Hill except Ice. All his hopes and dreams were flush away when Meeks body was found. The other bodies found only reaffirmed his suspicion. He had snitched and his partners in crime didn't get a pass. The day he escorted Cookie to identify and claim his body was so disheartening. After reading the medical examiner's report, she screamed out in agony and horror. "Who could do such a thing to a human body?" she continuously asked while hugging him tightly and crying. Half of his face was burned with several knuckles and fingers broken along with his jaw. Whatever they used on him he willingly surrender every piece of information they desired even some that didn't matter. Who could have sustained their silence under such torture? He knew he couldn't.

"Who could do this to a human body Ice?" she asked staring up into his eyes or an answer.

How could he tell her a lion seeking retribution? The disfiguring of his body left no doubt that he talked. He knew he and the others were marked for death. What he needed to do was get with the others and decide their next move? Deep inside of him, he wanted to gather up all his shit then empty his bank accounts and get the fuck out of town. If he did run, Cookie would want to know why the sudden move? She was educated not just in school but in the streets and far from a dumb bitch. A sudden move would make her very suspicious of him especially since she would be seeking revenge over her little brother. She asked him to be honest and tell her the truth if he knew anything while staring into his eyes. "Was her little brother involved in something that cost him his life and that was why he was trying to reach out to him?" He stared deep in her tear-filled sorrowful eyes and replied, no. How could he confess to hiring his junky ass to kill someone and got caught up? How? She would never forgive him and would come to despise his presence. No, he would never confess his involvement. The meeting was finally set at one of Black's houses off North Avenue on Appleton Street.

Lion was living a double life. Most Thursday, Friday, and Saturdays evenings after eleven o'clock, he could be found with T.T at a jazz spot getting to know one another a lot better over the past last month. They would find a nice table and enjoy the scenery around them. Every time a slow song came on, he would request a dance.

"What's up with you and these slow dances?" she asked rubbing his back while inhaling his cologne.

"I can't talk to you if we are gyrating and hopping around but having you in my arms is another story" he replied grinning.

"Is that all?" she asked with a smirk.

"Of course, not. Who wouldn't want to feel your embrace or the heat from your breathe on their chest? Not, me" he answer smiling down at her.

"Did anybody tell you that you are very attentive and so romantic?"

"Am, I really?"

"You know you are" she said pinching his side. "I'm surprise you're not married yet?"

"There is so much more of life I want to explore and if I had a wife, I wouldn't be here exploring you and I'm definitely enjoying this journey."

"So am I, Malik" she stated staring up into his eyes. "May I ask you something?"

"Sure, if you can handle my answer" he warned her grinning.

"Oh, I think I can handle it" she replied staring up into his eyes. "How come you never press up on me?" she asked.

"I thought I was" he replied with a coy grin.

"You know what I'm referring to Malik" she said poking him in his ribs. "Why haven't you press up on me? I really need to know."

"I haven't decided if I wanted to make love to you or not" he replied.

"What?" she asked seemingly confused by his comment.

"You heard me" he replied grinning. "Every day men are vying for your attention and who could blame them? I'm guilty myself. Don't you contemplate if a guy is worthy of your most prized possession?"

"What, my love?" she asked smiling.

"Na, yawl surrender yawl love too freely for me" he corrected her lightly laughing. "Na, I'm referring to your most prized possession in the whole wide world. Your garden of love."

"Garden of love?" she reflected feeling him suddenly thrust himself gently against her then she suddenly started giggling. "That's so cute."

"I'm sure she is" he replied staring into her eyes and causing her to openly blush while averting her eyes. "So, I want to assure myself that we can communicate after the initial act of making love. The last thing I need is doubt in you or me. I desperately need to know our friendship can endure such an emotional adventure. So, I take my time."

"That is very admirable, I must confess. Almost, cavalier" she compared openly smiling. She had never experienced the conversations he would initiate or the things that they have experience together. She would have never consider going to a jazz club, but now, she rather listen to some live jazz and float away in his alluring eyes than shake her ass. The script of being careful and patience was being displayed by him had caused her to doubt her own natural beauty and sex appeal. Now that was a first. "I honestly think that our friendship could endure it" she shared slightly blushing. She was openly revealing that she wanted to make love to him, and this was another of those first for her watching that coy, little smile come to his lips. "I love that impish little grin on your face" she shared slightly shaking her head. "Do you know you never invited me over to your place?"

"Of course, I do" he replied grinning.

"When are you going to invite me over?"

"When do you want to come?"

"How about you cook, dinner for us tomorrow night if you're not busy?"

"If nothing is jumping off, we can do that" he told her causing her to smile again and resting her head against his chest.

"You really feel good" she whisper.

"You feel as soft as cotton candy" he replied lightly pressing at the small of her back causing her to giggle. "And yes, I would eat you up."

"I don't think I can handle such an erotic and passion filled night, but I'm willing to try" she stated looking into his eyes.

"And, I would have great patience throughout our blissful and erotic night, my beloved" he whisper staring sincerely into her eyes then leaning down and kissing her passionately.

Over by Appleton Street, the six gentlemen were sitting around a table expressing their concerns and trying to decide how to handle their dilemma?

"What are we going to do?" inquired Sunshine revealing his nervousness. He hasn't had a good night sleep since the bodies were recovered from the Patapsco River. Slightly dark rings were starting to form around his eyes while the whites were now reddish in coloration.

"Since Ice didn't want to take care of business with those loose ends, we have two options. Hunt him down or run" stated Byrd.

"I vote we run" Sunshine mentions instantly without caring what the fuck they thought about him.

"I do too" co-signed Mookie.

"We have more than a hundred people working for us" Ice stated looking around the table. "We can hunt this motherfucker down and deal with him."

"We wouldn't have to take care of him if business was taken care of in the beginning" Byrd reminded him.

"Okay, okay! I fucked up! My fuck up is not the issue, Lion is."

"You want to put a contract out on him, don't you?" Byrd openly smiled over at him.

"Hell, yeah! I do!" he admitted taking a sip from his scotch.

"We should run" Sunshine reiterated.

"You run! You high yellow motherfucker!" Ice snapped staring at him coldly.

"Fuck you, Ice!" he snapped back returning his cold stare. "You are so worried about what Cookie would say if we had touched him. Well, he still got touched and you can bet, your name came out of his motherfucking mouth first" he assured him slightly grinning with a small snarl. "We wouldn't be in this shit if we did what Byrd suggested."

"Well, we didn't bitch, so let's just move the fuck on" he said staring at him.

"You're a bitch especially when it comes to Cookie" he counter returning his cold stare.

"Keep my bitch name out of your mouth, motherfucker" he warned.

"Ice!" called Black grabbing his attention. "This shit been going downhill ever since you plotted it. One thing I'm not is a bitch, but if you decide to go after Lion, it would be a big mistake especially if you miss," he warned him taking a hit from the blunt he was smoking. "The only person that might know where he's resting his head is Misty or that other fine as little bitch, he's been seen with at several jazz clubs."

"Na, we can't do that" objected Byrd. "Asking either woman about Lion's where about would be a grave mistake. Misty would definitely pull his coat."

"Let's snatch her little ass up" suggested Ice staring around the table. "We can use her as leverage."

"First of all, nobody is touching Misty" Byrd stated adamantly staring around the table. "Nobody" he reiterated staring directly at Ice. "This shit has nothing to do with either young lady. You are so quick to grab a woman up but not Meeks. Keep your motherfucking hands off them. Besides, I owe her brother much love so hands off."

"He still got another nickel to do."

"I don't give a fuck if he had a day to do Ice" he declared staring at him with venom in his eyes. "Nobody had better fuck with Misty. Touch her and I'm taking out your family from the roots" he warned him. He wasn't making a threat. He was making a promise. "Besides, what makes you think Lion should give a fuck about a girl that once abandon him?"

"What?" replied Ice.

"Do your motherfuckin homework, stupid" he replied shaking his head. "Do you even know who the fuck she is? Do any of yawl?" he asked staring around the table.

"Na, we don't" replied Ice.

"Monster's little sister. What the fuck do you think five-o will do if she turns up missing or dead? Huh? One and one equal two Dummy. You don't want to create any connections to her and Monster and definitely not to Lion."

"So, what do you suggest?"

"The obvious Ice. You need to bounce. He could never connect us without you,"

"I'm not going no got damn place!" he insisted snarling at him.

"So, you rather jeopardize our lives again huh?" Byrd replied staring at him.

"Wait a minute, he might already have yawl names" mention Bash trying to increase the peace between the two enemies.

"How Bash?" interjected Byrd staring over at him then back at Ice.

"Even if he don't" interjected Ice before Bash could think about his question. "I'm not going no motherfucking place" he reiterated while glaring over at Byrd.

"You choose a junky over us before now you're putting yourself before us. You made one serious mistake don't make another."

"What motherfucking junky?" Black inquired staring at the two men.

"Tell him Ice" Byrd invited him.

"Nobody know if he's getting high or not" he lied avoiding Bash eyes.

"You are a damn liar" Byrd called him to his face still snarling. "You really need to bounce Ice."

"Like I said, I'm not going no motherfuckin place" he remained adamant. "We can do this Byrd" he insisted trying another tactic. He didn't want to keep looking over his shoulder for the rest of his life. Eliminate the problem was his mindset.

"You're a piece of work Ice" he chuckled. "Fuck what is logical, huh? Suppose I just decide to take you out and dump you somewhere for five-o to find you. I bet that would shake things up, huh?" he asked pulling out his Glock and chambering a round.

"I can't let you do that Byrd" Bash interjected pulling out his .357 Magnum and pointing it at him.

"So, this how it's going down Bash? You're actually pulling your baby out on me."

"I'm sorry Byrd, really" he apologized. "We're all in this shit together, man."

"You pulled your baby on me" he reiterated openly shock that he would do that. "I would never have thought you would flip on me, man especially for a bitch ass motherfucker like Ice. We go way back Bash" he declared unable to hide the hurt in his eyes as he slowly lower his weapon.

"Since elementary, I know but you know I got nothing but love for you. We can't allow Lion to divide us."

"Ice did that when he choose a funky ass junky over us and you're doing it now by backing a bitch ass motherfucker like him."

"Fuck you Byrd!"

"Na, whore! Fuck you!" he said venomously still clutching his Glock while watching him squirm as fear creep into his eyes while putting the blunt he held in his other hand in the ashtray. "I might not be able to bust a cap in your punk ass, but I can damn sure can come around this table and put my foot up in it" he threaten glaring over at him.

"Chill Byrd!" insisted Mookie. "None of us wants to run but Lion have to be dealt with man."

"I'll have my men on the streets tomorrow sniffing him out" Bash informed them.

"You can't touch him in public" Ice informed him ignoring Byrd's stare. "It would have to be some-place secluded or private like a bathroom in a club or movie theater."

"Byrd" Bash called to him. "Come on man, fight with us. We have a better chance with you than without you. Who knew how vicious Lion could be but you? Maybe, we can snarl him. Do this for me brother and I'll try to make it up to you."

"We wouldn't be in this shit if Ice had just listened, Kazandu (You are a young man)" he said still looking at him with venom in his eyes.

"You haven't called me my government name since middle school, Byrd" he replied staring over at him.

"That's because I can't believe you pulled your girl out on me" he told him returning his harden stare.

"I'm sorry man. I'm sorry" he repeated softening his eyes. "I need you to stand with us. With, me! Will you?" he requested.

"Okay Bash, I'm down but this will have a profound effect on our relationship. You understand that, right?" he asked staring at him with slightly softening eyes.

"And rightfully so brother" he confessed returning his stare.

"If you didn't tell Meeks who are involved, you're the one under threat" Byrd informed him. "If you didn't tell Meeks" he reiterated his statement while staring in his eyes.

"I didn't tell Meeks shit except what he needed to know" he insisted but Bash was peeking at him closely.

"What-ever, your lying piece of shit" Byrd said waving off his comment. "Like I was saying, if you boasted to Meeks as it's your nature to do, run your motherfucking mouth, Lion already has some of our names."

"If he does, Meeks didn't tell him" he offer.

"Gotcha" Byrd said, grinning over at him.

"What the fuck do you mean, if he does?" Bash snapped staring at him coldly not liking his answer. "He shouldn't have any of our motherfucking names. Did you boast to Meeks? Was you stupid enough to give him our names too Ice?"

"No, I didn't tell him shit!" he insisted returning his stare, but he did. He boasted how they were going to rip a new ass hole in the city after Road Block and Monster were out of the scene. He was going to step him up personally so they could control Cherry Hill also, but the script got dramatically flipped on him. Who in the fuck would give away keys of drugs to motherfuckers they don't know unless this was their intention in the first place? To block any attempt from outside motherfuckers from trying to infiltrate his brother's territory without bodies getting stretched out, he never thought he would do something as crazy as that. Cunning motherfucking, just like a lion he had to admit. Just like the shit Road Block did for his community over the years was straight out of the Robin Hood story, he provided for those same families he was fragmenting. So, why shouldn't his younger brother be any different than his mentor? He was now providing for his brother's once employed corner boys and are keeping them and their families feed. With his options being marginable, now, he needed all of them to help take out Lion before any of them get touched and then they would know, he did foolishly boast to Meeks about all of them.

"I personally don't believe you" Byrd stated flatly. "I don't see a zebra changing it stripes.

"I don't give a fuck about what you think" he countered staring at him coldly.

"Let's suppose you did jump out of character and didn't tell Meeks our names, who in here believe you won't tell Lion our names?" he asked with a smirk on his face.

"Fuck you Byrd. I'm not a snitch!"

"Tough words coming from a motherfucker with no pressure on him. Lion used a got damn butane on Meeks not because he had to" he told him shaking his head. "He wanted to Ice. I heard how fucked up Meeks was. His toes and knuckles dislocated from a blunt instrument" he shared with those that didn't know. "He already had the names of Meeks accomplices. He was leaving a message for us" he replied getting to his feet. "We'll see how much of a soldier you are, once Lion gets his claws in you since you aren't going anywhere" he shared downing his drink and sliding his Glock back into the small of his back then grab his hat and adjusting it. As he walked towards the door, he paused. "I'm really disappointed in you Bash" he said throwing his words over his shoulder then opening the door and walking out.

"Fuck him, Bash!" Ice smiled over at him.

"Na, fuck you Ice!" he counter getting to his feet. "I pulled a gun on my closest friend because you choose a motherfucking junky over our self-preservation. If any of us gets touched first, you did boast to Meeks and that won't be healthy for your motherfuckin body" he warned him walking towards the door. He pause at the door to stare him in his eyes before opening it and stepping outside.

Ice sat there, stun for a moment still looking at the door. He heard what Bash said and he knew he meant every word also. Consider psychotic by most motherfuckers close to him, Byrd was one of a very few that liked the quiet side of him. Looking into his eyes, they appeared to be the absence of a soul. The streets is what made him ruthless, but Byrd was always able to calm the storm inside of him. He's been rumor to twenty bodies around the city. If Lion isn't touched first, Bash will touch him if any of them are touched first. "Hit the streets tomorrow. Now, get the fuck out" he instructed pouring himself another shot of Gray Goose. "Move motherfuckers! Get the fuck out!" he snapped not liking how slow they were moving.

"You need to check yourself" Mookie told him getting to his feet then adjusting his hat. "We don't work for you motherfucker" he reminded him. "Come on, yawl. Leave this tire ass motherfucker to his thoughts" he said walking towards the door then opening it. Sunshine slowly closed it behind himself as Black and Boo-Boo walk through while staring in at Ice. He could see the intense expression on his face and in his eyes. Fear was slowly engulfing him. The same fear he had since those bodies were recovered in the Patapsco River.

It had been over three weeks since Misty cancel their dinner engagement. He started to call her twice to make sure things between her and the mysterious man's was cool but thought better of it. He have never been an intrusive person. He had seen several times how brothers run to the aid of a distress woman only to have her flipped her script on them. Making the protector the villain. He would not join the ranks of those black men. Honorable but feeling foolish in the end. All he wanted was to complete his business then bounce out of this drug infested, urine smelling allies and violent city. After completing his business, he was going to cut all ties associated with this morally degenerate and rat-infested city called Baltimore.

Lion was just leaving Forman Mills on Belair Road from buying a couple more pairs of jeans, a couple of pull over hoodies and flannel shirts. He needed to dress more appropriate for the things he needed to do than his usual casual attire. Earlier, he had went to Shoe City on Monument Street to buy a pair of Rock Ports and Butter Tim's. Exiting the parking lot on Belair Road, his cell suddenly rang.

"Hello?"

"Hey Lion" Misty's sultry voice greeted him. "I'm sorry for canceling our date" she apologized.

"No problem is everything alright?"

"Some fools just don't accept that it's over" she shared.

"How long was yawl together?"

"Three years" she admitted. "From the time we first hooked up, he had wondering eyes and couldn't keep his zipper up."

"Why didn't you just step off?"

"I've asked myself that same question several times" she confessed. "The answers I keep coming up with is I'm a fool or have a self-esteem issue. There aren't a lot of good men in the city, so we tend to put up with a lot of bullshit than usual."

"Is that's your explanation?"

"Well, it's the truth."

"Na, I can't accept that" he denounced. "Men are only going to do what you allow us to do. If he disrespected you and you didn't give him his walking papers, you're creating your own personal hell and deserve everything that happens."

"Damn. You have never been one to put a cut on the things you say" she slightly giggled. "Straight no chaser."

"You can hear bullshit anywhere. Let me ask you something, do you think he would forgive a single indiscretion on your part?"

"Of course, not" she replied adamantly while slightly hardening her eyes.

"Yet, women surrender their love so easily even to those you know is unworthy. That trait, yawl can keep."

"Have you ever been in love?"

"Na, I rationalized that I was infatuated with you when we were younger, but I met a lot of women over the years since graduating Morehouse" he revealed slightly grinning.

"Morehouse?" she interrupted. "You graduated from Morehouse?"

"Damn, I'm not that dumb Misty" he chuckled. "Yeah, I graduated fifth in my class. I haven't considered my personal life. I do know I want children. How many I don't care? Besides staying in my law books, I'm usually just chilling."

"Law books? Are you a lawyer?"

"Sshhh, don't tell everybody" he teased placing his index finger over his lips. "I work for a very prominent black firm."

"In Atlanta?"

"Na" he lied not offering any more information.

"Well, I'm very impress" she complimented. "So, what are you doing Friday night?"

"Nothing specific unless I get a call."

"Well, I hope that call don't come. How about us hooking up and going to 5 Mile House to get our boogie on?"

"How about us going to this new jazz spot on Charles Street?" he counter.

"I'm not into jazz but if that gets me time with you, I'm down. What time?"

"The last set starts at ten. I can pick you up at nine."

"Okay."

"I'll call you Thursday to confirm everything."

"No need, nothing is going to change this time" she replied. "I need to ask you something."

"Ask away."

"Who is the young lady you've been seen running around town with?"

"Her name is Khatiti."

"I saw yawl a couple of times when I was cruising through in a friend's car. She is extremely attractive?"

"Yes, she is."

"Are yawl an item?"

"An item" he suddenly burst out laughing. "I've been home a little more than a month and I'm supposed to be in a relationship" he lightly chuckled. "Na Misty, she's an acquaintance but we are definitely feeling one another."

"I don't doubt that" she replied reflecting how he used to clutch her fingers when they were kids. He never cared how it might appear to others especially his friends and he was only thirteen at the time. When she saw them walking into Smooth Jazz over in Northeast, she almost spilled her drink on her date. The place seem to slightly pause as everybody glance towards the entrance, they looked gorgeous together and the sister was wearing the fuck out of a red form fitting stretch dress that hit her in the middle of her thighs. "Okay" she sigh shaking off the thought. "I'll holla at you Friday Lion" she said hanging up before he could respond. She sat there with a silly smirk on her face.

When she got his cell number from her brother Monster, he was adamant about not giving him a call. Road Block had trusted him with the information. "You blew Lion off for a punk ass motherfucker like Derrick" she heard herself say. Monster's last instruction are still engraved into her memory bank. He stress that the number was to be used only if something happen to him and Road Block together. Together, he had stressed hardening his eyes and it wasn't the first time she saw the menacing stare that he gave motherfuckers when fucking with their business. She started to defy his wish, but she never forgot what had transpired the last time she ignored his words. It cost a person their life, she was constantly told by him and some of her girlfriends not to fuck with those boys around Collington Square. Yet, she did when she was seventeen and starting to smell herself. A little too much to drink and smoke then she uncharacteristically became very promiscuous especially in her style of dancing. At seventeen and still a virgin, the aggression of one of the guys and feeling their erect dicks against her had frighten her. She had shoved the guy off of her then ran home like a little girl crying while their laughter and taunts filter into her ears. The last person she wanted to run into she did, Monster. Forcing her to tell him what happen, he went home to get Lucy against her pleads and tears. He went straight to Collington Square and air the area out. Killing one and hitting two others as the other guys ran away screaming like little bitches. She caught the stares from several of the guys and girls from around that way in school. Their stares wasn't a friendly or flirtatious either. Their stares were menacing and filled with venom. So, as much as she had wanted to hear his voice, she wouldn't disobey her brother ever again.

It was almost five months before she realized that she hadn't heard from him or seen him, and she found that very unusual. They were like Bonnie and Clyde growing up. She was enjoying her instant new lifestyle with her new drug dealing love interest Derrick that time had slip pass. She casually asked Monster one day how he was doing, and she did not expect the cold stare that he suddenly shot her. She found herself slightly repelling from him while looking at him perplex. Did something happen to him, and she was now asking like she had some genuine concern? His eyes slightly soften before informing her he left Baltimore three whole months ago then shook his head and walked away. Three whole months. The time frame fucked her head up. What does that say about her and the alleged affection that she claimed over the years to have for him? She had broken many promises with him while he was incarcerated and her not missing him confirm what the song had advocated. "Love don't love nobody."

When Monster status instantly changed from security to distributor overnight, she always wondered how? Did he and Road Block make a big score somewhere out of town? The first thing he did for her when the money started turning over was buy her a brand-new Lexus. He was giving her money fist over hand. She had acuminated ten Gs in her saving account and drove up to Philly with her girl Diamond to get herself a new wardrobe. She placed four G's in her girl's hand. She hooked herself up with the latest fashions coming out of New York and so did Diamond. What they were buying would not reach Baltimore for another six months to a year at least. They roam the streets of Philly for five hours getting acclimated to the fast pace. Stumbling upon South Street, they could not believe the mass congestion of people. A smorgasbord of men. It was almost six o'clock in the evening when they forced themselves back to her car, they would drive back in B-More two hours later talking about their adventures in Philly and making promises to return.

Her senior year at Lake Clifton High, she knew she was the shit. Besides driving her own whip to school, she wore clothes that constantly got her compliments even from the other girls. Even more guys than before were trying to hollow at her, but what were they bringing to the table? Most did not possess a job and that meant they didn't have nothing to offer her. Only about five of them had their own cars and it was not new, they couldn't do nothing for her. She did not even notice how pompous and pretentious she was becoming then she stumble upon Derrick slick talking ass whipping a 750 Beamer and her life was never the same. She did not care that he was almost ten years older than she was. He was talking some real Casanova bullshit and she found it extremely flattering. Rereading some of Lion's letters years later. He was writing and expressing some erotic shit, but she did not understand them because she wasn't mature enough. She now understood his confessing of loving her, but she realized it much too late.

It would be years later that she would find out that Lion had won a settlement against the state and gave Road Block five-million dollars to get his business out the gate. He had the money when he first approach her but did not reveal he had it. He wanted to see would she come willingly journey with him into the unknown, and she failed his test again. Yeah, she would have leap at the opportunity to disappear with him if she knew he had the money. What woman would not have? Wouldn't you? She realized that the Audi he was driving that day was his not his brother as he told her. He jumped in his car three days later after being told she would not go and headed out of town. She had thought about him often especially when she lost her virginity. Something she promise she would preserve for him, but it was just another promise of many she did not keep concerning him. She had gotten pregnant twice within the first year of fucking with Derrick and had abortions until the words he wrote to her in a letter hit home when she asked how did he feel about abortions? He said babies were life yearning. After aborting her two children from Derrick, she was not going to abort Nia and he had the nerve to get irate. Punk ass motherfucker claim he was not ready to be a father. How was she to know he already had four daughters out there by three different women? She had chosen Baltimore and these worthless ass men over Lion. Because of her decisions, she have been paying for it ever since but something else that was bothering her. Why haven't she mention her six-year-old child, Nia (purpose) to him yet?

Who would have thought he would become a lawyer and a prominent one at that? Damn. She could not help but wonder again if he still have a small flame or ambers for her? Foolish thinking maybe, huh? The answer that always came back to her was one in the form of a question. Why should he hold a flame for her? Was she blowing jail house rap to him instead of it coming in reverse? With a minimum of five pages in his letters, his words always sounded sincere and express with an admiring love from his heart while it took her days to complete a single page letter. Didn't she abandon him while incarcerated and refuse to leave with? If a guy did that to her, what would she do? Would she still hold a flame for his abandoning ass or allow the love she had to dissipate like the dew on grass?

He appear to have adjusted to the loss of their love as she have done, but if the script were flip, she would still harbor some animosity over a person subliminally saying, "fuck my love like Derrick did" and he probably still does hold some animosities against her. The thought made sadness come to her heart. The one person she actually feel in love with growing up was the same person she abandon once their love could not be displayed or materialized for all to see. She had some heart felt conversations with Monster about him. He constantly asked the same plaguing question. Why didn't you go with him especially since you claim to love him so much? She never could answer the question honestly, but she could now. At least, to herself. He did not have nothing to offer her but his love. No true plans or prospect for employment. He could not even tell her where they would be going except down South. She had cast aside his love and now she was wondering, could he ever love her again? The thought made her subconsciously laugh.

Lion had achieved a lot over the past six weeks. Although he had to admit to himself if not to anyone else, he was worse than his brother could ever be. He had murdered four guys like it was nothing and seeking the others. As speculations flowed, homicide detectives never came knocking on his door. How could they when they did not have the vaguest idea where he was staying. Constantly crossing different communities looking for his marks, a routine of his was slowly developing. Cruising down Monroe Street from Mondawmin Mall on Wednesday evening around eight-thirty, he spotted one of his marks car parks in front of Maceo bar and lounge at Walbrook Street. He continued to North Avenue then turned right and took the first immediate right again. He eventually parked on the corner of Walbrook at Payson Street. He sat staring in the direction of the lounge through the passenger window. He reached out to Bunkie and told him where he was. Twenty minutes later, he pulled up in his Cadillac STS he brought from the money Lion gave him from Meeks and park on Payson. Climbing out, he peeked at Lion as he proceeded towards the small community lounge sitting on the corner. As he enter, he allowed his eyes to adjust to the dim lights before going to the bar and requesting a glass of wine. As he sat staring in the mirror, Sunshine was at a back booth with three gold digging young girls. The two guys were more interested in the entertainment that would be jumping off later than watching his back. He watched him for another fifteen minutes before getting to his feet and walking outside. He stood on the corner talking on his cell before walking back up the street and climbed inside Lion's car.

"I got somebody coming that's going to bring him straight to us" he informed him grinning.

Watching the corner for about twenty-minutes, a bronze complexion girl wearing a jean skirt much too short for her muscular thighs and phat apple bottom ass suddenly appeared with two of her girlfriends. Looking to be just over twenty-one, she was a pure knock out as niggers on the corner instantly started salivating and was not embarrass begging like Keith Sweat. If she told you to come to her, oh you would definitely excuse yourself and come. Her chocolate girlfriends was dressed just as provocative and as sexually alluring like a Venus flytrap. They casually enter the lounge being escorted by three of the aspiring guys.

"Post up on those steps" he told Lion pointing to a vacant house. "I'll be further up the street" he told him as they got out the car. Bunkie headed towards his car and backed it up around the corner before posting up. With the sun rapidly descending and forcing the light pole lights to come on, they sat in the shadows patiently waiting. About thirty-minutes later, they eventually came out of the lounge with his mark. As she led them up towards Payson Street, they walked right past Lion without giving him a second glance or thought. Their minds were focused on what they were going to do to these three young vibrant gold-digging teenagers. They had foolishly told their bodyguards to meet them at their cars on North and Payson. Bunkie was leaning on the corner smoking a cigarette with his back to them like he was looking down towards North Avenue. The group was about twenty feet away when he suddenly turned displaying his .45 and a menacing snarl. Shock instantly gripped them as two of the men struggled to free their weapons from their waist band, the ladies instantly duck then took cover between two park cars and kept their heads down. A single shot rang out hitting one guy center mass. The force knocked him off his feet. Lion recognize the other guy as one of his marks. They did not need two for the information he needed. So, he put one round in the back of his accomplices head as he walked past. His body instantly went limp and collapse to the ground. Sunshine looked on in horror.

"Do not shoot! Do not shoot!" he insisted raising his hand and shocked by the whole ordeal.

"Put your damn hands down" insisted Lion smacking him in the back of his head with his Glock then controlling him by his collar.

"Here you are ladies" Bunkie said giving the girls five G's to split between them.

"Holla at me later, Cuz" the bronze complexion girl said as she stuff the money into her bra then they disappeared up Payson Street.

Lion snatched Sunshine and threw him in the trunk of his car. He secured his hands and legs while placing a stripe of electrical tape over his mouth while Bunkie stared out at the those peeking out their windows. Lion gave him a menacing stare just before he closed the trunk. They was last seen hooking a U-turn then heading up Payson heading towards Mondawmin Mall and turning right.

Ring! Ring! Ring!

"Hello, who is this?" he asked not recognizing the number.

"Hey Byrd" the voice was barely audible.

"What the fuck do you want Ice?" he snap.

"Just got word five-minutes ago that Sunshine was snatched coming out of Maceo by one of his bodyguards."

"What the fuck you mean snatch? Where the fuck was his got damn bodyguards?"

"Waiting at his car for him."

"Waiting at his damn car! What kind of motherfucking security is that?" he asked staring, perplex at his reflection. "How come they wasn't with him?"

"He was escorted out by some bitches."

"Okay but that still does not tell me why they didn't at lease follow him to his car. What kind of dumb shit is that!" he declared piss.

"There's more."

"What is it?"

"Boo-Boo and Blank was killed on the spot."

"What? Shit!" he declared slamming his fist on the coffee table. "You know who got him, right?"

"Yeah" he answered solemn.

"So, you did boast to Meeks. You are lying motherfucker and he now have our names. What in the fuck be running through your stupid ass motherfucking head? Damn!"

"What are we going to do?"

"What are we going to do?" he mock lightly snickering. "Our options are still on the table" he reminded him.

"I can't run, or Cookie might put things together about Meeks."

"Meeks, fuck him?" he snarled through the phone. "You are worried about what Cookie would say? Motherfucker do you realize that your life, our life is in imminent danger. Fuck what Cookie will think. I hope you are not concern about your image?" he suddenly chuckled. "Do not. You never had an image. What you need to be thinking about is self-preservation."

"I am but I can't run."

"You mean you won't run" he corrected him.

"I can't."

"Then your only other option is to tighten up on security. Was Bunkie with him?"

"Yeah, people said the first shot sounded like a fucking cannon going off" he describe.

"Yeah, that was him and his baby, Lucy" he confirmed shaking his head grinning.

"I think we should take him out of the equation" he suggests.

"Who? Bunkie? You obviously do not know who the fuck Bunkie is" he chuckled. "He is the last motherfucker you want to go at and miss. He would dissemble your family tree from the core. Do you understand what the fuck I am saying? Do you?"

"Yeah."

"Then take heave, motherfucker" he advised him. "Lion is deadly alone. Do not even consider fucking with Bunkie. He is the last motherfucker you want to wake up. Like I said, we have two options. Since you are not running, tighten up on your security."

"I'll double my security."

"You sent ten at Road Block and you see what happen? Two of them even had AK's. Lion is nothing like his brother. Are you hearing me now? He is stealth."

"Yeah, I hear you" he said. "If I knew where Road Block lived, I'll send a squad through both of the doors."

"You need to focus on laying low."

"Fuck that!" he replied snarling into his cell phone. "I'm not keeping my head on a damn swivel."

"You won't have to if you stay low" he reiterated. "If you walk out of your front door, you better have your head on a motherfucking swivel. You better because no matter how many motherfuckers you think you got covering your back, they will not be enough. Do any of your bitches know where you rest your head away from home?"

"Hell no, they only know about the apartment up from Coldspring and Reisterstown."

"Good, I got some arrangements to make, and you should be making them too. In the meanwhile, watch your back" he said hanging up then sighing. He had begged Sunshine to leave town, but his dumb ass would not listen. I bet he wish he had now. Well, Lion is going to get from him everything he need to know including their locations and their tendencies. Everything he want he will get before rocking him to sleep. The others can do what they want. If Lion wanted him, he would have to come into his den.

Darkness had consumed the city as three figures were walking through a rat-infested alley near Patterson Park Avenue.

"Oh Shit!" he said as a rat the size of a cat wobble into the darkness.

"Shut your high yellow ass up" whisper Lion smacking him in the back of his head with the butt of his gun, again. "In there, move" he told him as rats squeal and scurried away. They stared up at the houses facing the backyard. All they saw was the reflections of television sets and no curtains moving. Once they were sure it was safe, Bunkie open the metal door that led down to the basement. Lion led the way into the darkness with a pin-flashlight. Once the door was shut, he walked towards the steps. He hit the switch and the basement became illuminated. There were a chair sitting on industrial plastic with at an old wooden table with a black doctor's bag sitting on it.

"Have a seat Sunshine" Bunkie offer him while bringing up another chair for Lion to sit on in front of him. He picked up the black bag that was sitting on the table and placed it at Lion's feet then back away.

"You know why you're here, right?" Lion asked opening the bag causing the clanging of the metals inside. He had his full attention.

"Na man, who are you?" he asked nervously lying.

Slam! A quick vicious right slammed into his mouth causing him to rock back and almost tilting the chair over as blood suddenly appeared from his mouth. His two front teeth were loosening by the blow. "I want answer from you motherfuckers not questions. Do you understand me?"

"Yeah" he slightly whimper as blood trickle from his lips.

"I am Lion. The same motherfucker you stared in the eyes of at my brothers funeral" he informed him reaching in the bag, pulling out the butane tank, and placing it on the table. The next thing he brought out was a pair of shears then holding them. "The butane is to coagulate the blood of your sever fingers" he educated him. "Now, do you know why you're here?"

"No" he persisted with his lie.

"Okay" he replied grabbing the electrical tape and bonding his wrist to the chair and strip across his lips. He gripped his right index finger and snip it off. The sound of his bone crushing, and his muffle screams from filled the basement as Lion lit the butane. Setting the fire to his sever finger, he scream again but the blood was not flowing. "Okay" he said grabbing the shears again. "Let us try this again. Do you know why you are here?"

"Yes" he acknowledged staring in his eyes then slightly at the blood-stained shears and his finger on the floor.

"Tell me why all this shit went down?" he asked leaning back in his chair.

Sunshine squeal like a true Baltimorean without subjecting himself to anymore of the medieval things that Lion had plan. Apparently, they wanted to lock the city down by forming an organization called The Enterprise, but Road Block was not known for joining anything especially with some west side niggers. The only one he vaguely trusted was Byrd. He was fine with the way things were set-up. Locking down the city as Ice wanted to do would eliminate the independent dealers and he was not feeling that. "Everybody deserve to eat" he told them. Byrd wanted to go forward without Road Block, but Ice Pick put a glitch in the plan by plotting the whole assassination scenario. By the time Sunshine was finished talking, they knew where the majority of their stash house was located and had their private apartment locations including personal addresses of their main side bitches. Byrd's address was not one of them because he kept them out of his private life. Sunshine surrendered shit they had not even considered like what they do on certain weekends and where?

"Lion, I am sorry for your brother. Really, I am. I am not about the violence and shouldn't have participated in Ice's scandalous scheme, but I did. If you give me a break, I swear by all that I love that I will leave town tomorrow. I promise."

"Didn't you have a chance to leave town?"

"Yeah" he admitted solemnly.

"You should have taken it" he told him still holding the shears.

"I'll leave to tomorrow man, and you will never see me again, I promise."

"You promise, huh?" he asked softening his eyes slightly.

"Yeah, man. As soon as the banks open at nine o'clock, I will make my withdrawal. I will be gone by ten o'clock" he told him as a ray of hope seems to exist. "I promise."

"Well, I can achieve both agendas tonight. You suddenly leaving town and never coming back" he told him suddenly leaning forwards and thrusting the shears into his esophagus then twisting while staring him in his eyes. Surprise was in them not the fear that once engulfed them as his blood quirked out with each beat of his heart. As he slowly closed his eyes, Lion did not snatch the shears out until his last breath escaped.

"I thought you was going to give him a pass" Bunkie mention grinning while shaking his head.

"Yeah, his dumb ass thought so too." Reaching in the leather bag, he pulled out some Clorox and poured it on the shears then his glove covered hands before wiping both clean. Retracing their steps, they slightly pushed the metal basement door slightly open then stared out up at the windows again. Not seeing anybody, Lion suddenly pushed it open and exited quickly with Bunkie then quietly closing it. Pausing as a junkie was turning a trick in the alley, she completed her business in five minutes then they were free to exit the yard and proceeded out the alley toward their cars. Turning on Biddle Street, Bunkie headed towards Cedonia while Lion headed towards Rt.40.

Monday morning, WBAL news started its 7 o'clock broadcast with the discovery of a black male's body being found in the basement of a vacant house. The contractors that were contracted to remodel the house remember smelling a stench coming through the vents all morning. Searching each floor for a possible dead rodent, they eventually venture down into the basement and made the gruesome discovery. They had just inspected the house on the previous Friday morning. So, the individual had to be murdered over the weekend. The victim's name was Walter "Sunshine" Wilson. Forty-five-year-old father of four. The coroner would not describe the wound or wounds. All he would say was it was unnatural and vicious in nature.

Byrd was sitting in the front room eating his breakfast when he heard the news. He felt pity for Sunshine. He should never have gotten in the game even if he was just a booky and damn sure shouldn't have patch into this fuck up plot constructed by Ice. Since talking to Ice, he had four additional soldiers around him constantly. If he wanted female company, he would have one of his men pick her up while the other five remained behind. He has not left his apartment all weekend and won't until Lion is either killed or leave town. He was seriously thinking about catching a plane to Seattle and getting lost in the forestry or going to Cali. With his luck recently, the slogan, "It's a small world" solidified that running to Seattle just might not be far enough. Lion would still keep sniffing him out. At that very moment, he had to check himself. He realized that he was unconsciously becoming paranoid. His fear was slowly gripping him. One thing he was going to do is keep his family safe. He did not confine in his woman what was transpiring but she heard the severity of it in his voice. Instead of chilling, she tried to get out the gate on him. The verbal tongue slashing he gave her was completely out of character to stress home his point. She never knew he could utilize such obscene language so eloquently while directing it at her. The person he absolutely loved. Something very haunting was transpiring and he was trying to keep her and their three children safe.

On the other side of town, Ice, Bash, and Black was hitting the streets hard. Road Block's car have not been seen in a month which meant Lion was utilizing another car and not the 300 he owned. Their hunt for him had just gotten more difficult. Nobody from their crews knew his real name so his MVA connection was useless. Misty know his real name but approaching her was off limits. He had more than enough trouble already on his plate. He didn't need Byrd on the list also. They had ten cars with four soldiers inside hitting every neighborhood trying to get a handle on him or Bunkie, but nothing have prevailed yet. Cruising through the East Side Boyz turf was definitely not happening, now especially since Lion kept them feed and their operations were flowing like usual. Getting caught being intrusive since Road Block's assassination, they would instantly set it off on them. Riddling their vehicles with large caliber hand guns and assault weapons, they do not venture into the East Side any more. Any alleged sighting of Lion was usually worthless by the time one of their crew they arrived at the location. He was moving like the wind and as stealth as an animal of prey. Bash was not hibernating like Byrd, but he was damn sure being careful when he was on the streets. His head stayed on a swivel and his two bodyguards from Ice needed to have the same perspective to preserve his life. Every car that passes should be considered a possible threat. So, he needed them to scrutinize every vehicle and everyone approaching. If he caught you eyeing a piece of ass once too often after the second warning, the person were cast out into the cold. Homeless and with no financial assistance. They could not even be a corner boy on the west side.

Bash decided to go to Melba's Place up on 32nd and Greenmount on Thursday, lady's night. He had not been out partying in a minute and his pockets were heavy. How the word reached Bunkie ears was scandalous, I guess? When Bash cut off one of his partners he knew since junior high and the guy had done two years for him while grinding, he took it personally being cast out into the cold and not being able to feed his family. He pleaded for Bash to give him just one more chance, but his words fell on deaf ears as he waved him off. Rage filled his eyes for being slighted by Bash like he was a piece of shit and malicious gradually darken his heart. So, he reached out to one of Bunkie's cousin's and gave him the 4-1-1. Around eleven o'clock, he would park at the fire hydrant up the street from the fire station and stay in his car until his security returned. They will all be strap until they reach Melba's. Only then, they would then surrender their weapons to two members in his clique who will rotate but remain outside scrutinizing everyone entering and every car that drove too slowly pass.

With the information Bunkie gave him, Lion had four days to survey the area and plot his attempt. Every evening after the sun had gone down, he would venture into the area. He stood on the corner of 31st and

Greenmount surveying the area as he casually walked. He had walked down 31st Street then nonchalantly walked into the alley inspecting possible access to the roof. One of two positions was good, but the one with the best shadow was diagonal of where his target would park. A mere sixty to seventy yards away. With Bunkie connection, he was able to purchase a Salty rifle off the streets and had set the sights. He had venture deep into Lincoln Park and set up a shooting range with four soda cans. He knew he had about fifteen minutes from the first shot before the first patrol car would come to investigate. In four shots at fifty yards, he had her sighted-in.

On Thursday night around ten-thirty, he parked his car on Brentwood then retrieved the duffle bag containing the Salty from the trunk. He walked through the alley scanning the back windows while staying in the shadows before he suddenly ascended a telephone pole to gain access to a garage roof. He walked over the top hoping that it will support his weight then leap for the roof top and lifted himself onto the main roof. His crawled to his position then assemble the two-piece rifle on the roof. He locked and loaded one .45 caliber bullet then waited for his intended target. Time seem to suddenly creep as the bewitching hour was nearing. At approximately eleven fifteen, a brown Mercedes Maybach pulled in at the vacant spot as two black Suburban turned left on 31st Street to find parking spots. Watching his six men coming back up the street, he slightly snarled. They never looked towards the roofs as they walked pass. They congregated on the corner looking around before walking across Greenmount then one of them open the back-passenger's door and Bash stepped out. He extended his hand back inside and a walnut complexion young lady barely over twenty-one stepped out. The white Gucci pants suit she was wearing fitted her to a T. He stood among them adjusting his tie and rolling his shoulders like a pure gangster. He reached into his breast pocket admiring the ladies checking him out that were walking pass across the street and pulled out a Havana cigar. Igniting his gold cigar lighter, he illuminated his face as he went to light the cigar.

POW! The sound was deafening and startled his men. The round struck him in the center of his forehead. The force took him off his feet and slam him violently into the wall he was standing next to as large fragments of his skull and brain particle splattered the wall behind him plus the young lady, he was standing next to. Her screams were deafening as shock engulfed her as she stood there appearing to be running in place while shaking her hands. She suddenly took off running down Greenmount towards 32nd Street cover in blood and brain particles while still screaming. His bodyguards never considered reaching for their weapons. They got the fuck down and stayed down while staring around in horror at their boss. Half of his face was missing from the large caliber weapon. The sudden flash of light revealed where the shot came from but none of them was willing to go investigate. What was their incentive? As five-o sirens could be heard and lights could be seen coming up Greenmount, two of the men had no option but to brave the unknown and hope they were not a part of the hit. They could not be there when five-o arrive because they had warrants. None of them could afford to be caught with a weapon on them not with their extensive criminal history and being on parole. So, the two men collected the weapons then took a deep breath before crouching over and scurrying away from the murder scene. Only when the area was flooded with five-o did they come up from behind the car they used as shelter with their hands held high while pointing in which direction the shot came from. By the time they climbed the roof, Lion was long gone. He had collected the single brass then retraced his steps to his car.

When Det. Ron and Shitty arrived about an hour later, Baltimore's finest had collected the witnesses' statements and personal information. Walking over and removing the sheet off the victim, both Detectives threw up their dinner.

"What the fuck!?" declared Shitty spitting out the last of his dinner. "What the fuck is going on in this psychotic ass city?"

"Do you recognize him?" Ron asked going through his pockets and retrieving his wallet.

"How? Half of his motherfucking face is gone."

"According to his driver's license, this is Marcus "Bash" Tisdale. He was an extremely dangerous individual with an extensive criminal record. He and Sunshine both attended Shabazz memorial" he reminded him. "Somebody is getting payback."

"Surely, you don't think Malik?" inquired Shitty.

"It is too early to suggest he would sacrifice his prestigious future for redemption, but somebody is. Two of the largest drug dealers murdered in the past two weeks and now one of the city's most notorious hit man. I do not call this coincidental. They have a connection to the murder of Shabazz. I can feel it, but I just cannot figure out why?"

"We need to press up on Mr. Tavon Smith at Hopkins" Shitty said sarcastically.

"Bright and early tomorrow morning," Ron told him staring down at the bloody sheet.

Saturday night, Lion had T.T over for a home cook meal. She wore a sexy pair of hipster jeans, a light brown silk tie-up blouse revealing her sexy naval and brown saddles. While she sat at the four-chair island sipping on a glass of red wine and watching him maneuvering around the kitchen, Jelly Roll Martin's "Creepy Feelings" played in the background. He was preparing a simple meal of brown rice, steam vegetables and a sirloin steak. As he was completing each aspect of his meal, he was washing the pans and utensils. He had her set the table so she would stop gawking at him.

"Have a seat" he told her as he brought the steaks and prepared her plate. After saying grace, they got to devouring their meal.

"Oh, my goodness" she said biting into her steak. "How did you get it to be so tender" she asked staring across the table at him.

"Like I'm going to tell" he slightly smiled.

"No, serious Malik. What did you do?"

"Nope, not sharing" he replied smiling over at her and causing her to suddenly giggle.

As the candles provided the light, they talked through their meal. She shared her aspirations, hopes and dreams with him. By the time he had everything place back in its places, he had an excellent perspective of her and what lie in her heart. Relaxing in the family room listening to the Moments singing "Just Because He Wants To Make Love" in the background and smoking white boys (joints). He asked her unique questions that surprised the hell out of her. Questions like, "Tell me about the man who first broke your heart?" He was not accepting any general explanations either as they dissected her every response. Arriving at the root of the situation, he would intrude further into her private life, and she willingly provided the information. It was well after three o'clock in the morning when he gave her the option of sleeping in one of the vacant bedrooms or be taken home, she chose to be driven home, of course. He rationalized that she just did not trust herself. What kind of image and impression would it give to make love to a somewhat complete stranger after three weeks, right?

Around nine o'clock the next morning, Detectives Ron and Smith were entering Johns Hopkin Hospital through the main entrance on Orleans Street then proceeded towards the elevators. Climbing aboard, they push the third floor for the ICU Unit and eventually felt the elevator elevating rising. Exiting on their floor, they spotted the patrol officer station at room 312 and approach displaying their badges. Pushing open the door, Tavon was sitting up watching Sponge Bob Square Pants while eating his breakfast. Seeing them this early brought a look of dread to his face. He had continuously lied about the night he had gotten shot twice. "He was just at the wrong place at the wrong time" he persisted but they weren't biting his hype. None of the weapons that were recover had his finger or palm prints nor DNA. Ballistic revealed that his hands and clothing were saturated in powder residue consistent with someone firing a weapon repeatedly. Yet, no weapon could be placed in his hands. Very circumstantial evidence at best, he rationalized. He made sure that the weapon he used would not be recover untainted. By tossing it in the storm drain down the street from where he was found semi-unconscious, all DNA would be tainted at the least if they did recover it. Yet today there was something different about their character and demeanor. The usual casual expression they usually possess was replaced with a stern expression and harden eyes. He knew it instantly that this was not going to be just another casual conversation, but an interrogation.

"You know Tavon" Detective Ron stated casually walking around the bed and grabbing the television remote then turning it off. "After a month, I'm tire of listening to your got damn lies."

"What are you talking about?" he asked returning his stare then looking over at Shitty. "What are you talking about Detective Ron?"

"From day one, you been lying through your got damn teeth to me and I personally don't appreciate it" he told him hardening his eyes. "I've been here trying to win your trust to assist you and you constantly keep bullshitting me" he slightly snarled at him.

"I still don't know what you are talking about, Detective Ron?" he reiterated averting his eyes and staring at Shitty.

"Do not look at me with your lying ass. He is talking to you" Shitty said. "I personally knew you was a damn liar and would have filed murder charges on your black ass weeks ago, but Ron wanted to wait."

"Murder charges!?" he repeated lightly chuckling. "I didn't murder anybody?"

"You're a damn liar" insisted Shitty.

"No, I'm not" he persisted. "I'm the victim here."

"Bullshit somebody else" counter Ron staring at him coldly. "How hard would it be to convince a jury with the circumstantial evidence we have to show that your hands had involvement in this murder?"

"What evidence?"

"This evidence" he said slamming the toxicology report on the table for him to inspect. "Although you had truly little residue under your right finger nails which can easily be explained especially since your hands were saturated in urine. Did you piss on your hands in hopes of eliminating any residue, Tavon?" he asked slightly smiling but did not expect an answer. "You, wiping off your hands on your pants was not intelligent either. The amount of powder residue on your clothing only collaborated what ballistic is claiming. It was your clothing that burned you. They were saturated in powder residue, also. Consistent with someone firing a weapon repeatedly especially your left arm sleeve. Are you left-handed, Tavon? Now, can you explain how that happen?"

"No, I can't but I didn't fire no weapon" he persisted.

"What about explaining the amount of powder residue in your nostrils after they were swab? How hard do you think it would be to prove that you knew and was associated with the gentlemen that were murdered a month ago? All of yawl coming from out of Cherry Hill is supposed to be a coincident also, huh Tavon?" he played his hands then stared over at him. "Talk or lawyer up. I do not give a damn at this point. I will have an arrest warrant for you by tomorrow for conspiracy."

"Conspiracy?"

"Yeah, conspiracy motherfucker" he snorted at him.

"I didn't conspire with anyone!" he stated adamantly.

"Tell it to the damn jurors" stated Ron collecting his papers.

Circumstantial evidence have gotten a lot of motherfuckers locked up dealing with this bias ass judicial system. With the things he openly shared, did he really want to take his chances with a jury? The last thing he needed was the prosecutor to start disclosing his criminal history and incarcerations. Na, that would not be flattering. Na, that will not do. Plus, most people in Cherry Hill know that they all got down together and if they start snooping for people to collaborate their association it would not be hard.

"Fuck all this bullshit!" snarled Ron staring over at him, contemplating. "Enjoy your Square Pants show" he said tossing the remote back at him. "I got better things to do than sit around here trying to help a motherfucker that do not want my help. Come on, Shitty. We got detective work to pursue" he instructed starting to turn.

"If I tell you what I know, what will you do for me?" he asked staring over at him. "I am still not admitting to a damn thing. I am just asking."

"What are you asking for?" Ron inquired returning his stare.

"Immunity from prosecution and nothing else" he replied staring at him with a slight smirk.

"You will tell us everything?" he asked staring at him coldly.

"Everything including how much we received as a down payment?" he revealed adding more mystery to the pot. If they try to play hard ball, he will disavow everything he said.

"We might be able to work something out."

"You need to get started" he advised him slightly grinning.

He looked over at his partner who was still slightly snarling at him then back at Tavon. "Okay, I will contact Charmaine Robinson from the prosecutor's office and run it past her. If she accepts the offer, I will get back with you."

"You do that detective" he said reaching for the remote and turning the television back on. "I'll be right here for the next two weeks and then I'm gone" he told him shoving a fork filled with eggs into his mouth while smiling at the cartoon Archer.

"Let's step outside Shitty" he said leading the way out the door. He pulled out his cell and spoke briefly with Charmaine. "She'll be here within the hour" he said placing his cell back into its case.

"I knew his ass was lying from day one" Shitty stated still snarling. "Now his punk ass is looking for an out."

"Most tough guys usually do when face with a lengthy incarceration" he replied slightly smiling. "His dumb ass is still not out of the woods even if the plea is successful. Somebody is eliminating all of those responsible for the murder of Shabazz and he is one of them. Let us go back inside and soften him up a little before Charmain's arrival. Some pictures just might accidentally fall out displaying what is waiting for him if he doesn't cooperate" he said with a coy smile.

"Seeing what happen to his friends will shake his memory especially when he view what happen to Meeks" he lightly chucked. "Come on, I can't wait to see his expression" he said smiling while leading the way back to his room.

"She's on her way" Det. Ron informed him as they walked back into the room.

"You need to get a public defender here to inspect any legal documents that might need my signature" he informed him slightly grinning.

"Charmaine will be bringing one with her" he replied allowing some pictures to mysteriously slip from his folders. The look that instantly engulf his eyes was priceless. Seeing the sever fingers and other displays of medieval torture of his previous partners, he stared up into Ron's harden eyes with absolute fear.

Word of Bash's assassination spread like the plagued. In the past two weeks, two of the city's main distributors and a known hit man were taken out while their bodyguards mysteriously did uncharacterized traits associated with being a bodyguard, but not a motherfucking punk. Mid-level dealers and corner boys were hoping whoever were committing these murders would spare them their wrath. Speculations started resurfacing again, most associated what was transpiring on the West Side main distributors to the murders of Road Block and Monster. Some thought that one of their soldiers were claiming revenge for them while others thought it was one of Monster's little knucklehead cousins. What no one wanted to mention the obvious? Where were Byrd, Mookie, and Ice? Speculations that they might have had a hand in the murder of Road Block and Monster resurface especially among the soldiers on the East Side? No one wanted to accept Byrd would have a hand in the murder of his once close friend. Yet, the question was now being ponder again with the sudden demise of Sunshine and Boo-Boo. Would Byrd really participate in the assassination of Road Block? The city homicide department was stump as CI's related the rumors running around in the streets.

"Byrd! We have got to do something" Ice said revealing his urgency.

"I am, I'm staying off the grid" he laugh at his fear and apprehension.

"How in the hell can you laugh at a time like this!? He is picking us off man one by one!" he stress causing Byrd to laugh harder.

"I tried to warn your dumb ass about him, but what did you say? Oh, yeah. Fuck that little nigger, right? Well, from where I am sitting, he's doing all the fucking" he burst out laughing again knowing that it would irritate the hell out of him. "From what I heard; he was accurate as a motherfucker with that rifle. He blew away half of Bash face according to witnesses and his bodyguards. I know Bash or you did not see that coming because I damn sure didn't" he shared still laughing. "Who in the hell did Bash piss off that Lion knew actually where he was going to park his car and on which night? I had to start keeping my blinds closed during the day time after that hit. When I am on the balcony at nights, you know all the lights are off behind me including the television. I cup my hands around everything I smoke which can cause an illumination to my face especially those blunts and cigars I like so much" he shared with him. "You foolishly thought he would have a gun fight out in the streets like the O.K Corral, huh?" he asked lightly chuckling. "Na, a lion stalks its prey and show patience" he informed him lightly laughing then becoming quiet for a brief second. "I will share my pessimistic thought with you."

"Pass a who?"

"Pessimistic, dummy" he lightly snicker. "My private wish or thought."

"What is it?" he asked hesitantly.

"I hope he gets me before he gets you" he stated shocking him. "Me because I am supposed to have been a friend. Someone who use to break bread with him and Monster at our parents houses back in the day. I got into the game because of Road Block and Monster before moving to the west side. Since elementary school, that is how far back we go together, and I allowed a piece of pussy to destroy our friendships" he shared with him. He never told anybody that story and yet he was sharing it even with a bitch ass motherfucker like Ice and wondering why he was confessing it now? "So, Lion is going to look at me as he should. A backstabbing pussy chasing worthless motherfucker deserving what is coming to me" he shared his fate. "You for constructing the whole plan and you can bet he knows this. They say the value of certain bullets are thirty-eight cents apiece. He will not invest that much in you or me, if possible, especially if he could get his claws into us. He do not want a bullet to take away his plans for you. Rest assure Ice, you will be begging him to allow you to purchase the bullet yourself, but retribution is what he is seeking not requests. This is not Burger King" he burst out laughing again then slowly coming under control. "The retribution he took out on Meeks, Boo-Boo, Sunshine, and Bash is just a prelude to just how vicious and medieval he can be. I thought I seen it all until he used those shears to penetrate Sunshine's esophagus."

"His esophagus! He shoved some damn shears into his throat!?"

"What, you didn't know?" he asked unable to contain his chuckle. "That was some vicious medieval ass shit. I do not want to be last. I honestly do not want to be last Ice" he reiterated in an eerie voice. "Being the last to feel his wrath will not be pretty. I will commit suicide before I allow him to get his claws in me. I mean this Ice. I will not allow him to get his claws in me if I'm last. I will holla at you" he said solemnly then suddenly ending their conversation.

Ice sat there, stun and remembering his last words. He did not want to be last. He knew the Grim Reaper was coming and he have already accepted his fate, but he has not and won't. Who in the hell can make peace with death? Surely, not him. Shears through his motherfucking windpipe, damn. There is no bargaining with this motherfucker. Money is not the restitution he's seeking. The color was wrong. He wanted red and blood is the only color that will suffice his thirst and nothing else just like a man eater would desire. Byrd has been on point from the very beginning, but did his words have any effect on him initially? No, but now they do. The arrogance he displayed previously was noticeably gone. He did not want to be last either now. He did not want to consider the things that Lion would do to him once he gets his claws into him. His mind could not conceive such viciousness or devious shit. Now, he was a dead man walking unless he flip his script and get the fuck out of Baltimore. Something that he really did not want to do, but self-preservation brings logic to the forefront.

At this point, if Cookie did not want to leave with him, fuck her. He was not a bad looking man for his age of forty-five. There are more women in the world and all he would need is just one. He had abused her trust years ago and figure that she was only staying with him for financial reasons for their children, not for love. Once their last daughter graduate high school, she would probably file for divorce the very next day and he would concede to her wishes. As for now, he could take the money he got stash and get the fuck out of the country by noon tomorrow leaving her the money in their private account in D.C. His pass port was up to date. He could easily find some Caribbean location like the Cayman Islands,

Guadeloupe, or Barbados where he could live like a motherfucking king off his money and really stay off the grid. Or he could move to one of those Scandinavian countries or Afrika. He could easily disappear among the thick bushes while being surrounded by wild animals. What-ever he decides he needed to decide and quickly. Time was running out. He could feel the walls gradually closing in on him. If he try to get into Lion's mind knowing the things he does, Black or Mookie could be next on his hit list. If that comes true, he knew he was on barrow time and escaping his wrath may be too late.

A little after one o'clock Charmaine Robinson was just arriving at Johns Hopkins Hospital accompany by public defender representative Mr. Wilks. Coming out of the elevator, she was dress in a beige color two-piece skirt set. The mid-level thigh skirt complimented her muscular thighs and calves. Standing about five feet seven with a deep mocha complexion, she could definitely turn heads.

"Excuse me" she softly spoke to the nurse.

"Oh, good afternoon" the young white female nurse smiled. "How may I assist you, ma'am?"

"Can you tell me which room Tavon is in?"

"He's in room 320."

"Thank you" she replied turning and searching the numbers as she walked. Pushing open the door, Detective Ron and Shitty instantly got to their feet. "Hey Ron. What's up Shitty?"

"Hey Charmaine" they greeted together admiring her body before resting their eyes on her eyes.

"This is Tavon and Mr. Wilkes from the public defender office" Ron introduced them.

"How are you, William?" she asked smiling.

"Just fine Charmaine" he replied returning her smile.

"Okay, Tavon" she said grabbing another chair and pulling it up next to the bed then crossing her legs. No cellulite was present. "As you know, I'm Charmaine Robinson of the prosecutor's office. These detectives claims you can shine some light on the rash of murders occurring around the city, is that correct."

"Yes ma'am" he proclaimed admiring her body and light brown eyes.

"Tell me what you know?"

"That is not part of the agreement" he interjected returning her stare.

"If the information you provide results in the capture and convictions of the individuals involved, you'll get your immunity."

"Na, that, won't work Ms. Robinson" he denounced her offer shaking his head while staring at her defiantly. "I have witness individual escaping a conviction charge that they shouldn't have escaped. Your office doesn't have a good track record in the streets especially with witnesses. So, your offer doesn't hold water with me."

She stared at him then over at the detectives. "Do you have anything connecting him to any of the murders?"

"A lot of good circumstantial evidence including individuals that will testify that he usually hang around with the gentlemen that were murder" Ron revealed to her and him while slightly smiling at the expression on his face.

"Oh, I could definitely use that" she replied returning his stare with a coy smile then focus back on Tavon. "Do you have his thumb print on any of the recover weapons or casing?"

"Na, we don't" he admitted returning her stare.

"No weapon, huh?"

"None" he replied. "Just ballistic revealing him having residue on his clothing and person.

"I could still use that" she replied, smiling at him then focusing on Tavon "So, what do you think Ron?" she asked in a personal tone.

"Honestly, Charmaine?" he replied as they took their respective roles. They have played this game many of times in their ten-year relationship.

"Yes, honestly" she replied containing her slight smile.

"I personally think we should go to trial with the evidence that we have collected and what I have shared with him willingly" he replied returning her stare before snarling over at Tavon. "There is no doubt with his criminal history we can obtain a guilty verdict on both counts of first-degree murder. I want to see if he still have that same little smirk on his face after being found guilty" he continued to snarl at him.

"Wait a minute!" interjected Mr. Wilkes. "I thought we had an agreement on the table. My client is willing to provide as much information as he can for immunity."

"I know why you are here Sam" he replied. "She was asking me for my opinion" he said still staring at Tavon. "Where is that little smirk, Tavon?"

"I don't know Sam" Charmaine shared peeking over at Tavon. She could see in his eyes that he didn't want to go to trial. "What do you say Detective Smith?"

"Personally, I say take his black ass to trial" he replied staring coldly at him. "But he could clear up a big mystery for us and clear our books" he told her then stared back at him.

She stared back at Tavon as though she was contemplating. "Okay Tavon, Kwanzaa is coming early for you this year. You have a deal."

"Write it up" he slightly smiled over at her as she got to her feet.

"I'll be right back" she said walking out the room with her brief case. She called her office to have an intern deliver the documents to her on the Orleans Street main entrance. Twenty minutes later, a young black male intern place the documents in her hands. She sat in the lobby for twenty minutes reviewing the pages and making sure that everything was in order. She got to her feet then proceeded towards the elevators. Pushing her designated floor, she eventually walked into the room with the documents with in her hand revealing them to him. "Here it is" she offered to him. He took the paper and pass them over to his public defender. After allowing him to read it, he pass it back to him nodding that everything was in order. Trust wasn't high on his priority as he tried to decipher what it was saying. The main thing it said through all the jargon and bullshit was granted immunity. "If you're please, sign at the bottom" she instructed. After acquiring his signature, they got started. She sat in front of him with her legs cross as he spoke into the tape recorder. He told them everything that he knew including who hired them for the contract. Why would an alleged renown drug dealer assassinate someone that's not in the game? That was still the mystery that even Tavon couldn't shine a light on. Still, with the information he provided, they did know where to search for their elusive answers. Ice Pick was the main character mention but so was Byrd. Now, all they needed was their government names and they would have their faces.

The next couple of days the city's homicide detectives and narcotic-squads disrupted the drug game. Instead of following establish rules of engagements, they would park their patrol cars at every known hot stop around the West Side and chill. This isn't how the game is supposed to be played. They are supposed to cruise the city and the look-out boys would chirp when they come into their neighborhood. Seeing them, they are supposed to bounce out on them and try to catch them dirty, but usually failing. Their new and unusual tactics started frustrating the corner boys. They would stand counter corner of five-o with their arms raised over their heads at them asking, "What's the fuck up?" Although they were feeling the crunch financially, nobody felt it more than the addicts. Unable to walk up and be served, they were now subjecting themselves to urine and rat-infested allies to get their daily fixes and gate shots. The possibility of a stick up occurring in the confines of an alley was greater than being served on a corner, less witnesses. Their tactic slowly started to work. Catching dealers stepping back out of an alley after serving someone or a mid-level distributor slipping and getting caught with a weapon on them. The tactic was working.

"You wanted to talk to me?" Detective Ron asked staring down at the perk with his hands cuffed to the metal table.

"The officer that arrested me said you're trying to put a face to the name Ice Pick. Is that correct?"

"Yes, do you know him?"

"Not personally, I have a cousin that does.

"Do you know his real name?"

"Yeah, but what's in it for me?"

"What are you here for?"

"I'm a felon in possession of a fire arm. Can you make that disappear?" he asked staring him in his eyes.

"That's a sure three and a half years vacation for you even with good behavior" he reminded him returning his stare.

"Oh, I know the law" he assured him. The last thing he needed was returning to Jessup or Hagerstown. Lifers would love to get their fingers around his throat or have him bending over to have the biggest dicks in the institution to fuck the shit out of him. He had stolen, swindle their commissary and invaded their homes while they were away. Going back to jail wasn't an option for him. "Help me Detective Ron so I can help you" he damn near pleaded returning his stare.

"If forensic reveals that the gun you was caught with don't have any body's, I'll let you walk."

"Oh, it doesn't have any bodies" he assured him seeing light in his darkest hour.

"So, what's Ice Pick real name?" he asked staring over at him.

"People say you are a straight up type of guy Detective Ron and that you won't fuck me after I give you the person's name" he revealed his apprehension and thought process.

"What you heard about me is true. I don't fuck people. I let them fuck themselves then I put my foot on their got damn throats" he told him with conviction. "Is that good enough for you?"

"Yeah" he said still returning his stare. "The guy's government name is Raymond "Ice Pick" Thomas" he snitched. "He runs Park Heights."

"Who is Byrd?"

"Never heard of the guy" he lied. That wasn't a part of their agreement, you don't give shit to five-o for free. That's basic snitching 101.

"Where can we find this Ice Pick character?" inquired Ron.

"This time of the day" he said staring up at the clock on the wall. "He could be found by the race track or sniffing around the young girls at Park Heights and Garrison's pool."

"What is he driving?"

"Usually, a pimp out Acura to attract the young ladies or his black Escalade but lately though, he's been seen driving his woman Cookie's lip stick red Caddy. She has monogram tags with her name" he shared. "Rumor coming through the grapevine is that someone is hitting high profile distributors on the west side."

"What high-profile distributors?" Ron asked staring over at him.

"Aren't yawl supposed to be po-po?" he asked shaking his head while grinning. "Sunshine and Boo-Boo got stretched out on Walbrook Street almost three weeks ago and then Bash got hit on 31st and Greenmount just before he was to attend ladies night at Melba's Place" he said tensing his eyes.

"Are you insinuating that that those three murders are related?"

"I'm not insinuating anything, Detective" he assured him returning his stare. "Something is jumping off on the west side, but the grapevine doesn't know what or why? Make no mistake, something is going on while the east side murders have damn near cease like they put away their petty little beefs against one another for a common enemy."

"Who's the enemy?"

"Nobody know but the sudden assassination of Bash got motherfuckers on edge. There are speculations starting to surface" he shared but hesitating.

"What speculations?" he asked hardening his eyes. "Kick it out."

"Some thinks that it's cops trying to extort more money from them. What do you say?" he asked staring at him like he expected an answer.

Ignoring his statement, he gather up his notes. "I'm going to have you move to a holding cell for a couple of hours" he told him. "When forensic complete their analysis and you're cleared, I'll cut you lose" he assured him opening the door and talking to the officer briefly. "You don't have any detainers or warrants, do you?"

"If I did, I wouldn't have helped you" he informed him slightly grinning.

Detective Ron placed Ice Pick's government name in the data base and his face filled the screen. "Well, well, well" he silently said recognizing his face from Shabazz's memorial. At the age of forty-five, he has an extensive criminal record that extends back to when he was a fifteen-year-old juvenile committing carjacking. Sending his face through the wire, a patrol car picked him up a couple of hours later standing on the corner of Park Heights and Belvedere Avenue flirting with a young lady then brought him to the Northwest station. He sat nervously waiting on the detectives. He wasn't nervous about the interview. He had endured several over the years and he could always lawyer up at any time if he didn't like where the interview was heading. He actually found interviews to be highly informative if nothing else. Na, his nervousness came from being unprotected. Even in a police station, he didn't feel safe or secure.

"You're a hard man to find, Mr. Thomas" Detective Ron informed him opening the door then placing a folder on the table as he and Shitty took a seat across from him.

"I didn't know you was looking for me."

"Our investigation brought us to you" Ron informed him staring in his eyes.

"What investigation?" he asked staring over at both detectives. "What is this about?" he asked.

"Simply put, murder" replied Shitty.

"Murder" he suddenly burst out laughing. "I thought bringing me to homicide was a mistake by the officers, but you're serious huh?" he inquired returning their stare but still smiling. "I haven't murder anybody detectives."

"According to our source, you contracted a guy name Meeks to assassinate Road Block and his right-hand man Monster."

"Bullshit" he snicker waving off his comment. "You have to come better than that Detective" he smiled crossing his leg. "We go way back together."

"So, you do know both gentlemen?"

"A lot of people know them. I paid my respect at his memorial like everyone else" he informed them. "What makes you think I had a hand in his murder."

"Not murder but assassination" Det. Ron corrected him staring into his eyes coldly. "Do you know a Tavon Wilkes?"

"No, should I?"

"Well, he's one of the guys from Cherry Hill that's at Johns Hopkins recuperating. He said Meeks told him that you hire them."

"Oh, he did, huh?" he slightly smiled. "I know he's pulling yawl legs. Unless you can substantiate what, he's claiming, I'm not biting your hype."

"Three awfully close friends of yours were murder in the past three and a half weeks. That doesn't trouble you?"

"What close friends and why should I be troubled?"

"Sunshine, Boo-Boo and Bash."

"They weren't no close friends of mine" he lied especially concerning Bash. His death still haunts him at night. "What makes you think that?"

"Didn't yawl attend the memorial together?"

"No, we just so happen to meet up there" he replied staying consistent.

"From where I was posted up, you seem to have a lot to say."

"Whatever I was saying was for them to hear and not you or anybody else" he counter returning his stare.

"You know what?" interjected Shitty forcing his eyes on him. "I'm still puzzle over one thing. Why didn't you take care of yours lose ends?"

"What lose ends are you talking about, Detective?" he persisted with his lie. His co-defendants had asked him the same damn question. "It's your job to speculate and that's fine with me, I don't have anything to hide."

"Do you know Meeks?"

"Yeah."

"Did you murder him or have someone murder him and his co-defendants?"

"What!?" he asked slightly shaking his head. "Why would I hire and then have him murder especially when he's the uncle to my children?" he revealed.

"What?" Detective Ron asked surprised by his statement.

"You heard me. He's family. His oldest sister is the mother of my three children. How do you think she would feel if she thought I had a hand in her little brother death?"

The revelation seems to take the wind out of their sails but Ron nor Shitty wasn't biting his hype completely. They knew he was involved somehow but proving it would be a challenge especially with the revelation he revealed.

"Who is committing these murders and don't tell me you don't know?" Ron insisted staring at him. "It's no secret that Road Block death and the available turf he controlled was up for grab, what went wrong?"

"There you go speculating again, Detective" he suddenly smiled. "Besides, who is claiming that Road Block was in the drug game?"

"We're wasting our time Ron" interrupted Shitty. "If he doesn't care or realize that his life is in danger, cut him loose. Let's see how long he lasts on the streets."

"Ice, we can help and protect you" Ron insisted.

"Detectives, I don't need any help or protection from anybody sir. I haven't done anything wrong to worry about somebody reaching out and touching me" he persisted. "Is this interview over? I really rather be any place other than here" he asked staring across the table at them.

"Yeah, this interview is over" Ron finally replied getting to his feet. He knew he was lying through his teeth, but how could they prove it?

"Have a wonderful day gentleman" he wishes them as he got to his feet. A patrol officer escorted him from the homicide department to the main entrance and left. Taking him back to where they had initially picked him up wasn't even a thought. Standing in the vestibule, he instantly started looking around suspiciously. Spotting one of his bodyguards leaning on his vehicle a half a block away smoking a cigarette, a smile creased his lips. He push open the double door then stood on the top step looking around before descending them. He scanned every car closely that drove pass as he descended the steps and headed down the street. His bodyguards took a more alert position after seeing him approaching. One of the guy's open the back-passenger's door while the other posted up monitoring everything and everyone until he climbed inside. He exhaled deeply then got comfortable as the driver pulled away from the curb. They hooked a U-turn on Reisterstown Road heading up towards Northern Parkway. He leaned back reflecting on what the two detectives had shared with him. They were right on point but his ace in the hole fucked them up. One thing he wasn't going to do was take them lightly. He foolishly took Lion as a nonthreat and look at the work he's putting in. He wouldn't make that mistake with these two detectives, especially Ron. As they drove on the outer perimeter of the Pimlico Race Track, Park Heights was his place of refuge even if it was just an illusion.

"Hey Lion."

"What's up Misty?"

"I ran into your mother about a half hour ago. Will you give her a call for me please?"

He found himself hesitating before replying. "What's it about?"

"I don't know. Will you please give her a call" she asked, softening her eyes as she made her request.

"Okay, what's the number?"

She gave him the digits then said, "Call me later so we can hook up."

"I'll see what I can do" he replied then ending their conversation. He has intentions of hooking up with T.T later if things fall into place.

"Alright" she replied hearing him end their conversation. Things between them haven't materialized as she had hoped. He never tried inviting her over to where ever he was staying for an intimate evening. She rationalized that it was because of whatever he was doing under the cover of darkness, but she shook that reason off. They could have just as easily went to a hotel some place. Na, he wasn't feeling her like she had hoped. The young lady she had seen him with often while secretly being with Derrick was a distraction for him. The kind of distraction she wish he didn't have continuously in his face.

He dialed his mother's number.

"Hello?"

"You told Misty you wanted to talk to me?"

"Malik?"

"Yes."

"Hi son" she greeted not trying to hide her excitement that he called. "It's good hearing your voice."

"What is it that you need?" he asked keeping their conversation informal.

"I know I don't have the right to ask you for anything, but I have to. Your brother took care of me over the years and now that he's gone, I don't know what I'm going to do."

Ignoring her statement, he asked "Is that your man that you was with there?"

"Yes, Milton."

"How long have yawl been together?"

"Pushing up on seven years" she admitted.

"Why doesn't he work?"

"His criminal background" she replied as an excuse.

"You're going to lay that lame excuse on me? You and I both know people with criminal records that works continuously especially Mr. Richie. He's been on his job since I was a child and he spent five years in prison. So, give me something that I can accept."

"I'm tire of making excuses for him" she finally admitted.

"Then get rid of him."

"I love him, Malik."

"You love him? When did you learn to love?" he asked lightly laughing. "You're in love with someone that can't bring a damn thing to the table. Do he get social service or anything?"

"No, he doesn't qualify."

"Not even for food stamps?"

"Nothing" she replied.

"Bullshit" he replied. "He's getting food stamps and probably selling them on you to privately get his drugs. I hope he doesn't have any children."

"Five."

"Na, I'm not feeling him" he shared. "You're asking me to not just finance you but your worthless ass man also. I don't think so. I'm not my brother."

"You must, or I'll get put out on the first."

"No, I don't!" he corrected her. "You're behind in your rent isn't a mystery or even how?" he stated not having to think about it. "You spent the money that Shabazz gave you and blew your monthly check also on your addiction and your worthless ass bum, didn't you, Monica?" he asked not expecting an answer. "Why should he not claim to love you when he has someone stupid enough to take care of his worthless ass like he is a damn child? Think about it Monica. He's more scandalous than you are and even more self-serving."

"I'm sorry baby. Really, I am" she started to cry uncontrollably. "I don't know what I'm going to do."

"You can start by packing up whatever you possess before the first" he offer as a solution.

"Malik?" she cried out to him. "Don't, please."

"Or" he stated pausing. "You can get your life in order" he suggested offering her another option. "If not for yourself, do it for Shabazz."

"I don't think I can do it" she admitted honestly.

"Nobody said it would be easy, Monica but I promise you a much better life is waiting after you complete the journey" he assured her.

"You promise to be there for me?"

"Even though you wasn't there for me, yes." he replied. "I would be there for you Monica if you graduate and successfully complete the steps. Who know I just might start calling you mom?"

"That would sound so much better than Monica" she admitted slightly giggling. "Do you know an out of state program?"

"Yes, I do" he replied. "Up in Philly, there's a program with a ninety percent graduation rate."

"Would you take care of everything for me?"

"Yes, I will, and I'll even drive you there" he offer surprising her and himself also. "I'll be over later to give you a few dollars then take care of that eviction notice for you tomorrow."

"Thanks Malik, thanks" she sigh with relief.

"Your so-called man, he has got to go" he insisted. "I'll keep your rent up while you're away, but I'll have someone watching the place while you're up in Philly. Tell his worthless ass, he don't want to be caught up in there by my soldiers while you're gone. The ass kicking he's going to get won't be pretty. Do you hear me?"

"Yes, Malik."

"I'm warning you to tell him, Monica or I'll tell him. I'll talk to you later."

"Okay" she replied hearing the phone go dead. Shabazz had tried to get her straight on numerous occasions, but she kept side stepping him. Malik was completely different. If she tried her antics with him, he would cut her the fuck off and disappeared back to his private life. All she knew about him over the years was through the pictures he and Shabazz had taken together. Did he finally graduate high school? Was he's a college grad? What type of profession he was getting into or any other questions concerning his where about were all shun by Shabazz? Any questions concerning if he has any children was also ignored? This was her first and only chance to do the right thing. She would hate to die from an over dose with no one there to cry over her. Her addict friends would only miss her for the abundance of drugs she could always provide or mentioning her in a passing conversation. Na, none of that will do. She needed her only child to allow her to be in his life. If this is the struggle and journey to assure that it happen, she must endure her demons to acquire a clean and productive life. She wasn't going to disappoint him again or herself.

Bunkie had been following Mookie movements for days. He watched him and his four well-dress bodyguards staring at a poster on a vacant house front window. A form of jubilation engulfed his face. When they finally left, he approached and stared up at the poster. Edmondson 10th Reunion was being given at Gentlemen Ten on Edmondson Avenue. Mookie was once a highly recruited football player while attending Edmondson High before his uncle introduced him to the drug game. He discarded all the colleges scholarships to obtain the allure of the quick money and perceived street power. He control certain areas around Edmondson especially at the Village and up to Popular Grove area since he was twenty-three years old. A ten-year reunion was just the stage he needed to display his success to those who knew him and those in the game who have only heard of him.

When the 396-number appeared on his cell, Lion had a good ideal who it was.

"Hello?"

"Mr. Mohammad?"

"Yes, what can I do for you?"

"This is Detective Ron. Can you come to my office?"

"How did you get my number?" he asked ignoring his question.

"I obtained it from the coronal office" he shared. "Will you come to my office?"

"Concerning what?"

"Some information has come to my attention concerning your brother and I would like to talk to you about it."

"You have me on the phone now. Start talking."

"I rather we discuss it face to face."

"Well, that won't happen. Unless you tell me, you have my brother murderers in custody, we really don't have anything to discuss."

"Did you know your brother was one of the biggest drug distributors' in the city?"

"My brother didn't sell any damn drugs, Detectives!" he denounced reverently. "If someone is claiming that then they are a damn liar. Have you ever known of any drug dealer that doesn't have any criminal charges? Any? Well, do you detective?"

"No, Mr. Mohammad. I don't."

"I don't even, sir. My brother was as model of a citizen as he could be living in Baltimore. Whoever told you otherwise is playing you?" he expressed adamantly. "Is the person responsible for these high-profile murders that's happening around the city connected to my brother's death?"

"No, I'm not saying or suggesting that" he openly lied.

"Then, what are you saying or suggesting Detective?"

"I can't reveal what I've learned during my investigation, but I assure you, the person murdering those high-profile drug dealers you been hearing and reading about isn't responsible for your brother's murder."

"Are you sure?"

"Absolutely" he assured him.

"Who is responsible Detectives?"

"We're still trying to piece together what's transpiring, but we're looking at two separate scenarios."

"Okay Detective Ron, I'm taking your word."

"Thank you."

"Please contact me if anything changes in my brother's case."

"I will, Malik."

"Thank you, sir."

"By the way, why didn't you mention you was an up-and-coming lawyer in Atlanta?"

"Would it have contributed anything to your case?"

"No."

"I didn't think so. Have a lovely day Detective."

"You too Malik."

Ron sat at his desk with a slight smirk on his face. No, mentioning his profession wouldn't have contributed anything to the case, but it damn sure surprised him. Coming from the Flag House and Collington and Jefferson area, he should have stumble as so many other teenage males have on the east side, but he avoided the traps and prosper outside of Baltimore. He needed a break in this case, but none came his way. None that was concrete except knowing Ice had a hand in this shit somehow.

Byrd had taken the past week to get all his personal business in order including the letter to his wife with his private-information that she will need to get his stash money from his personal off-shore accounts in the Bahama's and the Cayman Islands. Sitting on the balcony watching the sun descend was a thing of the past. When Mookie suggested attending the Reunion, he advised him to ignore it, but he knew his words were going in one ear and out the other. If he knew Lion, he would be waiting in the shadows. Hoping that one of them would play their hand. Well, he wouldn't be one of them. With his Glock on his hip at all times and his Remington 870 shotgun never too far from him, if Lion wanted him, he would have to kick in his front door then get past his four bodyguards before obtaining any form of restitution. His cell ringing interrupted his thoughts.

"Yeah, what's up Ice?"

"Hey Byrd, I just spent the last hour talking to homicide detectives" he informed him.

"Yeah, I heard they snatched your ass up" he shared. "What did they want?"

"To protect me" he nervously chuckled. "With the help of the only possible snitch in Hopkins, he piece together what happen, but I blew his speculations out of the water by revealing that Meeks was the uncle to my children."

"What did you just say?"

"That Meeks is the uncle of my children" he snicker into the phone.

"Do you think you convince him?"

"He can easily verify what I said, and I know he will, but my name still filtered through his lips, and I know why?" he shared. "I'm not putting shit pass Ron" he assured him.

"You know you can't touch that motherfucker in the hospital, right?"

"Won't have to" he replied. "As soon as he step out of the hospital, Lion will get him."

"I hope his stupid ass realize that. Lion is not leaving town until this shit is completely over" Byrd informed him.

"Are you thinking about going to the Edmondson Reunion?"

"Are you fucking serious?" he asked shaking his head. "You must have been talking to Mookie's dumb ass. I told him not to go, but I know he will."

"You think Lion will try something there? There will be a hell of a lot of people attending" he informed him.

"Including, Lion" he informed him. "Was you thinking about going?"

"I was."

"Don't, if you want to see the sun rising." he advised him. "As a matter of fact, you're not even from the Village" he lightly chuckled. "Listen, do what you want, but I got to go. My steak is finish cooking."

"Alright, Byrd. I hear you."

"Yeah, I hear you too" he said hanging up. He heard the sarcasm in his voice. You can lead a horse to water, but you can't force the dumb motherfucker to drink. If Ice felt that he had to display how successful he has become, who was he to tell him otherwise? All the wealth they have acuminated over the years didn't happen without using some common sense. Byrd was the only one that didn't flash his wealth as Road Block had advised him even after they went their own way. They were the only two that didn't get caught up in the hype and that prevented them from obtaining a rap sheet like the others. One thing he knew, Lion was doing his homework. He knew about Sunshine's affection for dark skin girls with a Toni Braxton hair style. Bash loved Ladies Night at Melba's and parked in the same spot every time. Lighting that cigar as was his habit, and that cost him his life. He was using their tendencies and weaknesses against them. Well, he didn't have any tendencies or weaknesses outside of his marriage. The love he held for Egypt and their three children was his only weakness. He knew the fate that awaited Mookie and Ice if they attended the reunion. Fate would reveal itself on the morning news.

Khatiti had asked Malik if he would take her to Atlanta while she was on her week vacation. She was presently surprised that the night before her vacation he called telling her to pack her bags because their flight took off at ten o'clock tomorrow morning. He picked her up in front of her apartment close to nine o'clock and drove to Thurgood Marshall Airport then parked in the over-night garage. Exiting the garage and entering the terminal, she was like a child admiring all the colorful and decorated planes. This was her first flight. Sitting by the window in first class, she felt the turbines elevating the jet into the air until it rise above the clouds revealing clear blue skies and a scenery a person wouldn't know existed from the ground. Descending at Hartsfield-Jackson International hours later, her eyes were still the size of a silver dollars and wearing a broad smile the length of the Mississippi River. After gathering their bags, they caught a cab to his home. She stared out admiring the landscape in the distance. Twenty minutes later, they were descending Rt.85. She stared at the houses in his neighborhood as the cab suddenly pulled up on a parking pad and stop.

"Who live here Malik?" she asked as they stepped out and walked towards the trunk to retrieve her luggage.

"I do" he replied looking at the astonishment look that engulfed her face causing him to lightly laugh.

"And you live here alone?"

"Yes, T.T" he replied paying the man then walking towards the front door carrying her luggage and opening it. "Make yourself at home" he told her as she walked inside admiring the exquisite environment. "Take any bedroom" he told her placing her suitcase down then retrieving his mail from the floor then walking towards the family room.

"Okay" she replied watching him disappeared. She grabbed her suitcase then ascended the stairs admiring the dark ebony color floors extending throughout. She methodically peeked in every bedroom until she came upon the rear one. He had French doors leading out to a balcony. "This will do" she said to herself smiling. She walked into the massive walk-in closet and hung her clothes up. She paused to admire herself in the full-length mirror before walking out of the room. Retracing her steps, she paused to stare inside his bedroom. Everything was neat and in their places. Nothing was on the floor except two rice paper lamps to illuminate the massive room. Curiosity had her walking in to view his on suite. Fabulous was all she could say. As she was leaving his room, a picture they took at Charles Street Jazz was on his night stand. A smile crept across her lips admiring the broad smiles on their lips. She left the room after hearing Billie Holiday voice singing "Ain't Nobody Business If I Do" coming from down stairs. Turning the corner, he was sitting on an over-sized beige color couch smoking a blunt and sipping on a glass of wine.

"You want one?" he asked as she walked around staring at the limited pictures he had.

"Yes" she replied giggling at a picture of him and Road Block when he was about twelve. "So, you always dress GQ, huh?" she asked smiling while walking over and taking a seat next to him. "You know I have a million questions floating around in my head" she admitted.

"Well, you have three days to ask some of them" he told her lighting her a blunt and passing it over to her.

"You have a beautiful home Malik, really" she express extremely impress.

"Thank you" he replied pouring her a glass of wine.

"What did you pay for it?" she boldly asked.

"This is what it looked like before I had it was remodel" he shared showing her a picture.

"Hell, no" she said laughing. "I would have never brought this" she said staring at the before pictures.

"Well, I brought it cheap and now it's worth easily nine-hundred G's. I actually had an offer of one point one million and damn near leap on it" he admitted laughing. "But this is home."

"And a beautiful one too" she said looking around then suddenly getting to her feet and walking towards the French doors then pushing them open. "Look at that pool" she stated walking out onto the colorful brick patio and Olympic size pool. "Oh, I'm definitely going to swim everyday" she said walking over to feel the water. Turning around after hearing the small out-door Infinity speakers, Malik was sitting at the patio table enjoying her acting like a school girl.

"So, what do you want to do?"

"I'm ready to see this city" she replied coming to sit next to him.

"We'll hit the streets around seven, but for right now, let's just chill."

"Okay" she smiled hitting her blunt. "How come nobody never snatch you up especially after seeing all of this?"

"You are only the second woman I ever brought to my home" he confessed.

"Are you serious?"

"Would you reveal your hand to a person before you actually got to know them?"

"No" she replied. "Somebody could very easily get a funny and scandalous ideal after viewing a home like this."

"Yeah, I know. So, that's one reason why I haven't been snatched up as you put it."

"How long have you lived here?"

"Believe it or not, but a little under nine years."

"Nine years?" she replied surprise. "Wow, you was young when you came down here. You wasn't scared?"

"Never of the unknown" he replied. "When a man and woman meet, they have an unknown journey they must share together to see if they are compatible. Well, I applied that same concept to life. If things didn't go as plan or too many things were breaking my peace, I would have moved to the next community or city just like lovers do when they go their separate ways. They could never stop loving because love exist inside of them. Right here, T.T" he smiled looking around at his massive backyard. "This is my place of tranquility."

"Yes, this is very tranquil" she admitted leaning back and enjoying the scenery.

They sat talking until they realized that the sun had completely set and the only light illuminating their faces came from inside the family room.

"Look at the time" he said peeking at his watch.

"It's eight o'clock already, damn" she giggled.

"Let's go and take a shower then get dress."

"Together?" she asked staring in his eyes grinning.

"You got jokes" he said getting to his feet and assisting her to her feet by her fingers then walked into the family room. He closed the doors as she started up the steps. When he climbed to the top step, she was just walking into her bedroom then looked back over her shoulder at him. They both shared impish smiles before she closed her door giggling, and he went into his bedroom. He hit the remote and Betty Carter asked, "How High The Moon?" The water felt invigorating as his body slowly started to relax for the first time in weeks. Although he could only stay for four days because of a special event was coming up back in Baltimore. He would enjoy these days and get to know T.T better. He wanted to capture her natural beauty before the lips stick and eyeliner. He wanted to capture the scent of her breath in the morning. He will take her on a journey to reveal her most frightful and alluring love. There were so many things he wanted to explore within her that he couldn't wait to get started.

Descending the stairs around nine o'clock then standing in front of him, he put his hand over his mouth slightly backing up and said, "Damn!" T.T was wearing a low V neck brown stretch form fitting dress that hit her at her knees. Her braless breast appeared firm and full. The full silhouette of her slightly flaring hips and apple bottom ass were high-lighted. Her stomach was flat and her locs were up off her shoulders. Wearing six-inch stilettos, she stood six-one easily and looking sexy as a motherfucker with her full glossy lips.

"I know I say it often, but you look not just sexy. You're beautiful" he complimented still shaking his head.

"Thank you" she replied slightly blushing. "You look as handsome as ever" she giggled admiring the brown Armani pin-stripe suit. Always GQ even when he wears jeans.

"I have a nice jazz club I want to share with you" he said grabbing his keys.

"I'm ready" she said grabbing her clutch purse.

As they walked out the front door, he hit the alarm and the remote to his Escalade then the engine came to life. Opening the door for her, the Five Stairs Steps "You Wanted Too Long" filled the night sky. As he pulled off his parking pad, he smiled over at T.T before pressing on the accelerator. Five minutes later, they were connecting to I-85 heading towards College Park.

"Exactly where are you taking me?" she asked accepting the blunt from him.

"A spot called St. James Live in the Princeton Lake community" he replied grinning.

Fifteen minutes later, he was cruising up Camp Creek Parkway.

"I would love to see these homes in the day light" she stated as they drove pass.

"That wouldn't be a problem" he assured her turning on Butner Road.

He found a parking spot then walked around and open her door then assisted her out. As they proceeded towards the club clutching fingers, their height made them very noticeable. As they proceeded into the club, guys were devouring T.T with their eyes while slightly ignoring the woman they were with then catching a cold stare from her once they catch themselves. He waved to several guys he knew and blew kisses to several women sitting around the club as he led her towards the right-side wall and found a table slightly in the shadows. He have never been seen escorting any young lady to the jazz spots he frequent although he usually met someone. They got a good look at a person that have his attention. They sat and talked until the house lights gradually descended then with one hand, he pulled her chair next to him all the while she was giggling and bringing attention to herself.

All night he did unsuspecting antics that had her embarrassing herself. Yet, her giggles or boisterous laughter couldn't be contained. With the illuminating of the lights, people would stare over at her, and she would burst out laughing again then lower her head still snickering.

She had never had such a joyous and hilarious weekend before in her life. They could blame it on the alcohol or just connecting and allowing their emotions to dictate their actions. Either choice, she explore a realm of love making that had tears freely flowing from her eyes and demanding more afterward during their interludes. She thought she hadn't lost her virginity when she was eighteen after exploring Lion. She found herself actually feeling like he was an aphrodisiac. A type of catnip that had her constantly purring. She didn't know if it was lust, desire, passion, or love, but she possess all of these desires for him. He is the man of her dreams and desires as a child but is she what he desire? Her intuitions say yes.

Before returning home, he haven't had the time to truly relax only breath. As subtle as he was in the streets of Baltimore, his head was always on a swivel when-ever he was out with T.T. Now that he was home again, his muscles could slowly uncoil, and he could actually relax. As he stood in his walk-in closet, he decided to wear a dark blue Armani with a light blue shirt and medium blue silk poker dot tie. As he was walking out the bedroom door, he hit the remote to turn off the CD player and hit the light switch extinguishing the recess lighting. He descended the stairs and took a seat in the family room. As he was smoking a blunt and sipping on some Parrot Bay coconut, Ella Fitzgerald was scatting on "Take The A Train" with Duke Ellington when Khatiti suddenly turned the corner. If looks could say a million words, she suddenly started blushing. She was wearing a white one-piece form fitting dress by Yves St. Laurent, and he was floor. He had peeked at her body occasionally, but tonight, he took in her full silhouette and seem to start drooling.

"Do you need a bib?" she asked giggling as she came over to sit next to him.

"T.T" he softly called while staring in her grayish eyes. "You are so beautiful."

"For some reason, I actually believe you" she giggled admiring the desire that crept into his eyes. "Are you comfortable with me wearing this?"

"Me!?" he asked suddenly laughing like he heard a funny joke. "Baby, I'm very comfortable with what-ever you choose to wear."

"Really?"

"Yes, why?" he inquired with a confuse expression on his face. "What's that stare and coy little smile about?"

"Malik, you are something else" she began smiling while taking the blunt from between his fingers. "I have worn certain clothing with you that made other men in my life extremely uncomfortable. Like what I wore last night. They were always trying to cage me in. Restrict my freedom."

"Including when you're making love" he interjected catching her completely off guard by the expression that suddenly engulfed her face. "Well, Miss?"

"You definitely say what's on your mind" she replied snickering but pausing before replying. "Yes" she confess.

"Have you ever instructed them about what you are desiring?"

"No, not really" she replied.

"Not really" he chuckled then slightly grinning. "Either you did, or you didn't instruct them, T.T."

"I didn't, okay" she replied staring in his eyes smiling. "I don't know if I like this lawyer side of you" she suddenly giggled.

"Oh, you do" he replied getting to his feet. "Come on before we start up another conversation, but we are going to finish this so-called provocative way you allegedly dress" he said extending his hand down to her. He grabbed his toothbrush holder to see how many blunts he had inside. Five was more than enough as he place it in his inside breast pocket and then they headed towards the front door. He press the security code to the alarm system then walked out the front door securing it behind himself. He press the button to the garage revealing his metallic gray Audi A7.

"Wow, she look sweet" she complimented as he unlocked the door then assist her into her seat. Climbing inside and staring the engine, Cannonball Adderley's "Mercy, Mercy, Mercy" filled the interior. They were literally cruising up Rt.75 connecting to I-85 as if they didn't have a place to go. He extracted a lot of personal information during their forty-minute ride. He exit the highway near 10th Street NE. "So, where are we heading?" she finally asked taking in the night life.

"Since we were discussing cloths and how some men felt like you was dressing a little too provocative, I'm taking you to The Compound" he said turning left on 10th Street NW.

"What kind of club is it?"

"Oh, if I have to describe it" he said with a coy smile peeking over at her. "I would say burlesque."

"Burlesque?" she asked staring over at him giggling.

"Yup" he replied with an impish grin on his face as he pulled up on the parking lot. He found a parking spot then headed towards the front door clutching her fingers. After paying the entry fee, they stood in the foyer admiring the atmosphere. "Come on" he said directing her by her fingers towards some empty tables. She definitely had everybody's attention.

"Damn, baby" a woman complimented her as they walked pass, but her girlfriend damn sure didn't appreciate it.

They found a nice table close to the wall and place their orders. They were quietly talking when the lights became even more subtle. He lean back and watch her. She would giggle and lightly push him while laughing at some of the skits that were performed. She found a love and passion for burlesque that she didn't know she possess.

It was well after three o'clock in the morning when they walked out of the club to the refreshing breeze to cool their moist bodies. It was a little after four when they pulled up in front of his house, they walked hugging one another as they went through the front door. They went straight up the steps departing way at the top. Hitting the remote as usual, Barbara Acklin "Am I The Same Girl" filled the quietness as he got undress then took a quick shower and climbed between the sheets. It was a little after five in the morning when T.T invited herself in his room and crawled between the sheets. He wrap his arm over her feeling her stomach rising and falling. Her perfume was very erotic to his senses. She wrap his arm with hers then sleep gradually over-whelm them. The weekend went extremely fast for them, so he asked if she wanted to stay a couple more days and she eagerly accepted. There was no one or nothing back in Baltimore that demanded her attention.

Monday and Tuesday were blazing with an unbearable heat index, but you would never have known by T.T. She wore a two-piece swim suit from Robin Piccone that made her sex appeal multiply by five. The red one strap by Gottex complimented her body even more than the one she previously wore. Her bronze smooth complexion got darker spending five days in Atlanta. Before they knew it, Wednesday was upon them, and he knew he had to get back to Baltimore. They reluctantly caught a late flight heading back to Baltimore. They whisper among themselves over the experiences he showed her concerning his new city. She found it very humorous watching under-cover bi-sexual men lusting after him and how he checked their asses. There was something about him that she just couldn't put her finger on, but what-ever it was, whenever it appears when a guy was getting ready to say something foolish or slick out of their mouths about her attire, his eyes always checked them. He never had to say a word. Not one word. When she was with other men, guys would say slick shit out of their mouths and her escort would ignore what they said, but not Malik. He almost had to step to a guy until he saw something in his eyes and openly apologized to him and her. Yeah, there was something about him. Something that she couldn't really see or put her finger on, but guys could see it very plainly. Just as the wheels touch down at BWI Airport, Lion could be heard growling very subtly.

For the past two weeks, Misty have been trying to convince Lion to escort her to the Edmondson Reunion. Being a cheerleader once at Edmondson High, she wanted to reconnect with some of her old friends, but Lion adamantly declined. He repeatedly told her to attend the reunion. He very subtly told her he was going to hang out at the Five Mile House with some friends on Saturday and just as he hoped, she invited herself and a couple of her girlfriends to join them. He placed two-hundred dollars in her hand earlier that day telling her they had an errand to run but would hook up with them later. Although slightly disappointed, the cash in her hands along with her girlfriends hanging out and probably flirt with every man in the place, she would keep herself entertained until his arrival.

Mookie and Ice was up on Garrison Avenue at their exclusive private single home they brought together three years ago to bring exclusively private young ladies. Remodel throughout, the place was exquisite as it should be. The three young ladies with them tonight were exquisitely dress from head to toe. Advised to accentuate their thighs, they all wore skirt suits. Two wore Louis Vuitton's while the other wore a Versace. On their ankles, they wore tennis bracelets from Mark Loren and Cartier. Avianne embrace their wrists. The fellas had paid for everything that they were wearing including Victoria's latest secrets. These were their very exclusive and private young ladies. They were surrounded by eight of their best bodyguards.

"Man, when we went to New York to get fitted for our suits, I didn't think they would have it done this quickly" Mookie chuckled.

"Money talks home-boy" replied Ice taking another sip from his Cîroc. "It will be nice to hit the streets again" he confessed staring over at the three young ladies staring back that them while giggling. "We should have done this weeks ago."

"The motherfucking walls was starting to close in on me too" he shared admiring the thick chocolate thighs of one of the young ladies barely twenty-one. "We haven't been over here since this shit went down. I didn't know how much I miss coming through this place until now" he lightly chuckled admiring the full lips of the honey complexion young lady with those Asiatic looking eyes. "I'm going to let motherfuckers see where I am and how I roll tonight. All those motherfuckers who thought I was stupid for walking away from those scholarships will be singing a different tune after tonight. This is like a home coming for me" he laugh blowing a smoke ring.

He had also thought how his life would have evolved if he had taken just one of those scholarships. Four years away from Baltimore, he didn't know if his system could have endured such peace and tranquility, but he would have love to have experience it. His path was already map out for him after being born a boy in his family tree. Certain characteristics were expected to be adopted and certain attributes were expected to be follow. He didn't quit school like his cousins but he damn sure eventually acquired those same nine numbers that will follow him eternally through life. He remember watching his running mate back in high school getting drafted in the late second round to the Cleveland Brown. He was instantly a millionaire while he was still operating on a corner. He used to smile seeing his boy operating on the football field. Family can be a motherfucker sometimes and a fantasy destroyer.

Across town, Lion and Bunkie was already inside the Gentlemen Ten. They needed to view the inside and do their recon since neither have ever venture into the spot. He needed to know where was the best possible exit except the front door and how many men are securing it? What's the best possible position for Bunkie to maintain both positions? Security patted down every guy thoroughly that entered while subtly peeking inside the women's clutch purses. If they were carrying over-size purses or crossbody bags, they wanted to see the bottom. It took some trials and errors before security realized that some guys were using their ladies like mules to carry their weapons inside, but not anymore. What does that say about that woman? What does that suggest about a guy suggesting a woman to do such an act? It's a shame they never tell the guys to lift their hats or look inside those that naturally took them off inside, Lion peeked at that neglect of professionalism in the performance of their duty then nodded to Bunkie. Staying in the shadows as he moved towards the front entrance, Bunkie peeked his movement and headed in the same direction. Meeting outside on the corner of Appleton Street and Harlem Street, they had gone back to the car to retrieve their weapons and then re-entered. Walking pass security again, they held their hats in their hands clutching their weapons while being patted down then proceeded inside. Separating and discretely placing their weapons in the small of their backs, Lion moved back towards the shadows to his left while Bunkie took up the position to watch their exit and those coming through the front door.

They were both sipping water from a plastic bottle. It was almost eleven-thirty when an entourage of twenty walked through the door. Most of the women wore expensive clothing and were ice out. From Armani to Gucci suits, white gold watches studded with diamonds, they better have the bodyguards that they did, or the undercover stick-up crew wouldn't have a problem confiscating it off of them especially if they catch one going to the bathroom alone.

As all eyes followed the entourage, Lion slightly shifted his position. Mookie looked just as Sunshine describe. Dark skin with gold fronts, flashy in his style of dress but laid back. The other guy was Ice Pick. He remember him specifically from his brother's memorial. His smile was scandalous, and his eyes were cunning. Yeah, the brain behind the whole shit that murder his brother. He stared at him through venomous eyes. He wanted to methodically walk up to him and blow the back of his motherfuckin brains out. Fuck this nigger Mookie, fuck Byrd just him. An impish smile crept to his lips listening to what his emotions were urging him to do, but he was not an emotional person. He would not be swayed for some instant gratification. Na, patience. He had something incredibly special planned for him and he would not alleviate from his plans or deny himself.

He watched them pay three tables for their position over-looking the danced floor then settle in on a little elevated stage and place their liquor bottles on the table. It was apparent that they had started partying way before they came there, five minutes at the tables, three of the ladies grabbed a partner and they were gone. Ice and Mookie remained seated profiling. As several people that remember Mookie from high school tried to approach him too closely, one of his bodyguards would impede their movement while wearing a menacing snarl or glare. Ice tap him nodding towards an exceptionally light skin young lady and whisper something to him then they burst out laughing. Ice suddenly got to his feet and approached the young lady while two of his men stood watching his back. Lion's eyes shot back to Mookie who was smiling his ass off then back to Ice. There was no doubt by her reaction at seeing him that they possess a history and haven't seen one another in a couple of years. When he escorted her to the dance floor, he unconsciously growled at how easy it would be to rip his esophagus from his throat. Mookie just sat back with his bodyguards and enjoyed the show. With so many women openly flirting and shaking their phat asses at him, his bodyguards found it hard to concentrate on their jobs. Mookie relish in the attention and the love he was receiving from so many old school mates that he didn't notice his bodyguard's inattentiveness. Lion couldn't believe his luck when he gave them permission to dance. As they eagerly walked towards the dance floor, Lion made his move. Pouring the contents of his bottle on the floor as he walked towards his target from his left, he stayed out of the full sight line of the video cameras. At twenty feet away, he pulled his Glock from under his suit jacket. Ten feet away, he glared at back of Ice's head as he walked pass less than three feet away while he forced the plastic bottle mouth piece over the barrel of the gun. Five feet away he stared Mookie straight in his eyes. At first, he was confused by the mysterious eyes and uneven smile until he notice his hands slowly rising. Fear and surprise instantly gripped him. Boop! Boop! Barely audible, he clutched his chest as disbelief consumed his face. Looking at his hands, they were covered in blood. He stared back up. All he saw was the cold stare and eerie smile of his assassin disappearing into the crowd. He stared out at his bodyguards who were unaware of what just transpired. Just as he cough and started to slump forward, a loud scream suddenly filled the air. Just as Lion and Bunkie were escorting two women out the front door. He took time for Ice to stare into his eyes before disappearing in the crowd.

"Meet me at Five Mile House" he told Bunkie as he climbed into his car and started up the engine. From Appleton Street, he turned right onto Edmondson Avenue to see the crowd scurrying out the front door then proceeded towards Hilton Parkway going pass Lincoln Park. He came out on Wabash Avenue then turned right onto Woodburn. He found a parking spot across Reisterstown Road then parked on the dark street. Ten minutes later, Bunkie arrived parking behind him with three of his partners. They enter the club and obtain drinks from down stairs before climbing the steps to the second floor. Lion spotted Misty on the dance floor. They moved towards the bar then posted up. After about three dances, she was back at her table where four of her girlfriends were sitting. Three guys were trying to get to know them. She was seated about five minutes when she scanned the room again and finally spotted him then waving him over. Walking over with his entourage, the three guys straighten up some while checking out the five well-dress individuals.

"How long have you been here?" she asked smiling up at him then giving him a kiss on the lips as they pulled up chairs.

"About forty-five minutes" he lied.

"It was closer to an hour" Bunkie cosigned his lie.

"Why didn't yawl just come over?" she inquired.

"Yawl was enjoying yourselves and we just wanted to sit back and watch the show" he replied smiling.

"And that's all it was, a show" she tried to assure him as the three guys excused themselves. She had been dancing very provocative all night. She could blame it on the alcohol or just enjoying herself but she knew he had witness everything or so she thought. The illicit things she had done to the guys she danced with wasn't very lady like to say the lease. How would any man feel about seeing their woman dancing the way she had?

"Lady's, introduce yourselves but I'm going to dance. Come on, Lion" she said getting to her feet as they gripped fingers and headed towards the dance floor. For six-minute and ten seconds, they dance to The Dells "Stay In My Corner." For the next two hours, the two groups vibe together. Their laughter filled the lounge area where they had retired to. They took several pictures together and reserved all dances among themselves. They didn't desire no out-side interferences. They were being well entertained by themselves. That night, two love connections were established but Lion wasn't one.

Early the next morning around six o'clock, WBAL morning news was announcing the murders from the previous night. Their main story concern Gentlemen 10-night club up on Edmondson Avenue. "In a crowd celebrating the 10th Edmondson Reunion, Maurice "Mookie" Savage was gun down as he sat next to several people. A once prominent running back from Edmondson High was struck twice by a Glock .40 according to sources. According to those sitting next to him, they never heard any shots. He just suddenly became erect and focus on something or someone before collapsing in his seat. Not until they saw blood on his hands and flowing profusely from his chest area, did they realize that he had been shot. The surveillance cameras clarity wasn't really worth shit. Homicide detectives was unable to find anyone who witness the crime. Court documents revealed that Mr. Savage started establishing a criminal record distributing drugs not long after refusing the college scholarships he had on the table. He was described as the main distributor in the Winchester and Popular Grove area where he was partying in when he was assassinated. It is speculated, the person who murder him could also be responsible for the murder of three previous high-profile distributors and a known hire gun. Homicide detectives are asking the community for their assistance in solving these murders over the weekend, of course."

"Two to go" Lion stated turning off the television. He knew Detective

Ron and Shitty would be contacting him for another interview. He would be extremely disappointed in their professionalism if they didn't. The pictures he took last night would cover him completely especially with five women able to verify the time they arrived and left. Are there any better alibies? An impish grin cross his lips thinking about Ice, he now realized how close he came to inhaling his last breath and busting his last nut. The thought of how he escaped didn't ration into his thinking only how lucky he was to be able to walk out of the club breathing. He lightly chuckled thinking how he's going to get low and try to stay low. He would eventually rationalize that Lion didn't want him and he would be right. He was putting his focus on Byrd next and that would make him last. He didn't have time to contemplate that thought. His mind was concentrating on getting the fuck away, not just Baltimore but the whole fucking state. He needed to take advantage of this opportunity. Byrd doesn't step out of his apartment without eight of his best soldiers around him. If Lion wanted him, he would have to jump out of character and not show the patience he have been displaying. Crashing his apartment door with gun blazing is a sure way of getting him or being gotten. Na, he wouldn't attempt such a foolish thing especially not knowing the setup inside. He conjure up shit that motherfuckers never anticipated like frying a motherfuckers' face damn near off or catching a motherfucker with a head shot while lighting a cigar about a sixty yards away. A prolifically accurate and deadly motherfucker. Silent like a lion stalking its prey.

"Hello" a rough sleepy voice asked.

"Byrd! Wake the fuck up man!"

"What the fuck is your problem!? What the fuck is all the fucking hollowing about!?" he snapped peeking at the clock. "Its six-fifteen in the motherfucking morning, fool! What's your damn problem!?"

"He killed Mookie last night! He killed Mookie!" he repeated shouting adamantly. "Shot him dead while sitting between two bitches."

"So, you took your dumb ass there anyway, huh?" he asked shaking his head while slowly sitting up in the bed.

"Nobody heard shit, man!" he shared ignoring his statement. "I was right in front of him dancing with this girl when one of the girls we were with started screaming" he shared downing his glass of scotch then refilling it. "I could be next!"

"Relax, dummy. I'm next" he told him. "If he wanted to touch you, he could have done so last night. Stretch your dumb ass out right next to Mookie or before Mookie. So, don't think that you're lucky. I am" he told him.

"You are, why?"

"I won't be last" he reminded him.

"What can we do man? What can we do?" he asked revealing his fear.

"Confess to five-o and take your chances negotiating with the prosecutor's office or leave town if you're able but I doubt if that option is still on the table" he lightly chuckled.

"What do you mean that option is off the table?"

"It's probably too late" he reiterated. "If I were him, I would have niggers posted up at all travel exits especially the buses, trains, and planes. Believe me, those boys on the eastside appreciate the love he showed and would have soldiers posted up, but you can try to escape."

"If you was trying to get out of town, what would you do?"

"Under the cover of darkness is not how I would approach leaving. I would leave during the day with an army of soldiers watching my back and head down towards D.C or up towards Philly to catch a flight."

"Yeah, that does sound better than creeping around in the darkness. He could be standing in any of those shadows salivating at my mistake."

"Yes, he would."

"Tell me your plans?"

"You're funny" he snicker. "I'm supposed to tell you my plans, huh? I'll tell you this. I should not have included my money in that fucked up hit you orchestrated. Who in the fuck hire a junkie for a job as big as murdering Road Block and Monster? And don't tell me you didn't know Meeks was a motherfucking junkie because I know you did, the only thing that comes out of your mouth is motherfucking lies?" he told him. "I found out much too late that you was going to use Cookie's little brother and his little habit he acquired while at Jessup. If I had known, I would have sat back and watch this shit unfold as it has. Prey that know a lion is on their scent will frantically try to find an escape route but will ultimately stumble straight into its clutches. Your fear is your scent and the closer he gets the more he is salivating" he couldn't control his eerie frightening laughter. Once he gain some control, he asked. "You said fuck that little nigger, right? Well, like I asked you previously, who's doing the fucking now Ice? Who?" his eerie laughter filled his ears as he hung up.

Ice sat stunned with his cell phone clutch in his hand. Everything that Byrd predicted has come true including the probable ending. I mean every motherfucking thing he predicted. Admittedly, he too had heard the exploits of Road Block's little brother. Being all the way up in Park Heights, there was no way he could have witness the viciousness he allegedly administered to three guys in their late teens from Popular Grove up at Mondawmin Mall while he was just fifteen years old. The shit that came through the grapevine less than an hour later appeared to be impossible. No fifteen-year-old is getting down like that, but if it's yellow, wobbles and quack, it's a damn duck. The little stories that reached his ears through the years almost had him call Road Block to get an eye on this wolf in sheep's clothing especially when he was twelve. Very humble and intellectual. In the years that has elapsed, he still hasn't laid his eyes on him not even in a picture until the memorial. He didn't have the vaguest idea he was standing that close to him at six-feet-five until last night. He was certain the guy staring at him after Mookie got murder was him. After all the shit he did over the years, Lion was now the last person he wanted to see in the world and if he became negligent in his actions, he would get his wish or nightmare.

Byrd warned them that he wasn't anything like his brother and now he's witnessing that first hand. Remorse and forgiveness wasn't a part of his character or DNA code. Restitution and stealth consumed his DNA. Byrd said you wouldn't see him coming and he was right. Meeks didn't see him coming. Mookie and Sunshine damn sure didn't see him coming. Bash only felt his wrath for a brief second. How fortunate was that? He could have walked right pass him on the dance floor and pop him in the back of his head then proceed to Mookie, but he didn't. Like Byrd said, he has special plans for them. Byrd stress that he was next and why should he doubt him? If what he did to Meeks was an indication of what he had planned for him, he needed to run. Right now, he was thinking about nothing but self-defense. Defense of one self. When Sunshine and Boo-Boo suggested running, he looked at them like a bunch of punk ass motherfuckers, but now, he understood what he refused to acknowledge. Sunshine and Boo-Boo both saw it. Death's personal assassin in Lion.

There is no amount of money to suffice death's retribution except for your soul. Since taking out four of his closest friends, the streets have become extremely violent especially around Popular Grove as independent corner boys were infiltrating once off limit corners. The corner of Edmondson and Popular Grove suddenly erupted into violence for control of the very lucrative corner. With four areas available for control, street soldiers maintained their new acquired corners with an iron fist. Detectives and narcotic officers were being swamp with calls of discharging fire arms, murders, and the openly mass distribution of narcotic. While the West Side had homicide detectives running around like chickens with their heads off, the East Side was as quiet as a church mouse even at the notorious C and J corner. Right about now, Ice had a decision he needed to make. Even if he talked to the prosecutor, incarceration was still in the cards, but he wasn't feeling that not even five years behind bars. Yet, that were the only two options that still existed, but neither wasn't too flattering. Incarceration or death? You make the choice or simply run if possible.

Around ten o'clock Monday morning, Lion was walking through the lobby of the Eastern District Police Station on Edison Highway. He casually walked up to the receptionist desk.

"Yes, may I help you?" the black female officer asked admiring his attire from head to toe. The light gray Brioni with a silk tie that match it to a T with a dark gray silk French cuff shirt. The cufflinks would catch your attention glittering from the light striking it.

"Yes, ma'am" he replied admiring her eyes. "I have an appointment with Detective's Ron and Smith."

"Mr. Malik Mohammad?"

"Yes, ma'am."

"Yes, he sent a message to allow you to enter" she said pressing a button and releasing the lock on the door. "Take that hallway and have a seat in interrogation room number three, please."

"Yes, ma'am" he replied causally walking towards the door then pulling it open. He walked down the narrow hallway until he came to the room then open the door and walked inside. He took a seat at the table across from the two chairs and peeked at the camera. He knew someone was watching him, especially his demeanor.

About three minutes later, the door suddenly swung open. "Hey Malik" greeted Detective Ron coming through the door first.

"Good morning, Detective Ron. Smith" he greeted them unbuttoning his jacket and crossing his leg. "You have information concerning my brother's case?"

"Don't know yet but I want to thank you for coming in this morning" he began adjusting a folder. "I'm sure you heard of the murder that occurred at Gentlemen Ten Saturday night, right?"

"No, you're wrong" he corrected him. "I really don't watch a lot of television or listen to the news. What does this murder you're referring to have to do with my brother's case?"

"Where was you at Saturday night?" blurted Shitty watching him closely.

"Pardon me" he replied staring over at the young Detective with slightly harden eyes.

"You heard me" he stated returning his stare. "Where was you Saturday night?"

"I don't know if I like what you're implying or the tone that you are using first" he stated snarling at his disposition and mannerism. "Where I was at is no damn business of yours" he stated snarling over at him. "But I'll excuse it" he told him staring into his eyes then focus on Ron. "I was out with friends."

"Where?" inquired Ron.

"At the Five Mile House."

"Is there anybody who can verify your claim?"

"Of course, if I'm out with friends" he replied slightly hardening his eyes. "Anglia Bliss, she works at Hopkins as a register nurse."

"May I have her cell number?" Shitty asked staring at him.

"You? Hell no" he replied instantly snarling at him. "I would love to give it to you Ron but I'm not in the habit of giving out my friends' telephone numbers, especially my female friends. You can call the hospital or go to Hopkins yourself and look her up" he offer as a solution. "I'm not in no hurry."

"I'll make that run, Ron" Shitty said getting to his feet collecting his notebook then exiting the interrogation room.

"Why would you assume I have a hand in these hideous crimes?"

"Three of the biggest drug dealers in our city that were killed conspired with two others to murder your brother" he replied.

"What?" he stated staring at him closely. "If you know who they are, why haven't you arrest them?"

"Because the only person that is talking is providing hearsay and you know it's not admissible to obtain a conviction. I did have an interview with one of the accomplices, but he wasn't sharing anything."

"Well, one thing he knows is that yawl are at least peeking at him."

"That we are" he assured him. "I was hoping the latest murder will shake him up and he reconsider talking to us. He knows who's murdering his friends" he shared his hand, but he didn't get the reaction that he thought he would get and desire from Lion.

"If the right offer is on the table, we can find out who murder my brother and maybe, whoever is murdering his friends" he said returning his stare. "Let me talk to the prosecutor and see if we can work out a mandatory ten-year sentence for him if he cooperate" he suggested.

"I'm not willing to give him a deal like that Malik if he conspired in the murder of Shabazz. If he values his life, he needs to cooperate" he told him slightly hardening his eyes.

"Good luck on that even a wolf would marl off his own paw to escape capture instead of just cooperating" he reminded him grinning.

They sat talking for another forty minutes before Shitty walked in holding a picture frame. He extended the picture to Ron who study it.

"You're very photographic" he complimented passing the picture over to him.

A faint smile cross his lips knowing that Misty would place their picture on her desk instead of inside her photo album. "Thanks" he replied extending the picture back to him.

"Na, you can give it back to her" Shitty said.

"You give it back since you got it" he replied still slightly snarling at him.

"Malik" Ron said getting to his feet. "I want to thank you for coming in. If we have any more questions, we'll contact you."

"I'll be in town an additional week or two. I'm taking my mother to Philly tomorrow. With the death of Shabazz, she's finally going to get clean."

"I'm glad for her."

"Good afternoon, Ron" he said ignoring Shitty as he open the door and walk out.

"He has a solid alibi, Ron" he shared watching the door close. "I must admit I thought he might have had a hand in this shit, but he might not have been as close to Shabazz as he first stated. It could be one of the East Side Boyz getting revenge but why?"

"That I don't know, but we can definitely cross him off this compact list. What the fuck was Shabazz about?" he asked closing his folder.

The next morning around nine o'clock, Lion was heading towards Dallas Court in the Perkins Project on Caroline Street to pick up his mother. He didn't know she had moved down there almost seven years ago. He thought she was still on Collington Avenue. He was pleasantly surprised pulling up in front of her house to see Misty sitting on the steps with her. Climbing out the car, adults that haven't seen him in over twelve years were shocked to see him. "Malik?" Someone asked as he walked pass ignoring them.

"Morning ladies" he greeted as they got to their feet.

"Morning Malik" they chimed together.

As his mother grabbed her suitcases, her neighbors was staring at her and wondering where she was going. She didn't share with any of her get high friends her intentions. She didn't want to see the look of doubt in some of their eyes even while smiling. They have all heard the stories of junkies vowing to get rid of their monkeys or full-grown silver backs and everything in between. She remember the slanderous things that were said when Sugar and Brenda who attempted the journey. Nobody was the voice fighting for them to succeed just reasons why they will fail. She admittedly was guilty of the same offense. They were back on the streets of Baltimore in less than three-months, but they had picked up some good weight and looking truly refresh. According to rumors that started to flow, they was struggling to pay their bills and found herself turning a few tricks to acquire the money they needed. Things went quickly downhill from there somehow. Today, they could be found on Eastern Avenue turning thirty-dollars tricks near Patterson Park.

There is no disputing that his mother had started fucking up her life when she was seventeen as he found out. Thinking she was mature enough to do grown folks shit while still in high school and ignoring the words of advice, or apprehension about the path she was flirting with, from those that genuinely cared for her. Did she listen? Na, she first dropped out of high school going into her senior year. As she continued on her self-destructive journey, she continued to fuck up her life while giving birth to her only child. She provided nothing to him but life itself. She would allow him to be coerce if possible or stumble through the traps on the streets and fuck up his life on his own, but he didn't. Somehow, he maneuver through the traps. Yeah, she heard little stories about him fighting when he was about twelve, but that's damn sure is better than hearing about him running away from a fight. She remember the first time she heard his nickname. A broad smile came to her face because he was known for walking lightly and stealth just like something on the prowl. A lion is a perfect descriptive of him according to the streets and the streets hold a lot of truths. If he were terrorizing the streets as her girlfriends sons were doing as a teenager, she could justify her actions of becoming an addict and for not visiting him while he was incarcerated, but she couldn't. In his most dire and vulnerable time, she abandon her only child for the syringe filled with heroin and try to place the blame of her addiction, but Sha wouldn't allow her to comp out that easily. She has seen that side of him twice. The first time was when she wouldn't go to Malik's trial even though he said he would provide her a ride and the second time was using her addiction as a crutch for not visiting him. She had never heard such vulgarity put so eloquently to say the least. He cut her off for two months after those incidents and she felt the sting of him not assisting her. A sting that had her living in the bathroom for three days.

Malik have transformed the life she gave him into something positive and productive. Now, it was her turn. Yeah, she is taking the same journey that most junkies have attempted or will attempt, hopefully but she has a motivating factor that most might not have. Her only child was giving her a second chance at redemption. If she fail at her attempt, all she would have, are the memories of him and her unwillingness to conquer her demon for him. She insisted that Misty sit in the front seat while she sat in the back with her thoughts. Cutting her man lose wasn't as hard as she thought it would be. She had been taking care of his worthless ass long enough. What was his motive to want to do more for them when she did it all? His anger was warranted considering he was losing his goose with the golden egg, but he had enough common sense not to put his damn hands on her again. Sha had lifted him off his feet and damn near slam the life out of him against a wall for giving her a swollen lip. Lion or one of his friends would have him dig a ditch and buried his worthless ass in it. She asked him for her keys, and he surrender them without any incident. Then allowed him to spend one final night together, but he was gone before the crack of dawn. He didn't want to be seen leaving by Lion. She didn't know what the future held, but it have to be a whole lot better than the past twenty-five years she was leaving. "How long will the trip take Malik?"

"Once we get on 95N, I will say ninety minutes but less if the traffic isn't too bad" he replied heading up Broadway to Orleans Street then turning right. He continued until it turned into Rt.40 East, and he saw the I-95 signs then jumped on I-95 heading North.

"How long you been into jazz?" she asked staring at the rear-view mirror.

"About ten years" he replied maneuvering towards the fourth lane then accelerating.

"Your father asked about you last month" she informed him.

"Why?" he asked staring into his rear-view mirror at her. "I don't know the man."

"You was incredibly young when he got locked up. Where do you live now?"

He slightly hesitated then replied. "In Atlanta."

"Here Ms. Mohammad" Misty said extending a magazine to her.

She stared at the cover in shock. "You're a lawyer!?"

"Yes, ma'am" he replied peeking in the mirror then focus back on the road.

"How?" she heard herself foolishly asked.

"Studying" he replied watching her from the rear-view mirror turning to the page containing his story then becoming quiet. As she read the article, he openly admitted to the world he was the product of including an addictive mother and a murderous father. Surviving the streets of Baltimore can be contributed to his older brother. Tears suddenly fell from her eyes. She used to boast to all her addict friends how Road Block took care of all her needs and desires. She never assumed her stepchild would have such an impact on their communities as he did. She didn't know the things that Shabazz was doing until the testimonies of so many at his memorial. Now, she was reading how her baby was a well-respected and admire lawyer in the criminal justice profession. Highly desired by those awaiting trial on drug charges and serious weapon violations. He adamantly refuses to represent anybody charged with a "short eyes" charge. A terminology associated with charges like child molestation or child pornography. A junior partnership was waiting for him upon his return to Atlanta. After reading the article, she clutched it to her chest.

"May I keep this?" she asked staring into the rear-view mirror at him again.

"Sure" he replied watching her clutching the magazine.

"Thanks" she smiled then stared out at the signs indicating that New Jersey was the far right three lanes while Philly was the left four lanes.

"So, have you considered my offer?"

"Still churning it" he peek over at Misty.

"Come on, Lion" she pleaded smiling. "If you allow me to come stay with you for a couple of months, I can stack my money. With my surgeon nursing experience, you know I'll get a job easy. Will you do this for me, please?"

"Still contemplating" he replied nonchalantly ignoring her eyes. They enter Center City from 5th Street then turned right onto Market Street until they ran into Broad Street. The addiction clinic was on the left-hand side. They found a parking spot then exited the car. As they approached the clinic, he could see his mother's nervousness and apprehension.

"I'm going to make you proud of me, Malik" she said staring up into his eyes as they ascended the steps.

He didn't know how to respond so he kept quiet. Walking through the foyer, they approached the receptionist desk.

"Good morning, may I help you" a middle age black woman asked with evidence of her past life on her arms.

"Good morning, Mrs. Mohammad reporting in" he replied staring down at her.

"Morning Monica, you're going to enjoy this environment" she assured her smiling while getting to her feet. "Everything is set and approved for you. You will have a private room with full cable television thanks to your son. You have to say your good byes here because no unauthorized personnel is allowed beyond this door."

"Well, son" she said taking her suitcase from him and Misty. "I got your number if I need anything."

"You have five-thousand dollars on your account" he informed her.

"Okay baby, I'll see you later" she said turning and slowly walking away.

"Mother!" he called walking over to her then surprisingly giving her a hug while whispering. "Be strong" he said before releasing her and watching her smiling as she walked through the door to her reprisal. "Let's bounce Misty" he said watching the door closing completely. They retraced their steps to the car. He open the passenger door for her to get inside then walked around. Starting up the engine, Big Joe Turner's "You're Driving Me Crazy" filled the interior. Pulling away from the curb, he was back on 95 heading South in less than five minutes. He reached under his floor mate and brought out his toothbrush canister with several blunts inside. Giving her one, they lit them up then lean back cruising with the early afternoon traffic.

"Is everything alright?" she asked breaking their silence.

"Yeah, why?"

"Five-o came to my job yesterday questioning me about you?"

"They just wanted to know where I was Saturday night."

"Why?"

"They never actually said" he replied never taking his eyes off the road.

They drove in silence for a moment before she started sharing her life with him including how she lost her virginity under the influence of weed and hard liquor to an allege worthless piece of shit? "There is nothing here for me, Lion. Let me come back to Atlanta with you, please" she smiled over at him.

"There is nothing here?"

"No, nothing" she replied before seeing his eyes and when she did, she didn't like what she saw. "What?"

"When are you planning on telling me about Nia (Purpose)?" he asked staring over at her.

"I don't know" she replied honestly slightly lowering her eyes.

"What about?" he stated then his words suddenly ceased.

"What" she asked trying to catch his eyes, but he never took them off the road.

"Listen, stop pressing up on me about Atlanta. I haven't made my final decision, okay?"

"Okay, thanks" she replied slightly smiling at the glimpse of hope he was providing her. Wondering how he knew about Nia would be a waste of time. There were more than enough people to give him the 411 on her personal life especially those jealousy ass bitches they knew while growing up. She was sure he knew about Derrick and that he was the father, but did he know she was still secretly seeing his worthless ass behind his wife's back. Did he?

For the next couple of days especially at night, he posted up on Byrd's apartment. He watched his men come and go without a routine. He had some East Side Boyz on him around the clock. He was never without eight men around him except when two of them went food shopping. He thought about making his play then, but patience told him to wait. They would be more relaxed when they call their freaks over. Under the influence of alcohol and weed, their reflexes would be slower, and their equilibrium will definitely be altered. So, he decided that would be the scenario when he finally make his move.

With no words coming from the streets on him or Bunkie's where about for almost two weeks, a false sense of security slowly started creeping into their minds. The two jazz clubs that he frequent was a thing of the past and so was the Five Mile House and Melba's Place up on Greenmount Avenue. He wasn't seen with Misty in a little over three weeks although she was seen out with her girlfriends regularly getting her freak on or sitting in a dark lounge with her baby daddy. The starling thing was his mother also had suddenly and mysteriously vanished off the face of the earth. Her closest friends weren't unable to provide any information even with the proposition of drugs. If that didn't produce any results, nothing would? The only information that they could provide that was consistent is that Lion came to get her with Misty, and she haven't been seen since. That was over a month ago. Could he have left town and taken his mother with him? Na, she admitted not deserving his love or respect at Shabazz memorial, but one thing was for sure, she had mysteriously disappeared, and her ex-boyfriend couldn't provide any information neither. Although some thuggish looking character enter her house periodically at various times of the day and night, they never stay longer than a few minutes.

Byrd nor Ice could accept the possibility that he just might have left town. He could be setting up another elaborate trap. This was a real possibility in their mindset. Although neither man would like to admit it, neither have slept peacefully since Lion acquired their names until the past couple of nights. Sleeping a straight six to eight hours was unheard of initially but now, they have slept eight hours three straight days. Before, the slightest sound would startle them awake and reaching for their weapons while staring into the shadows of their bedrooms. The ability to sit back out on the balcony and breath fresh air was invigorating. Could he have really left Baltimore?

Friday night, Byrd and Ice got together for the first time in months. Sitting inside the Sugar Hill Tavern on Druid Hill entertaining their entourage felt good. Observing the girls openly flirting and jockeying for position did wonders for their egos. Mid-level dealers were sending drinks to their booth as a form of respect. Both men took deep breaths, sigh then laugh. They haven't felt this relax in ages. With security around them extremely tight and alert, they felt comfortable to get on the dance floor to get their boogie on. When the last call for alcohol was made, they filed out and stood on the corner socializing. Although their shit, was now tight as far as security was concern, the core of their security would be just four later. They never paid the Crown Vic pulling away from the curb up the street any attention as it drove pass.

"Where are we headed?" Bunkie asked staring at them as they pass.

"To Byrd's apartment" he shared pulling out his cell phone to make a quick call. Twenty minutes later, he was pulling up and parking on the rear parking lot. The emergency exit door was ajar. They enter taking the stairs up to the third floor then pausing before stepping into the main hallway. Slowly opening the third-floor door, they peeked outside, and the hallway was clear. Briskly walking to 312, he slowly twisted the doorknob, and it swung open surprising Bunkie. "Inside assistance, brother" he smiled over at him as they stepped inside. Placing their gloves on their hands and masks on their faces, they stood quietly then went through the bedrooms before staring out the kitchen window at the front parking lot. A half hour later two cars and a black Suburban were pulling up like he hoped. As they found a parking spot then walked towards the front door, it was evident that they were highly intoxicated and still in a festive disposition. The four occupants of the SUV hooked a U-turned and left the apartment complex. As they enter the building, Bunkie stepped inside the closet in the living room while Lion proceeded down the hallway to Byrd's bedroom. He open the door closing it behind himself then walking over to the closet and stepping inside. With his Glock held tightly in his hand and a round chamber, he peeked through the blinds. He could hear the chatter of voices and laughter until the music drowned them out.

"Enjoy your night, gentlemen!" he wished them at his bedroom door hitting the light switch and illuminating the room with a soft glow before closing the door. "Go jump in the shower sweetheart" he told the honey complexion girl while palming her phat firm looking ass. He hit his remote and Curtis Mayfield's "People Get Ready" filled the quietness. He took a seat on the bed watching her peeling herself out of the white stretch dress then pulled the string over her head revealing the absence of a bra to support her 36C breast and red thongs. He smiled at her as she stared back at him. "I'll be right there" he said smiling at her while admiring her body.

"Don't have me waiting too long" she replied stepping out of her thong and twirling them was she walked into the bathroom. Her young vibrant ass was jiggling like Jell-O.

"Don't worry, I won't" he assured her as she partially closed the door. He eagerly untied his shoes and removed them before taking off his shirt. The good life had taken a toll on his body physically as he removed his wife beater. Just as he was about to unbuckle his belt, he felt a sudden chill run down his back from vaguely hearing the closet door opening. He never turned around. "Lion?"

"Hey Byrd."

"Caught a nigger slipping, huh?"

"Just a little."

"I guess apologizing for what I was a part of is senseless, huh?"

"I don't know" he replied softly pulling back the hammer and locking it in place. "When you get to where I'm sending you, send a text message back and I'll let you know. Turn around."

"No" he replied defiantly. He didn't want to see it coming.

"Turn the fuck around or I'll blow your brains out the front of your scandalous ass head then touch one of your family members" he threaten.

Reluctantly, he turned and stared into his eyes. It has been too many years since he first stared into them, they still held a calm about them even though he knew the opposite existed. "When you was about twelve, I told Road Block you would be a beast if you were in the game" he lightly chuckled.

"Byrd, I'm waiting on you!" the young lady called from the bathroom.

"Be there soon baby" he replied staring at her silhouette through the steam then stared back at Lion. "He thought you didn't have what it takes to be in the streets. He's a perfect example of someone standing to close to the tree to see the forestry" he lightly chuckled. "I warned everybody about you, but they waved me off."

"So, did you apparently or you wouldn't have put your money in the pot" he reminded him.

"True that" he admitted slightly sighing. "As they started falling like dominoes, they witness just how vicious and medieval a lion seeking restitution can be for a loved one. What they saw scared the shit out of them worse than any horror movie they might have seen. Will you do me a favor?"

"What is it?"

"Give that envelope to my women" he requested pointing at it on the night stand. "The address is on the front."

"I can do that.

"Thanks man" he slightly smiled.

"Byrd! You better hurry up baby!"

"I'm coming" he lied while staring into Lion's eyes.

"You're not coming yet!" she giggled.

"I got to go" Lion said starting to raise his weapon.

"Later, Lion."

"Later, Byrd" he replied grabbing a pillow to muffle the sound. The round discharging was louder than expected in the confined area.

"What was that Byrd?" the girl asked pausing.

Hearing the single shot, his bodyguards rushed towards the bedroom while reaching for their guns. Bunkie stepping out of the closet caught them totally by surprise as he sprayed the small hallway as Lion remained still until the last round was discharged. Their bodies did a familiar dance as the rounds struck their bodies if you know what I'm talking about. Hearing the rapid fire of an automatic had the girls in the front room screaming including the one in the bathroom as she took cover in the bath tub. When silence filled the apartment, Lion stepped out of the bedroom still clutching his Glock and stared at the bodies stretched out along the hallway leading towards the bedrooms. Walking past the girls cuddling in a corner, they approached the door peeking through the peek hole before slightly opening it. Lion extinguishing three of the hallway lights with his weapon then retrieve his casing before fully opening the door and stepping out into the diminishing light. Descending the stairs and exiting at the fire exit, they pause slightly before opening the fire door. Hugging the wall, they turned the corner and climbed back into their ride and left the area with their headlights off.

By the time five-o had arrived, they were long gone. Opening the apartment door and noticing the number of casings that consumed the floor, they were extremely cautious as they made their way through the apartment. They checked each individual that was stretch out for any sign of life before continuing their search of the apartment. They came upon Byrd with a single shot to the fore head. The slight sounds of whimpering from the bathroom had them on high alert as they push open the door.

"There's one in here alive!" a man's voice startled her. "Are you alright, Miss?"

She was found in the tub butter ball naked by five-o in a fetal position with her eyes closed tightly and in shock. As she slowly open her eyes and focus in on the blue uniform of the Baltimore City Police Department, she suddenly leaped into his arms ignoring the fact that she was naked. Covering her with an over-size towel, they escorted her into a vacant bedroom to get dress and to wait to be interviewed by homicide detectives when they arrive. By the time they arrived, she was fully cloth and somewhat under control. She was unable to provide the homicide detectives with any useful information not even the names of the young ladies the three decease men apparently had as company. No other witnesses existed as they got low once they knew they weren't being targeted and retrieved every dollar in the deceased pockets including their expensive jewelry.

"At approximately two-thirty last night, gun fire erupted in a usual quiet neighborhood in an apartment near the Garrison Apartments. Neighbors reported being startle awoke after hearing approximately twenty to thirty shots from an assault weapon. Another one of the cities alleged high-profile distributor was found gunned down in his apartment bedroom by a single shot to the head while three others were gunned down in the front room and hallway. Andre "Byrd" Thompson, a reputed Kingpin and three of his associates were partying when the incident occurred. An unidentifiable woman who was found at the crime scene was unharmed, her name is being kept confidential as the investigation commences. Although the lead detective won't answer any questions concerning if these murders were related to the apparent unjustified assassination of Shabazz Mohammad, they continue to refuse to associate the two. As an investigative reporter for over fifteen years, I know a connection when I'm witnessing it. The mysterious deaths of several high-profile distributors isn't a coincident and all this started transpiring after the assassination of Mr. Shabazz Mohammad. You still want to call it a drug deal that went wrong and this is the result of that alleged deal or still accept it as a coincidence, huh?

Two days after the murder of Byrd, a special deliver envelope was signed by Byrd's woman, Pudding from FedEx. Receiving the envelope and opening it, all the pain she felt initially resurfaced as tears flowed from her eyes uncontrollably as she groan as though in extreme pain or anguish. In a hand-written note, he confessed that if she was reading this, he paid with his life for something scandalous that he was a part and rightfully so. He gave her the codes and passwords to his two off shore accounts. He apologized for all his indiscretions and lies. He never stopped being in love with her exclusively even though he threw my dick around like a school boy. With the money in the off shore accounts, the four hair salons and ten housing properties, leave this crazy ass city. I don't need my sons or daughters hearing how I was and am. If any of our sons tried to emulate me in any fashion, slap the shit out of him and show him this letter that I said to slap the shit out of him again after showing it to them. If any of my children get hurt in the streets, I would never forgive myself. Go baby, please. Leave this psychotic and heartless ass city. I need our children to always think of me as Daddy and Pops. Since I didn't appreciate and love you as a woman should be loved, the next man will surely appreciate you. I will always love you exclusively, Pudding.

Ring! Ring! Ring!

"Hello, Detective Ron. May I help you?"

"Detective, this is Ice."

"I thought I would be hearing from you" he told him slightly smiling over to his young partner. "What can I do for you?"

"I do know who is responsible for the murders" he confessed.

"Do you want to come in and make a statement?"

"That all depends."

"On what?"

"What type of deal I can get with the prosecutor's office?"

"What are you requesting?"

"I'm open to suggestions."

"Did you personally shoot Shabazz or Monster?"

"No, absolutely not!"

"Did you conspire?"

"I'll take the fifth on that" he replied slightly smiling into his cell. "I'll talk to the prosecutor not to you if the deal is sweet enough, but you need to hurry."

"Why?"

"Because I'm next, got damn it!" he shouted hanging up. He was willing to be incarcerated for up to ten years for his part. He could easily get out in seven years or earlier with good behavior. If they offer twenty-years with the possibility of parole, he will tell them to kiss his black ass and take his chances on the streets or move. He made up his mind he was leaving if things went further south for him especially if the prosecutor office isn't offering refuge. He refused to live or walk another weekend on the unforgiving and brutal streets of Baltimore. He would bounce then send for his family.

Cookie was cruising around the city without a care and unaware that she was being followed by a black Crown Vic. From the time she left her house to drop off her two elementary age children at school to the hour and a half she spent in the hair salon at Rogers Avenue on Thursday, they were her shadows. Even the two hours she spent having lunch with a strange man, her shadows were watching her. When she pulled into Mondawmin parking lot, one of the occupants made a call.

"She's at Mondawmin. What do you want us to do?" He listen intensely to his instructions then hung up. About twenty minutes later, another car pulled up next to him. "Park next to her facing out" he told the late model Cadillac driver with a co-pilot. They took up their position. Both occupants stared at the main entrance and at the Burger King exit. She was inside for only a half hour when they spotted her exiting from the Burger King door. Occupants of both vehicles exited but the two guys from the Caddy remained stationary as though they were talking while the other two from the Crown Vic took an angle that would bring them up behind her. She was so indulged in her conversation that she didn't take notice of the trap into which she was walking. Just as she finish her conversation and was placing her cell phone in her Michael Kors cross-body bag to retrieve her car keys, she stared into the eyes of the two strangers talking near her car. Her intuition started banging as her peripheral vision caught a slight movement. Just as she moved to her right to avoid the strangers and peek at who was coming up behind her, her lights went out. She felt her body floating not realizing she was being placed in the trunk of a car. One of the guys scanned the parking lot to see if they were observed. After placing her packages next to her, they closed the trunk. One of the guys leaped into her Caddy then all three vehicles left the parking lot heading up Liberty Road.

Ice in the mean-while have been trying to reach out to Cookie, but she wasn't answering her phone. "Answer the got damn phone! Shit!" he heard himself say staring around the apartment. He had two suitcases in the closet by the front door and his pass port in his coat breast pocket. If the conversation he's hoping to have with the prosecutor's office doesn't fan out, he was bouncing. The only two stops he had to make was to the bank then he was jumping on 95N heading to New York's LaGuardia Airport or John F. Kennedy International. "Come on, Cookie. Call me back bitch."

In a vacant house up near Lochearn off of St. Luke's Lane, the faint sound of music being played could be heard. Gradually stirring, Cookie open her eyes. "Damn" she whispers gradually waking up while rubbing the back of her head. Looking at the blood on her finger tips, she stared around in a strange and dimly lit environment. She gradually spotted four guys with masks staring over at her. "What's this about?" she asked staring at them.

"Ice and Retribution" a voice behind her answer.

"Ice?" she asked turning too quickly and causing her head to ache to see two more mask guys. "What the fuck have that no-good motherfucker go and do now?" she asked hardening her eyes.

"Got himself killed" he replied pulling a chair up and taking a seat in front of her. "I apologized for the abduction and the small lump on that pretty head of yours" he told her slightly smiling. "I've been trying to get my hands on him for a minute but he's a slippery and elusive motherfucker. I need you to do something for me, but I need you to be motivated to do it."

"What's that?"

"Get him here."

"He won't come."

"Here's my motivation" he said staring into her eyes. "When was the last time you saw Meeks?"

"Meeks?" she asked staring at him curiously. "What do my brother have to do with this?"

"Have you seen that sudden change in Meek?"

She didn't respond right away. She had to cut him off two years ago after finding him in one of her bathroom's, sniffing dope. Seeing him a week before he got killed, there was a drastic change in his appearance. He was dress fresh from head to toe with the new Jordan sneakers and a fresh haircut. He resemble the little boy she once raised. Of course, she asked him where he got the money? He told her from an accident claim. She never challenge what he told her as usual, but her intuition told her, he was lying through his teeth again. When word reached her about him putting a small package out on the streets in Cherry Hill, she knew he had done something illegal to get what he had acquired. "Yes, there was a substantial change in him" she replied honestly.

"Have you ever wondered how he obtained the money he got to put those packages out there?"

"Yeah" she replied staring into the stranger's eyes.

"Would you like to know how?" he asked in a soothing even voice.

She stared into his eyes then at his manicure hand. She wanted to know but fear and apprehension had her unconsciously hesitating. She already had her suspicions, but did she want to know for certain? She could barely hear herself say, "Yes."

"He got it from Ice."

"From Ice" her assumption was answer. She had asked him repeatedly did he give Meeks any money and he sworn that he didn't. Now, she's hearing he did. "For what?" she asked returning his stare.

"For something that he wasn't man enough to do himself, sweetheart" he replied watching her anger slowly materializing.

She stared at him trying to read between the lines. What has occurred in the streets recently that cause her baby brother the opportunity to make such money to put a package on the streets? She had to reflect long and hard on what shook up the city? As she started reflecting on his sudden money flow, a revelation slowly materialized. A revelation that she refused to accept but must ask. She took a deep breath then slowly exhaled while keeping her grayish eyes fixed to his. "Did my little brother have anything to do with Road Block's and Monster's murders?"

"Regrettably, yes."

The weight of the world seems to fall on her shoulder as she sigh while lowering her head, and her tears suddenly flowed. "Ice is the cause of this, huh?"

"He and those who have already met their Maker."

She stop to listen to what he said. And those who are already meeting their Maker, he was talking about Byrd, Sunshine, and the others. "That lying son-of-a-bitch, he told me he couldn't find no information concerning his death" she said as vengeance enter her eyes and heart. "I knew he had something to do with Road Block's murder and for what?" she asked staring over at him.

"They had aspirations of expanding into the East Side Boyz turf."

"Are you for real!? Really!?" she asked surprised by the answer. "Those boys aren't going to lay down for no one especially motherfuckers from the West Side! If they thought they could just walk in and set up shop, they don't know shit about the eastside apparently" she shared while hardening her eyes.

"Can you bring him to us?"

"I don't know" she answer honestly returning his stare.

The stranger became quiet as he sat contemplating something then an impish grin came to his face. "Excuse the intrusive question, but have he ever shared a sexual fantasy with you that he would like to experience?"

The question caught her slightly off-guard as she thought about the question. What one thing that most supposedly monogamist men desire their woman to explore? A coy smile creep across her lips. "I'll get his scandalous ass here" she said. "May I have my cell?" she asked as he extended her crossbody bag to her. She pulled it out and seen that he had called her four times in the span of an hour and that was very unusual. Pressing a pre-set number, she waited for a response. "Hey, do you know who this is?"

"Cookie" the voice answer.

"Yeah, I'm ready to set this thing off, but I need your assistance in something."

"What-ever it is I'm in?"

"I'm going to text you an address. Come as soon as possible."

"Getting dress now, just hit me off" the person replied ending their conversation.

"I need this address" she stated staring at the mouth piece and he surrendered it to her. She sent the text and lean back in her chair as Lion extended a blunt to her. About twenty minutes late, there was a light tapping at the door. She open the door and a sexy ass honey complexion girl enter. She was initially startle by the six men wearing mask, but Cookie assured her nothing was going to happen to her.

"If anything, young lady. You could be walking out of here five thousand dollars richer" Lion informed her extending the money to her.

"What do you need me to do?" she asked staring into the eyes of the mask men.

Cookie explained her intensions while they shared a blunt and it was set up. She dialed Ice number. "Yeah, why are you calling me so often. Is everything alright?"

"Yeah, I just need to have a serious conversation with you."

"About what?"

"Our future" he replied.

"Our future" she repeated slightly giggling. "Since when?"

"I've been doing a lot of soul searching lately" he replied lying.

"Soul searching" she repeated again with a coy grin. "Have your soul searching found out who was responsible for my little brother's murder?"

"No, nothing is being said. Not even in Cherry Hill" he replied softly. "Where are you at?"

"Actually, that is why I was calling you until I seen that you have been blowing my cell up. I need you to come to a girlfriend of mine's house."

"For what?"

"Come and see" she replied.

"Na, I can't make it" he replied flatly.

"Ice get your sorry ass over here or never ask me about doing this bullshit again" she stated adamantly.

"What shit?"

"I'm talking about what we discussed a couple of times over the years."

"What!?" he asked leaning forward in his chair. The only thing he tried to convince her to do was experience a menage trios. "Bullshit!"

"Bullshit!?" she snapped. "Motherfucker you asked me to consider something, and I have. If you're not interested in this honey complexion young lady, just tell me and I'll never mention it to your sorry ass again, but your black ass damn sure better not bring it back up to me either" she snarled into her cell.

"You're serious, huh?"

"No, I'm blowing smoke up your ass."

"The offer sounds intriguing, but I have to decline. Why don't yawl come to me?"

"Oh, you want your cake and eat it too, huh? You're funny" she burst out laughing. "If you think I'm going to try to take her out of her comfort zone just to appease you, you, done bump your motherfucking head. Fuck you Ice. This conversation is over" she said suddenly ending their conversation.

"What the fuck!" he stated staring at his cell then try calling her back, but she wasn't being receptive. On his fourth try, she answer.

"Don't fuck with me Ice! Goodbye."

"No! Wait! Wait!" he insisted. "Text me the address."

"You know what time I pick up the kids so take your time if you want" she said ending their conversation.

"You don't like him very much, huh."

"He's a motherfuckin dog" she described him. "Why would he want those chicken box eating bitches out there when he got this at home?" she asked. With her smooth ebony complexion, shoulder length locs, on a medium five-foot-five frame and full lips, she couldn't understand why she wasn't enough for him? There was nothing she wouldn't willingly explore sexually with and for him except sharing him with another woman. His fantasy but what does that say about the love he allegedly have for her? He's always going to resemble a dog, wondering around marking his surroundings. "What do those bitches have that I don't have?" she asked sincerely staring over at Lion's concealed face for an answer she could live with.

"Sister" he began in a soft voice. "Do not ever deny your beauty or self-worth. You have both qualities in a woman that I personally admires. Your strength revealed itself by you not freaking out" he suddenly smiled at her. "Beloved, we do not truly control who we fall in love with although we think that we do. Not until you or I have had enough and step away do we realize the person you loved doesn't or didn't deserve your love. And, when they come crawling back, we can dismiss them as easy as a gentle breeze and with no remorse. Didn't you do that before?"

"Yes" she replied suddenly returning his smile and illuminating her beauty at the memory. Through all of Ice's indiscretions and two outside children, she remained faithful. But those two outside children destroyed their marriage years ago. Don't ask her, why did she stay? It damn sure wasn't for the children sake, he was absent more than he was present. She did convince his dumb ass to take out a life insurance policy for the children. The one-million-dollar policy and whatever he has in the bank accounts will sustain them including getting them out of Baltimore to a surrounding suburb. Secretly, she wish she could witness what they had planned for him. One thing she was certain, she wouldn't have to look into his lying, scandalous, cheating ass eyes again. When she witness the morning sun tomorrow, it won't represent just a new day, but the beginning of a new life.

Ice couldn't believe what his ears just heard. A ménage trio with Cookie. She finally summited to his wishes. Witnessing a woman eating her pussy while fucking a honey complexion girl doggy style would complete his sexual fantasies. Watching the pleasure, the girl would induce on her face would not only heighten but intensify his lustful desire. She was quick to hang out at the stripe clubs down on Baltimore Street with him and her girlfriends. Watching how she flirted and willingly throw her money at those working girls, he knew she was curious. Once she gets a taste of another woman licking her chocolate clique, she will be requesting more. A light chuckled escaped him.

"What's up Ice? Is everything alright."

"Couldn't be better" he smiled at him as the text came through with the address. Included was a honey complexion young lady approximately twenty-three with shoulder length hair sitting up on a bed completely naked. Her full breast had him unconsciously smack his lips. "I need you and Dink to take a ride with me. The rest of yawl continue to enjoy yourselves. Bonnie, I got a run to make but I won't be too long" he smiled getting to his feet. He grabbed his suite jacket then headed out the door. The thought of Lion never entered his mind. Only, the mirage he envision finally coming to a reality. His cell phone ringing brought him out of his thoughts. Seeing who it was, he gave himself some distance from his men as they walked towards the stairs.

"Hello?"

"You have a deal" Detective Ron announce feeling Ice smiling from ear to ear. "Can you come down to the station to make your statement?"

"Sorry, Detective" he apologized following his men. "I have an urgent appointment to keep."

"Will you answer just one question for me?"

"Maybe, what is it?"

"Does Malik have anything to do with this?"

"I won't answer that question, right now."

"Alright, can you be here by three o'clock?"

"No problem."

"And Ice?"

"Yes."

"Be careful" he urged him before ending his call.

"Ron, there's something about Malik's eyes I just can't put my finger on it" mention Shitty.

"Do you really think Malik would throw away a promising career to spend the rest of his life behind bars? I love my brother too, but I'm not spending the rest of my life incarcerated. I know he wouldn't do it for me. If Malik had any solid evidence, I'm sure he would turn it over to us. Our snitches in the streets don't know what the fuck is happening and that's very unusual? I thought if he couldn't supply a solid alibi on the night Mookie got murdered, I would have kept him on this steadily diminishing list, but his alibi was rock solid. The cameras inside Gentlemen Ten caught an image of our assailant leaving around 11 o'clock. He couldn't have made the trip that fast with the abundance of cars trying to leave the area."

"I know, I know" he admitted shaking his head. "But there's something about him Ron, I'm telling you" he persisted staring into his eyes.

"You know what it is Shitty" he smiled over at him while getting to his feet. "From your Caucasian perspective, you just can't see a guy from his background succeeding as he has but that's okay. You can't always be right just because you are privilege" he said grabbing his jacket snickering then leading the way to another homicide scene.

Staring through the curtain, someone announced "They are here."

"Move" ordered Bunkie as three of the guys went towards the kitchen and exited the back door to a small walkway leading to the front porch then took their position.

Inside, they watched as Ice got out of the back seat then stood on the sidewalk looking around. The front door opening suddenly revealing Cookie and the young lady was standing in the doorway. Lion hoped this ploy would convince him to allow his bodyguards to leave or stay in the car. He could catch a ride back with Cookie if necessary. If not, he wouldn't have his way with him. Slow and deliberate. He would have to stretch out two more people than he wanted plus bring attention to the otherwise vacant house. He wouldn't enjoy just busting a couple of rounds in his scandalous ass. He needed and desired time. Time to share the pain he brought into his otherwise tranquil life. Seeing him pointing at them and saying something to them adamantly, brought an impish smile to his face. The ploy had worked. They would wait outside for him. The prey was walking straight into the lion's den.

"Damn baby, you look sexy" he said smiling at the white spandex pants she was wearing that slightly accentuated her camel toes while climbing the steps of the porch.

"I have always been sexy" she replied turning and walking further inside.

"Yes, you have" he said stepping inside then noticing the young lady from the picture standing near the steps wearing a broad smile. He step fully inside keeping his eyes fixed on her while closing the door. When he finally notice the two mask men, he knew it was too late. A vice like grip clamped down on the back of his neck forcing him to submit to the person behind the door. A wicked right to his kidney knocked him to his knees gasping and groaning as his .38 was taken from the small of his back. He got snatch to his feet then slammed viciously into the wall. He focus on the menacing eyes.

"Lion!"

"Sshhh, let's not get Cookie or this young lady caught up more than they are, okay?" he snarled.

"Yeah" he replied solemnly then stared over at her. "Why baby?"

"Baby?" she lightly snicker with hardening eyes. "I always knew about your two outside children Ice" she informed him. "Bitches couldn't wait to tell me. Do you know how embarrassing that shit made me feel? Do you? Apparently not motherfucker because you did it a third time and with no motherfuckin remorse" she snarled. "Do you know this young lady?" she asked.

"No, I have never seen that girl in my life Cookie" he stated staring over at her.

"No, you haven't but if you look at her closely. You will know her" she offer with a faint smile.

Staring at her closely, he was certain that he never gotten with her sexually, but there was something about her enchanting eyes. Something awfully familiar. The longer he stared at her the younger she gradually appeared until recognition finally came to his eyes. He had placed a date rape drug in her drink after starting to back out from a sexual rendezvous she initiated for a couple of dollars. How was he to know she was a virgin? She damn sure didn't look like she was seventeen. Telling him three weeks later that she miss her menstrual, he denounce her claim that he was the father until the DNA test proved differently.

"So, you do recognize her, huh?" she commented starting to snarl at him, but he never confirm or deny it. "I saw your daughter from her younger recently turned eighteen-year-old sister conceived fucking with your cheating ass. She look actually like Jamilah (beautiful)" she continued to snarl at him with menacing eyes.

"So, you set me up?"

"Set you up! You set yourself up when you plotted against a good man like Road Block. I told you from day one. I'm not a ride and die bitch especially not for a cheating motherfucker like you. I got kids that depends on me not you" she informed him staring at him coldly then asked. "Are you responsible for getting Meeks killed?"

"Watch your answer" Lion warned him catching his eyes.

A lie here would only inflect instant pain from Lion. "Yes, baby" he admitted lowering his eyes slightly.

"So, you're why Byrd and everybody else are dead?" she said realizing what he have done and the violence he initiated across the city. Did he ever consider that restitution would have to be paid? A restitution that caused her baby brother's life. "You are a worthless piece of shit, motherfucker" she stated punching him in his mouth and he took it like a champ.

"Do you know what you have done, baby?" he whimper staring over at her in shock as tears started to fill his eyes.

"Stop calling me baby! I am not your motherfucking baby as I told you years ago" she reminded him. "Yeah, I know what the fuck I have done.

I'm returning my children's mother back to them. What did you do for them, Mr. Scandalous?" she asked glaring at him with malice in her eyes.

"Excuse the intrusion, Cookie" apologized Lion. "You got a half hour before school is out."

"Did you hear that?" she asked shaking her head at him. "They even know what fucking time our children gets out of school, and you didn't even consider the danger you placed them or me in. Did you motherfucker? I actually got snatch up on Mondawmin Mall parking lot" she shared shaking her head. "So, you really thought I was the type of woman to share my man, any man, with another woman then you're a bigger fool than I thought" she lightly giggle while shaking her head at him. "Good bye, Raymond" she said staring in his frightful eyes as she walked pass ignoring the plead in them. "Are we free to go?"

"Definitely" he replied extending five G's to the lure and five to Cookie as Bunkie open the door for her.

"Wait here for a second" she told the girl walking out by herself. As she descended the porch steps, she address the two bodyguards then they looked at one another then climbed back in the car and eventually pulled away from the curb. Cookie acted like she was returning to the house until they turned right onto Fox Manor Road. She waved the lure out. They paused on the sidewalk to discuss something then she pass her five G's to the girl also and hugged one another. The young lady walked up the street as Cookie climbed into her Caddie. Starting up the engine, "Oh How It Hurts" by Barbara Mason filter out as she pulled away from the curb.

As soon as the door had closed, the masks came off.

"Can we bounce Bunkie?"

"Holla at yawl later" he told them.

"Bye Raymond" the chimed together laughing as they exited by the back door then walked down the alley.

"Have a seat" instructed Lion slamming a right into the side of his ribs.

"Aaggghhh!"

"Shut the fuck up! You are a whimpering ass bitch" Bunkie snickered while reaching in the black bag and pulling out a roll of electric tape, a ping hammer for his toes along with a butane canister and other tools of Lion's hidden skill.

"Take his shoes and socks off before tying down his legs" Lion requested reaching in the bag and bring out a pair of shears and some long needle nose pliers. "You plotted the death of a very important person in my life" he said taking the long nose plier. "He was the only one to keep me calm and you took him away. Now you are going to experience what you unleash upon this city. I heard from several of your acquaintances that you thought I was a joke" he said gripping the pliers on his right index finger. "Do you still think I'm a joke?"

"No Lion" he tried to assure him.

"I don't believe you" he said suddenly squeezing the pliers causing his finger to become disfigured.

"Aaahhhh, shit! Fuck! Got damn!" he cried out before a right hand slammed into his mouth.

"Shut the fuck up! This isn't shit motherfucker" he assured him. "I started to take you out at Gentlemen Ten with Mookie but that wouldn't have satisfied me" he admitted gripping the next two fingers and squeezing again. As he cried out in agony, Lion slammed another right into his stomach cutting off the wind for his cries. "Byrd got it quick because he was once family" he shared. "But you don't mean shit to me, nothing" he explained gripping the ping hammer and bringing it down five consecutive times on his knuckles then on his two big toes. Blood splattered everywhere.

"Aaahhhh, shit! Damn, Lion! Stop please!" he cried out as snot started running down of his nose.

"This isn't Burger King, so you can't have it your way. Make as much noise as you want" he invited him bringing down the hammer four straight times as blood splattered from his toes. He cried out in agony while pleading for mercy.

"Please, please stop" he cried as tears flowed from his eyes and mix with the snot from his nose. "I'm sorry Lion."

His pleads fell on deaf ears. Lighting the butane, he commence to severing his fingers with the shears then using the butane to coagulate the blood. His screams continuously filled the air. "Kill me, please. Kill me!" he begged for relief, but none came. He didn't possess a tolerance for pain. Yet, he like to dish it out especially to the barely legal young girls sexually. Lion couldn't get to the third phrase of the medieval things he had planned. Bunkie couldn't contain his laughter. With his constant begging and whining for death, a single shot to his forehead gave him his wish and relief he beg for. Brain particle mixed with skull fragments splatter on the floor behind him. Lion stared down at is lifeless body with venomous and vengeance filled eyes. They packed up his tools and equipment then proceeded out the back door.

For days, Detective Ron tried to get in contact with Ice with no results. Word from the streets and his snitches didn't provide any pertinent information either. Speculations started surfacing about him leaving town with one of his tricks while other denounce such rumors. Although he was a dog as described by others, he would never leave Cookie for a trick. They had an interview with Cookie. She didn't show a concern about his absence since it was only a week. Him not being seen by her for even a month wasn't anything strange either although they may conversate. Some of their neighbors stated that they haven't seen him in approximately two weeks while others claims longer. All collaborating that he was like a ship in the night docking at one strange port to the next. Ron didn't want to assume the worse, but with a deal on the table from the prosecutor's office that assures him of walking the streets again, he couldn't believe that he just got low or walk away. Was he simply missing or killed? They would have to wait until his body finally surface one way or the other.

After a week of waiting, Detectives called Lion down to the police department. He informed them that he would be back in the city by tomorrow afternoon. He arrived a little after twelve o'clock dress professionally in a blue Armani suit and a white silk shirt with French cuff links displaying his initial on the cufflinks. Walking through the main hallway, his swag revealed a man filled with confidence. He sat waiting for Detective Ron to escort him. Hearing the elevator bell brought his attention to it. As the door slowly open, Det. Ron stepped out.

"Good afternoon, Malik" he greeted admiring his professional attire.

"Good afternoon."

"Follow me" he requested leading the way to a vacant interrogation room where Shitty was waiting them to take a seat. "We called you here to tell you what we have learned."

"You have my full attention" he said crossing his legs and fingers.

"The person responsible for your brother murder was a guy named Ice."

"Was?" he asked staring at him then over at Shitty. "What, you don't have him in custody?"

"Regrettable, we don't. He told us he would testify against the individual that's responsible for the nine murders if a plead could be worked out, but we're unable to locate him."

"Nine murders" he repeated staring at him puzzling.

"The four guys from Cherry Hill including the high-profile distributors. To clear up the mystery, we worked out a plea bargain for him."

"What, you set up a deal with him, but he vanished?"

"Yes."

"Come on, Detective" he slightly whined unfolding his fingers and legs then slightly leaning forward. He stated, "If I was connected in something that got all my associates killed and a deal was made, why disappear?"

he asked looking for some clarity. "Okay, Detectives" he said staring over at them. "All of that is fine and dandy but what does that have to do with the murder of my brother?"

"We believe they both are connected" shared Shitty.

"How?"

"That's the puzzling thing Malik, rumor has it that your brother was also a high-profile distributor in the city, but there aren't any evidence or persons to substantiate those claims" interjected Ron. "Anybody associated with this crime are demised except one."

"Detective, it don't make sense to me. Why didn't they just tell you who was committing these murders after the first one? You could have set up a sting operation or something."

"I don't know Malik" he replied honestly.

"This, shit, excuse my language," he apologized placing his hand over his mouth. "This don't make sense, Detectives. How am I supposed to get my mind around my brother's death when things just don't make sense no matter how I or you twist it? I would have called the prosecutor's office myself if my life was in danger especially if I knew who was coming for me."

"We agree" Shitty said. "You know, there has not been one drug related murder on the east side since your brother's death" he shared.

"What?" he said staring at them closely. "If my brother were some high-profile drug dealers, I would have suspected a surge in violence to try to control his alleged territory. Wouldn't you agree, Detectives?" he asked staring across the table at them.

"Yes" they replied.

"What-ever the reason for the lack of violence, I'm glad. But somebody said something to those East Side Boyz to make them increase the peace. Perhaps, who ever committed those murders might have given them the warning he didn't give this Ice character and his associates." he said slightly hardening his eyes.

"Never thought about connecting the two" admitted Ron staring into his eyes.

Shitty suddenly chuckled unexpectantly while staring over at Malik. "I would hate to be cross examine by you" he said while continuing to smile.

"This guy Ice wife couldn't tell you anything?" he asked ignoring Shitty comment.

"She said she wouldn't be surprised if he got with some younger girl and bounce."

"Are you serious?" he asked shaking his head in disgust. He sat there briefly before saying. "So, my brother case is put on hold until this Ice character raises his head, huh?"

"I'm sorry to say, but yes."

"Okay, Detectives" he said suddenly getting to his feet then pulling out a canister containing his law firm information and his cell number. "If you catch up with this Ice character, you have my information. Please contact me. I need to know why my brother was murdered?"

"We will" Ron assured him taking his card then shaking his hand.

"Enjoy your day Ron" he wished while ignoring Shitty again then exiting the interrogation room and retracing his steps. Walking through the main hallway towards the entrance, the bright sun forced him to grab his Dita retro sunglasses as he walked up towards Federal Street to get back in his car.

"So, what do you think now?" Ron asked as they watched him walking down Edison Highway.

"Na, I don't have him doing this" admitted Shitty. "What I saw in his eyes was conviction?" he shared. "If we have come after him, the questions he asked alone would have blown our case out the window" he lightly chuckled. "He's one hell of a lawyer right now. If I ever need one, I will definitely call him" he said watching him turning the corner.

As he climbed into his car and started the engine, "Since I Lost My

Baby" by Luther Vandross filled the interior. He pulled out a blunt then lit it. As he pulled from it, he checked his watch. It was early and he didn't feel like going back towards Columbia, so he decided to go to check out The Place on Franklin Avenue. Ten minutes later, he was creeping up the block and searching for a parking spot. He was fortunate to see a car pulling out and he swoop right in the spot. He stepped out securing the car then proceeding up the street. He pulled the door open and step inside. He greeted those that he was somewhat acquainted with from attending the spot with T.T. He brought himself a slow gin fizz then headed towards his usual spot to socialize.

Misty was just leaving her crib when she suddenly had the urged to see and talk to Lion. She needed to press the issue with him. She was wearing a white stretch fabric that truly accentuated her anatomy. As she drove her used Camry that Derrick had brought her for her birthday four years ago, she could only hope that he was at the location that she was heading. As she cross Orleans Street bridge, she took a deep breath. She could only hope that she could recite everything that she had to say in hopes of convincing him to take her to Atlanta with him. She spotted The Place on her left side then spotted Road Block's Beamer. She turned left at Eutaw Street and found a parking spot. After climbing out and securing the doors, she proceeded back to the quaint spot. She knew she wasn't dress appropriately for such an environment, but she didn't care. She was on a personal mission. Pushing open the door, the place was filled almost to capacity. As she squeezed pass several men, some took time to whisper compliments on her attire. Specifically, her phat little ass. When she finally spotted him conversing with several people, that didn't deter her especially since none of them were T.T.

"Excuse me, yawl" she apologized grabbing everyone's attention including Lion. "Can I speak to you Malik?"

"Sure" he replied surprised to see her. "Excuse me" he said getting to his feet with his drink then following her towards a corner. "Yeah, what's up?" he asked staring down into her eyes. "Is everything okay?"

"Everything is okay except I need to get out of Baltimore Malik" she shared returning his stare.

"Yeah, you have been saying that since I got back in town."

"That's because I really do. There really isn't anything here for me. I should have left when you invited me instead of being scared of the unknown. I wish I could take that decision back because I knew you would have done the best you could for us, but I can't."

"No, you can't" he cosigned. "But that wasn't the reason why you didn't leave Baltimore with me, you are in love with Derrick."

"I was but not anymore" she replied staring deep into his eyes.

"Since when?" he inquired surprising her with his question.

"For a couple of years now" she replied trying to return his stare, but her eyes were slightly hardening by the question. "What we had Malik is a thing of the pass" she reiterated.

"Since when?" he inquired again staring at her perplex. If she really knew him, she should had checked him out closer, especially his eyes.

"Since when?" she repeated staring at him closely now. "For a minute" she persisted but her intuition told her told her that he knew something but what? "You don't believe me?"

"Would you?" he flipped the question.

"Yeah" she replied adamantly staring into his eyes with her slightly hardening eyes.

"You know, deception is the core essence of a liar" he informed her. "I am supposed to be a friend Misty."

"Supposed?" she interjected staring up at him even closer.

"Yeah, Misty. Supposed" he reiterated.

"What are you implying Lion?"

"Nothing" he replied. "I caught you with Derrick five times and I wasn't even looking over the past two months ago" he informed her never revealing an untruthful expression to her because there were people peeking at them. "I was truly hoping that you would have introduce me to Nia by now also, but I guess, you are keeping your daughter safe from strangers as a mother should, right?" he inquired causing her to avert her eyes.

"You knew I had a daughter?"

"Of course, people still got mad love for me and watching my back. Why didn't you tell me about Nia?"

"I don't know Malik" she replied solemnly with her head slightly lowered. "I guess I was embarrassed."

"Na, no parent should ever be embarrassed about their children" he denounce her explanation. "If you have come clean with me initially, I would have seriously consider bringing you with me, but not now. How can I? Is Derrick the father?"

"Yes" she admitted softly then stared up at him.

"I don't mean to be rude, but I have friends waiting on me."

"When are you leaving town?"

"I haven't made up my mind yet" he replied honestly.

"I would like to see you before you leave."

"You won't" he replied never averting his stare from her eyes.

"Please" she requested stepping closer to him. "I'm sorry I wasn't honest with you, and I should never have kept a child of mines as a secret" she apologized staring up into his eyes.

"No, you shouldn't have and compounding it by deceiving me wasn't cool also. I have to get back to my friends."

"At least call me before you leave, okay?"

"I'll think about it. Later Misty" he said suddenly turning and leaving her standing there staring at his back until he disappeared in the crowd.

She caught herself staring at him then got herself trying to stay under control and proceeded towards the front door. She ignored the dumb shit that a few men was whispering as she walked out the door. She proceeded up Franklin Street not realizing that she was silently crying until a woman asked if she was okay. Once inside her car, she privately cried for five minutes before starting her car and pulling away from the curb. She deserved everything that had just transpired. Thinking that she was being slick got her exactly what her hand called for, nothing.

Lion arrived at Sha's house close to eleven o'clock. Pulling up on his parking pad, he was surprised to see T.T car and her sitting up on the porch. He had surprised her with his 300 as a birthday gift since he was returning home soon. She was genuinely surprised and appreciative.

"What are you doing out this late young lady?" he asked smiling at her as he came around the car.

"I needed to talk to you" she replied giving him a light kiss on the lips.

"You could have simply called me."

"Na, I needed to stare in your eyes as we talk. Besides, I wasn't doing anything at home and with the convince of your gift, I don't mind driving to you" she replied as he unlocked the door and push it open for her to enter.

"You are paying for your own gas" he replied smiling while watching her heading towards the family room. "Do you want a drink?"

"No, thank you" she replied taking a seat on the couch.

"What's on your mind?" he asked pressing the remote of the stereo and the Crusaders "Lilies of the Nile" filter out the Devialet Phantom speakers.

"In my previous relationships, I actually thought I had an emotional problem, but socializing and getting to know you better was exactually what I needed as a form of therapy. Although I have only known you for just over three months, you don't inhibit or restrict me, and I truly admire you for that. You freely allow me to explore my sexual fantasies and seem to enjoy yourself just as much as I do."

"Oh, I definitely do" he assured her with his impish smile.

"Yeah, I know" she confess blushing then gripping his fingers and staring deep into his eyes. "I might be wrong for saying this but I'm falling in love with you. I don't want this journey of ours to cease Malik. So, I've made some inquires in Atlanta. I have a position waiting for me, but I need a little help from you in locating a place to stay. I've looked at several apartments using the internet, but I don't know which area is safe."

"If you are moving to Atlanta to be with me, why don't you live with me?"

"No, Malik" she adamantly denounced his suggestion. "I don't want to impose on your private life."

"You won't" he replied slightly smiling.

"No, Malik. Let me move by myself."

"Why T.T?"

"I told you why baby."

"You won't be intruding really" he tried to assure her.

"I believe you but I'm still moving by myself" she remained firmed returning his stare.

"Well, can I assist you financially?"

"You better" she replied smiling fully. "That's why I'm falling in love with you, you allow me the independence that I crave and desire without any childish outburst or animosities" she lightly giggled. "Who couldn't love you?"

"Not me" he replied causing her to burst out laughing then she lean in and kiss him passionately.

"When are you heading home?"

"Very soon."

"I might not leave with you, but I will be coming."

"And I will be waiting" he replied returning her stare and smile.

A few days later, he called Bunkie thanking him for his assistance and if he ever needed him, don't hesitate to give him a call. In a matter of four months, Lion had set him up financially. During those conversations they shared watching their prey, he shared some aspirations and Lion made them a reality. There was no reason why he couldn't attend auto-mechanic school to give his two children a better quality of life especially since Lion paid for the trade school.

It was easy for him to obtained Tavon's release date from Johns Hopkins especially since Misty was working there. Bunkie was sitting in the main lobby peeking at the elevators while reading the sports page when Tavon suddenly walked out carrying a clear bag with his personal effects. He hoped that no one was there to pick him up and there weren't. Bunkie informed Lion what he had on and in which direction he going to catch the speed line to go down town. Bunkie entered from the Monument Station side and descended the steps; he climb aboard the train and sat several rows behind his target then felt the train slowly pick up speed. Most of the people exit at the Lexington Market stop including the target. Walking down Lexington Street towards Howard, he was being shadow, but he was naïve to it. He spoke to several people while bumming a cigarette. He looked to his left on Howard Street to see if the trolley was approaching, and it was. He never paid Lion any attention as he picked up his pace. Lion nodded to Bunkie then gave him the deuce sign as he continued in the opposite direction. He pick up the tail as the trolley gradually came to stop at Fayette Street. He climb on board with the others heading towards Cherry Hill and points north including to Thurgood Marshall Airport. He position himself near the rear door and took a seat as others were preparing to exit at Camden Yard.

In the reflection of the window, Lion saw his mark get up and approach the door with others preparing to get off at the next stop, Cherry Hill. As the trolley came to an eventual stop, the door swung open, and they shuffled out the door except Lion. As Tavon walked pass, he whisper in his ear "Gotcha." Turning to see who said it, he stared straight into Lion's eyes and his slight snarl as three slugs hit him center mass knocking him off his feet as the door closed. He stared into Lion's menacing eyes with shock from the ground until he disappeared. Arriving at the airport ten minutes later, he disassemble the Glock and discarded the pieces in separate storm drains as he walked pass then discarded his rubber gloves in a trash receptacle. When he enter the terminal, he collected his belongings from the locker he got earlier then hook up with T.T at the gate to catch their flight. They were going to spend another weekend together before she had to leave to complete her business in Baltimore. Of course, the news of Tavon's death shocked the hell out of Detectives Ron and Shitty. They thought he would be okay. Fooled again.

MONOLOGUE

He TALKS TO HIS MOTHER TWICE A WEEK NOW. IN THE SIX MONTHS THAT SHE HAS been in the program up in Philly, she requested to stay an additional three months for assurance, but she really didn't need it. She feared the unknown especially going back to her old neighborhood. When he and Misty went to visit her six months from her initial arrival, he couldn't believe the transformation. Her glow was starting to shine again, and her weight picked up tremendously eating healthy and working out. He would be proud to introduce her to his bosses and associates at any function as his mother. She looked that good. And because of her accomplishment, he rewarded her with the deed to Shabazz house and his cars. She completed her RN two years ago and boasting about some doctor sniffing after her. She also been reaching out to her old friends. Doing what-ever it takes to help them get clean. She even open her home to them upon completing the minimum six-month program because she understood their fears concerns returning to their previous environment. Shabazz would be proud of her because Lion was now.

As far as Misty is concern, the revelation Lion revealed broke her heart. She found herself crawling in the arms of Derrick for emotional support but all he desired was her getting naked. His insensitivity caused her to finally cut him off and explore other guys. Whatever she was searching for she never found. She found herself thinking more and more about Lion as her life slowly spiral out of control and deteriorated. She now have four children and the last daughter was by Derrick.

T.T finally accepted his invitation to join him. After forcing her to finish getting the college degree she started years before, they settle into a very romantic relationship. They have the joy of their lives in a three-year-old son named Shabazz, of course. Zion will be born next month. Marrying her completed his journey and put Lion to rest permanently, hopefully.

.

DEDICATION

To the families that have lost family members and loved ones to the senseless violence that plagues our streets and communities, I feel for yawl. One of the disheartening things is how our babies have now become innocent victims by those claiming to be soldiers but have never properly been trained in handling a firearm. How do you miss someone ten feet away while striking a child playing innocently in front of their homes? Put the guns down, please. If you don't know how to use your hands to handle disputes as men used to do, stay in your lane, and stop perpetrating that you are a soldier, or learn how to defend yourself. Even a coward can pull a trigger, are you one? Malcolm X said, "A man that don't know his limits are likely to make a mistake." Imagine spending twenty-five-years to life incarcerated because you murder someone over something completely foolish like getting your ass kick in a fist fight. Gone are your family. Gone are your responsibilities to watch over and protecting your children as they grow up, especially the young girls. Do you think your woman will be there emotionally for you after you choose the streets over your family? Or do you expect her to put her life on hold because of you? Do you? Would you if the script were flip? Life as you know it would be gone and why, because you thought murder was your only option. Immature and foolish thinking.

*Special message to a reader: You asked the question why would I attend Camden High knowing the repercussions that I would face and endure coming from out of North Camden?

*Answer: I wanted to see if the rumors were true filtering down to us in North and it was. We sang the Black National Anthem every morning.

FUTURE BOOKS

* "ATM AND J-LO"

* "ATL"

* "SEXY EYES"

* "SHADOW"

* "PRIVILEDGE"

Printed in the United States
by Baker & Taylor Publisher Services